Losing Lauren

Jordan Deen

BLACK ROSE writing™

ISBN: 978-1-61296-285-6

PUBLISHED BY BLACK ROSE WRITING

www.blackrosewriting.com

Printed in the United States of America

Losing Lauren is printed in Perpetua

"To the me I was, the me I am and the me I will be-
Life is about the journey."

much love -

With love.

Losing Lauren

<u>D a n n y</u>

Three more days until senior year starts and the countdown to real life begins. The past few months have flown by and were filled with more pain than joy. My application for the explorer program was accepted, but I withdrew it since I'm not really sure that's the future I want anymore. Working for my dad full time isn't nearly as interesting as working for Uncle John; not to mention the money is nowhere near what I used to make, but it's an honest living. Mr. Hyde is in check ... for now. There are a few things that haven't changed. Again, I guess some things never do.

Morning light streams through the bedroom windows of the lodge, waking me from a restless night filled with demons, regrets and a certain set of green eyes that won't let me move on or be happy in what I've settled for as my new 'norm'. I stretch and twist, feeling each vein pulsating through my aching muscles. I hadn't been hiking or climbing this much in years, but this week away with my friends has given me a much needed break from the scrutinizing eyes that seem to get more intense the closer the first day of school gets. But, it's not as though I can blame my folks. Last year was hard on all of us, and the situation with Lauren... well; it helped no one, least of all me.

The bed creaks as my feet reach for the cool wooden floor to head into the bathroom to take a shower. Jackie is sleeping peacefully on her stomach with her platinum hair cascading over her bare shoulders and down her back. We've been together one month and five days; at least that's what the bright pink, heart-shaped note taped to the mirror said. I peel it off and look back at her nestled so trusting in the bed I just slid out of. One month ... five days, and in three more days, she'll join me at Mountain View High School since her parents decided to move to our city last month. The first time Lauren sees us the masquerade will be over. I haven't spoken to her since the birthday party after I decided walking away was better than tearing her apart. And while Jackie is entertaining in her own way, she's not Lauren and she'll never have my heart. Mostly because I never got it back nor have I given up on my own sappy fairy-tale ending ... but that seldom happens for the jerks in most stories. I realize I was too intense with my feelings for Lauren, but the fact is, the moment I met her I dreamed I could have better and be more than what I had settled for. The problem is, now that I have more of a life than ever, I'm not sure I want it because it's not what I had envisioned.

"Hey sunshine," Jackie whispers and wraps her velvet arms around me in the shower. "You're up awfully early," she purrs with a hint of excitement and frustration in her tone.

"Sorry, once the sun comes through the window, I'm toast." I can't tell her that dreams of what happened at the party are haunting me. Mrs. McIntosh promised me Lauren was ok after the fight at her birthday party, but I won't truly believe it until I see her myself. I tried to see Lauren at the hospital, but her dad had me thrown out by security. I guess he drew the line in the sand and he's daring me to cross it. I know he can control her at home, but he can't control her day at school. Hopefully, she'll at least talk to me. Maybe then I can move on, although that's not what I really want. I really want Josh and his stupid games to be a thing of the past. But Lauren has had all summer with him and they've probably just gotten closer like they did when I was in rehab. I know I've made some bad decisions, but that one was probably my worst, even though it was for her.

"Hmmm ... what's the plan for today?" Jackie asks seductively, oblivious to the battle going on in my mind as she runs her hands down my chest, and then pulls my body tight to hers. Less than one week and I'll have to come to terms with a few things: technically I've *moved on* with Jackie; Lauren is probably still head over heels for Josh; and my future is dancing in the unknown.

"I promised Jeremy and Evan I'd do one more climb before we

leave tomorrow morning." She looks at me disappointed and it doesn't kill me like I know it should if I had real feelings for her. I feel guilty, so I offer, "we can go swimming and out to dinner later."

"Okay. Sara, Vanessa and I will hang out while you guys go." She pouts. "But I don't think it's fair that you brought all of us up here and keep ditching us. Doesn't Vanessa mind that Jeremy hasn't spent a lot of time with her?" The reason for his absence is apparent: Vanessa isn't Jenn and Jeremy can't wait to get back and steal her away from Mike. Jess and Sara need to stop meddling; they are setting up their friends with emotionally unavailable guys. Then again, we keep falling for the same emotionally unavailable girls ... so I guess it's fair.

Jackie is head over heels in love and totally devoted to me. I wish I could say I return those feelings, but honestly- she's just another step on the nameless-rehabilitation plan that Dad, Bev and Sara want me to follow. It's only because of Sara that she's been around as long as she has. Sad to say, but it's the truth. She's taken my mind off Lauren, but only temporarily. Monday morning will come soon, starting the merry-go-round all over again. Jackie will probably fall off once she realizes how tainted I am by my feelings for Lauren and my criminal past, both of which I've failed to disclose to her. She'll hear the rumors and find out soon enough about all my previous transgressions. Maybe she'll run away from me like Lauren did. That would be for the best, but it'd be my luck she'd run to Josh Miller too. Jerk.

"Do you promise to take me to dinner tonight? I don't like how you bailed last night." Jackie wraps a plush white towel around her after we've finished our shower. "I mean, why can't you just talk to me? I don't understand why you get all moody like that and close me off . . ." she continues, but I have no idea what she's saying. Her lips are moving but it's more like *blah blah blah.* I continue to dry off, barely even glancing at her.

"I hate when you do that," she says and storms out the door, referring to the fact that I don't hide when I'm tuning her out. I don't know what she's so upset about; our relationship hasn't been anything more than what it is right now. She has set her expectations too high. We haven't had a real date in the time we've been together and the first time we had sex, I slipped and called her Lauren and then convinced her she was hearing things.

Our relationship is pretty much the only reason her family moved to Mountain View. They had a great house and lived in a great town before, but she threw a fit and her parents gave in. She has too much control in the family being the overachieving, self-indulged, only child. She has always gotten everything she's ever wanted, all the way down to her brand new BMW, pampered AKC teacup Pomeranian (that annoys the hell out of me), full ride to the Ivy League college of her choice and designer clothes. She'll fit right in with Mountain View's social elite—after we break up, which, I'm expecting, will be on day one.

Some things never change and some things… well… they only get worse.

L a u r e n

Things definitely got *intense* after my party. Luckily, I just had a few cuts on my arms and back and some bruising on my ribs from trying to save Danny from Josh and Mike.

I know that was a big mistake now, but my mom says hindsight is always 20/20. Plus, my parents felt it necessary to blame one of the boys for ruining the party and starting the fight, but they couldn't agree which one was more at fault, so both boys were off limits for the *entire* summer. Needless to say, I'm looking forward to school tomorrow—back to my life and freedom from the confines of my overbearing, completely heinous parents.

On the upside, most of my girlfriends weren't off limits. Surprisingly, Jenn, Mandi, Jamie and I got really close over summer, as the events at my birthday party bonded us together in sort of a sisterhood. Whatever or however it happened, it just felt good to finally belong somewhere and have a life of my own and not to be trapped living in the shadow of my brother or sister.

We spent the summer going to the beach, the mall, and to the movies and stayed over at each other's house. More impressively, when it was time for school shopping, my mom let me go with my friends instead of her tagging along and inspecting everything I picked out or making me try everything on. Ultimately, she didn't like everything I bought, but most got her finicky seal of approval. I'd like to think she's finally lightening up a bit—but I know that's too much to ask for. My parents still have a small town mentality even though we don't live that life anymore.

Josh and I...well... we are *technically* still together; after I begged him to forgive me and swore I'd never even *think* of Danny again. Josh and I haven't seen much of each other over summer, but we did sneak talks on the phone and emailed each other at least once a day. He spent the entire summer helping my dad run the high school's football camp for the freshman class. I tagged along a few times to cheer him on—under my dad's watchful eye—without Mom's knowledge since she was at work. Devious, I know. But a girl's got to do what a girl's got to do. I don't want to lose everything I worked so hard for last year.

Unfortunately, neither Jenn nor I made the cheer squad. Not surprisingly, since tryouts weren't long after my party, we couldn't remember the routine and being in front of all those people made us nervous. At least training with Mandi and Jenn helped me get into the best shape I've been in my whole life. The summer has definitely changed me—for the better—or at least I think so although mom thinks she needs to buy stock in lip-gloss and hair products since I've picked up dozens during my recent excursions to the mall. After the last trip we made, she brought up the idea that I should get a job … I think it's mostly to defray the costs because neither of my siblings, James or Lynn, worked in high school. She probably wasn't serious anyway; she really wants me to focus on getting into an Ivy League school, not working at the local burger joint, although a job might be a good idea to get me more freedom and my own car.

Things at home definitely changed after mom started working outside the home for the first time in her life. It's been a saving grace since she's focused some of her energy on something else other than fighting me about my future and trying to get me to embrace my differences. *Ugh.* She really doesn't need to point out how I'm not popular like my sister, or athletic like my brother. I know she's having a hard time embracing some of the changes going on—while others she seems perfectly okay with. I don't get adults sometimes, but at least some of the changes have been for the better. And considering all the crap that went down last year, I'll take what I can get.

Mandi calls just after 9 on Sunday morning while I'm ironing my shirt and pants for the first day of my junior year. Mom really messed with my thinking last year. I have to get back on track to what I want; not what she wants. Even though I didn't make the squad, Josh and I can still rule the school. And with only two more years to get through, I'm hopeful we can get past everything that happened with Danny and my meddling mother. I guess it really depends on whether Josh and I can get back into our routine or not. He doesn't know about the squad yet, and after all the talks we've had, he's going to be disappointed. Hopefully it won't sway his decision to stay with me after everything else that's gone wrong between us. I hope he doesn't have his heart set on marrying the head cheerleader... because that's not me.

"Hey, I just heard you didn't make the squad. Jenn said she didn't either. I'm so sorry. Crystal said she would've loved to put you guys on, but there were just others that were... better than you guys. Sorry." There's no way that Crystal really wanted us on the squad. She's the head cheerleader this year and has always been a major witch to my group of friends, including Mandi.

"Don't worry about it. I was so busy last year with Josh's games and rallies. I don't think I could've fit cheer in too. It's no big deal." Josh may feel differently, but I would never admit that to Mandi. I don't want her to know there might be problems between Josh and I; telling Mandi would be like telling the whole school.

Jenn is concerned that Mike will be upset too, so we decided telling them in person would be best. I guess it never dawned on us that they were on the football team and people talk. Dad already knows, but Mom doesn't—I didn't really want to hear her gloat about it. She never wanted me chasing the cheerleading dream as she or Lynn did. Instead, it has always been about me "having more opportunities" than they did. Whatever.

"At least Josh is cool about it. He says hi and he'll miss you today."

My brain scrambles. "Wait. What? Josh already knows? What's going on today?"

"Yeah, Mark and Ben both already knew because Jamie told them. Ben told Josh and Mike." Ah—the high school super highway. It's my luck our failure was someone's status update.

"We're going to the beach today, wish you could go." Somehow, I don't believe her. It's no secret; if Josh is included that means I can't go. As it is, if mom knew dad let me see Josh over summer, she'd be pissed and it would spark another week-long argument.

"Well, I hope you guys have fun," I mumble and twist the cord of the iron around and around my finger until the tip turns hideously red and then purple. If the cord gets tight enough, it will cause permanent damage or my fingers will fall off, giving my mother yet another cause to complain about.

"Lauren?" Mom interrupts the silence on the phone. "Who are you talking to?"

"Hi Mrs. McIntosh, it's Mandi. I was calling Lauren to offer her my condolences."

"Condolences?" mom asks with a hint of sarcasm in her voice. Dad already told her. Figures. I have zero privacy.

"Yeah, she didn't make the squad ..." Mandi stops abruptly, realizing my mom may not have known. Mandi can't keep a secret just like my dad.

Mom chimes in trying to mask the happiness in her voice. "Lauren, I'm so sorry. I know you worked so hard." Silently, she's celebrating my defeat. Witch.

"Yeah. I know." I unravel the cord around my finger as the tip turns the purply reddish color again.

"Mrs. McIntosh, Jenn, Jamie and I are going to the beach to celebrate our last day before junior year. We're going to play volleyball and have a BBQ. I was thinking that Lauren could use some cheering up. Can she go with us?" I almost drop the flaming hot iron on my foot. It misses, but it does land sizzling side down and singes the carpet. A burning plastic smell consumes the room. I yank the iron off the floor hoping the smoke isn't enough to set off the smoke detector hanging over my bathroom door.

"Is *Josh* going?" Mom asks. So much for the possibility she'd feel bad enough to let me go without worrying who would be attending.

"Ummm ..." Mandi stalls. *Say NO!* "Yeah, but a lot of the

players are going. Ben and Mark are going and a bunch of cheerleaders are going too."

Mom snickers. "I'm not sure that's a good idea. Lauren's not allowed to associate with Josh ... or Danny right now."

"Please, mom. I really want to go. I have to start school tomorrow and I haven't been able to go with everyone together," I say, as if she cares I haven't gotten to go anywhere with Josh.

"Let me talk to your dad. Mandi, she'll call you back." Then her line disconnects.

"I can't believe you just asked her," I squeal. "You're crazy."

"What? I knew you wouldn't ask her yourself and you never know what she'd say. Besides, we are all back at school tomorrow and don't you want to see Josh before then?"

"Yeah," I say because Mandi has no idea that I really want to see Josh to solidify that tomorrow will go as I plan. It may be silly, but I need that reassurance. I need to see him, to look into his eyes and see our future again. Not this strange half-girlfriend, half-buddy kind of relationship that we've had since my party. I just need him to look at me as he used to and tell me he loves me. That's all.

"Lauren?" Mom pokes her head in my door.

"Mandi, I gotta go. I'll call you back."

Three hours later—and after a boat load of begging—Jenn, Mike and I climb out of Mike's very tall and very messy Chevy Truck. A truck that reminds me of a certain person that will remain nameless, except there are huge football stickers plastered all over the back and a huge push bar across the front.

"You made it," Jamie squeals as she runs across the parking lot to us. The breeze is gently wafting off the ocean and the smell of bonfires and seaweed is soaking into my skin. It was worth leaving Illinois, my friends, and our family, just for the experience of smelling the ocean and feeling the sand between my toes. There is seriously nothing that compares ... except maybe love. And that was worth leaving Illinois for, too, because there would've been no way I would've gotten a jock to date me back home. They were all too friendly with James. Here though, they are my friends, not James's. In fact, I'd like to think that Lynn and James would be the outsiders here ... not the other way around.

Mike pulls the two ice chests from the bed of his truck. He picks up the heavier one and heads towards our group of friends on the beach. Jenn and I pull off our tanks to reveal our newly toned cheerleader wanna-be bodies; thankfully I finally got out of my training bra. I can't wait to show off my new deep purple string bikini to Josh. Speaking of, I thought he'd be at the truck the moment we pulled up, but he's not with any of the people around the picnic tables. His brothers are tossing a football with Mark and Ben. Some of the boys from football camp are playing Frisbee. But, I don't see Josh anywhere.

Jenn, Jamie, Mandi and I set up lawn chairs close to the water. The water looks perfect lapping against the shore with the sun gleaming off the surface, but I refuse to get in until Josh can see me with my hair, make-up, and bikini looking perfect.

Jenn and I are laughing and talking to Mandi when a couple in the waves down the shoreline catch our attention. The sun perfectly shadows their bodies as they play in the surf. The girl laughs several times and dunks the boy. I can't wait until Josh comes. The first thing I'm going to do is run into his arms, play in the waves, and make him hold me as close as that guy is holding his girl. They look like two perfect shadows becoming one.

"I wonder where Josh is," I think out loud feeling a little jealous and anxious that he is wasting what precious little time we have left in the day.

"Do you want to get into the water?" Mark asks when Ben comes to coax Jamie out of her perfect spot for tanning.

"No, I want to wait to get in until Josh gets here." I smooth back a piece of flyaway hair. Ben yanks Jamie out of her chair and throws her over his shoulder to head to the water. We laugh and hoot as she screams and he runs down the beach with her arms and hair flailing everywhere.

"Are you sure?"Mark asks again, watching Ben and Jamie go.

"Definitely not,."I laugh. "Especially like that,."I point to Ben tossing Jamie into the water.

"Okay then."After a few minutes of silence, he takes off down the beach to play Frisbee. Maybe I should've told him yes—at least then I wouldn't be sitting here acting like a manic girlfriend wondering where the hell Josh is. It's not like we've gotten to come to the beach together everyday this summer. You'd think that my presence would be of some importance.

"So, you and Josh didn't get any of the same electives this year huh?"Jenn pulls out bottles of water from the ice chest and hands me one. "You got drama and choir with Jamie though?"

"Yeah, isn't that cool? Jamie was in choir last year and she said she had a lot of fun. Josh really wanted to take shop and he gets to TA for my dad fifth period then sixth is football. He basically gets to spend half his day at the field."I try to keep the conversation going while scanning up and down the beach. Jenn knows what I'm doing, but she doesn't seem to mind since Mike pretty much ditched her the second we got here.

"Mike does too, but he isn't assisting any of the coaches. He said ..."The couple playing in the waves start running our way and my eyes lock straight on them. Jenn turns to see what I'm wide eyed about. I use the palm of my hand to block some of the sun from my eyes because it seems they are deceiving me as the couple comes closer. "Is that...," Jenn starts to say.

My breakfast threatens to invade my mouth as my stomach does back flips. "Josh?" I whisper. As he gets closer, we see that his arm is wrapped around the scantily clad, well defined, and *very* well endowed, Crystal Thomas—head cheerleader—and aka total bitch to Jenn and I.

Their sides are touching and her arms are thrown around his neck pulling him sideways towards her. Her humungous breasts are practically popping out of her two sizes too small push-up bikini. My face has to show every ounce of jealousy and heartbreak that is rushing through my body and the fact that I'm dangerously close to blowing chunks all over my new bikini and Jenn's fresh pedicure.

The second Josh locks eyes with mine his face goes from being happy to a strange dull look, to shear panic. "Hey, Lauren…" Josh pushes Crystal's side away from him, "what are you doing here?"

"Maybe I should ask you the same thing." I glare at Crystal as she swings her hips past me, making the jewels dangling from her bikini strings shake like hypnotic beads waiting to suck in every teenage boy within a ten mile radius.

"What are you implying?" he asks with a slight eye roll that makes me want to smack the slight smirk off of his face. "We were just playing in the water. Nothing else."

"That's not what it looked like." I bend over and pick up my tank top and snatch the towel from the back of my chair. I look good, but nowhere near Crystal's league and there's no way I'm staying now that one of my worst fears have been realized. Josh wants the head cheerleader… not the wanna-be with the tenth of her body.

"She's like my sister. Besides, you were the one that cheated, not me remember?" He glares down hard at me as if he is giving me an unspoken ultimatum to drop the issue. Jenn and Mandi pick up their drinks and head towards the picnic tables leaving me to fend for myself in the argument that's been threatening to come to the surface all summer. I'm not sure I'll get through tomorrow if this doesn't go my way.

<u>D a n n y</u>

This year has to be better than last. At least I'm back on track after taking summer school with Mr. Claymore, the Theater Tech teacher, and Ms. Nelson, the Drama teacher. Well, that and the extra credit units I'm getting for taking Advanced Drama and Advanced Theater Tech this year. No, I'm not excited about having to spend so much time after school for the plays, but I'll be in charge of the set building crew since Ms. Nelson appreciated all the hard work I did for her over summer. Just ten short months to go and I'll have my diploma and be done with Mountain View ... for good.

Sara and Jackie jump from my truck in the school parking lot. Jackie really wanted to drive her BMW today but I refused ride with her, so she parked her car at our place and rode with us. She should've driven her own car, considering the fact that she probably won't want to ride home with us after what she finds out about me today.

Alexis and Justin pull into the space next to us. If you ask me, that's not a relationship I thought would last, but six months later they are still happy.

"Hey guys!" Alexis calls out to Sara and Jackie. Alexis hates Jackie, but she puts up with her because of Sara and I. "How was the rest of the week at the lodge?" The girls start talking and giggling about hiking and shopping. I tune them out just as I did most of last week. I'm barely participating in my own life anymore. Zombies? Yes—they exist in senior high school guys that don't want to put up with their cackling sisters or girlfriends. My previous life may have been made up of a lot of illegal activity, but at least it was ... entertaining.

"Hey." Justin and I walk towards campus, just in time to see

Josh Miller pull into his usual parking spot, sans Lauren, and my heart skips more than a few beats. Maybe they've broken up. Maybe she's ready to start over. Maybe she finally realizes she should've chosen me all along ... or maybe I'm just getting ahead of myself again. Old habits are hard to break. "You okay?" Justin asks pulling my attention back to him and the out of control thoughts in my head. Sometimes even I don't know when to let things go or to give up. I hate giving up—especially when my gut points me in a certain direction.

"Yeah, I'm good."

"You look good man. Have you seen Brandon?"

"Nope, not since he decided not to go to rehab."

"That sucks. I thought he was getting things in order for ..." He stops abruptly and looks at Sara. He's thinking that Brandon would get clean for her like I did for Lauren—a lot of good that did me, though. I guess I can't be bitter; technically my life has never been better than it is right now. I have a roof over my head, my family's support and a good job and I'm on my track to graduate. There are really only a few things that can make it any better.

"Obviously, she wasn't as important to him as, well, you know." Jenn pulls into the parking lot in the new Honda her parents bought her. Jeremy is already talking about ways to steal her away from her football-moron boyfriend, Mike, but he hasn't broken it off with Vanessa yet and Jess is begging him not to, just like she doesn't want me to end things with Jackie. And don't get me started on Sara's point of view on the whole situation. She ate up three hours of my sleep time last night chiding me on the importance of senior year, perceptions and most of all, how to avoid Josh and Lauren. If Lauren made cheerleader, and Josh is the captain of the football team, they are going to be Mountain View's golden couple this year and practically untouchable. But, have I ever said I didn't like a challenge?

Mike pulls his pile of crap truck into the parking space next to Josh; Mark's Jeep and Ben's Ford pull in shortly after. We all grew up together and lived only a few blocks apart for most of our lives.

Mark, Josh, Ben and I used to be the best of friends but Josh ruined all of that the day he destroyed my sister and her reputation.

"Danny?" Sara clenches my hand and yanks hard on my arm towards school. It doesn't take long to see the reason for her new found urgency. Lauren's lean body is uncurling from the backseat of Mandi's BMW. Her dark hair is sun-kissed like her skin. Her form fitting tank top shows fresh bikini lines encircling her perfect neck. Powdery pink lip-gloss accentuates the heart shaped pout of her lips. She looks like Barbie's brunette best friend—fake and plastic and in need of a serious dose of paint thinner to get the caked on make-up off. Two things are for sure: she made the squad since Mandi drove her today and she's still with Josh. Neither is good news and I really want to wrap my fingers around those perfectly bronzed shoulders and shake some sense into her.

"Danny, no..." Sara grinds her teeth and yanks again.

"What's up?" Jackie's overwhelming perfume brings me back to reality. I've made a commitment to her and the thoughts that just raced through my mind about kissing Lauren's perfectly pouty lips, well, they are wrong and out of line and I need to get control of them if I'm going to make it through this year. I may not like the path that I'm on—but it's my path and my future and I need to take control of it.

My hands start shaking as I walk into the theater for Drama class. This class is the only thing standing between me and a much needed forty-five minute break. You would think after a summer vacation that the rumors from Lauren's party would be old news, but it seems that wound hasn't healed and someone felt it necessary to pick off the scab just to flick it in my face. In every class there has been at least two or three students mumbling and pointing at me. The old me would've yanked them out of their seat and pounded them to a pulp—but it's a new year and I'm trying to turn my shoulder to the haters instead of beating them within inches of their life. However, today I'd really choose the latter if I could.

Luckily, Ms. Nelson isn't mad that I'm a few minutes late and I'm thankful Alexis saved me a seat. At least I'd have one person on my side in the class, or at least I thought she was on my side, until I realize she sat us directly behind Lauren.

What the hell is she thinking?

"Hey," I say to Alexis and lock eyes with Lauren. I can't do it. I look at Ms. Nelson to save me and start the class. I hadn't seen Lauren all morning, and now, she is in my class. So close that I can touch her, smell her; but I can't do either. So I just nod, giving her a confident, cocky smirk, betraying the three-ring circus in my stomach that's making me want to skip lunch all together. This is going to be the longest class in the history of high school.

By the end of class, I've stolen more glances at her than necessary and the same soft vanilla scent she had last year has brought back memories that I haven't allowed myself to indulge in. Thankfully, Ms. Nelson didn't put the two of us in the same improv group, but being in the same class with her is going to be agonizing. It's like my own personal prison and she's both the guard and warden.

The first play of the year is in October, so auditions are this Saturday. Every student has to attend to get credit for the class. Then again, I have to audition anyway since being in the play means more elective units towards graduation and guarantees me a spot in the set design group—right now I wish this wasn't the only class available that would help me make up the fifteen units I'm missing to graduate. I'd rather cut off my right arm at this point, but the school won't see that as penance.

When the bell rings, I'm thankful it's over. Lauren and Jamie practically fall over each other trying to get out of the theater seats and rush up the walkway to escape the theater doors. Lauren didn't utter one word to me. In fact, the two times she did look at me I could've sworn she was going to burst into tears. Not exactly what I wanted or expected out of my first day of senior year. There's only one thing that could make today anymore depressing.

"Hey sexy." Josh has his hands all over Lauren as I walk out of the theater doors. At least I have the satisfaction of having one class with her, but the look he gives me says everything from her party isn't water under the bridge. It's a can of worms just waiting to be ripped open.

Just as I'm about to pull out my can opener, Jackie intercepts me, wrapping her long, lean arms around my stomach and jumping into my unsuspecting arms. Not exactly what I want Lauren to see. Even though she's hurt me, I don't want to return the favor.

L a u r e n

Josh, Ben and Mark are waiting for us outside the theater. I wish they hadn't decided to meet us at our classes. The smiles they have diminish the minute Danny comes out of the doors behind us. I knew Josh wouldn't like this, especially after the promise I made him.

"Is he in drama with you?" Josh asks wrapping his arm around my back.

"Yeah." I pull him to me, trying to distract him from the nasty thoughts I'm sure he's having.

"I want you to stay the hell away from him. You promised," Josh says through gritted teeth.

"I know." I want to tell him to stay the hell away from Crystal since he is throwing out ultimatums, but I don't. I'm walking on eggshells to keep him happy right now. I just want things to get back to the way they were before Danny. I'll do anything to get there with Josh again. I want him to trust me and to look at me the way he did before we had all the drama. I just want to fully feel his love and attention again and I don't know if that will ever happen... at least not while Danny's around.

Josh pulls me away from the theater, like a child being pulled away from a toy store. I can't help myself. I look back at Danny just in time to see a blonde girl jump into his arms. Sara is clapping and laughing next to them. Danny looks at the girl as though she were a rare flower: delicate and irreplaceable. Maybe this year will be easier since he's moved on. I look back again, and damn it if Sara isn't staring straight at me. My feet skip a few steps and Josh tightens his hand on mine and tugs.

"What's wrong with you?" he asks, clearly annoyed.

"Nothing," I mutter and refuse to look back again. The past is past and I need to focus on my priorities—not on Danny.

We claim our regular place in the quad and immerse ourselves amongst the other football players and their girlfriends. Josh goes straight to Mike and Jenn sits next to me on the table. She pulls out celery and carrot sticks for us to share and that blonde in Danny's arms won't get out of my mind. She looked similar to the girl at Jess's house. It can't be the same girl, can it? I shake my head trying to get the thoughts to stop coming in waves. It seems the more I try not to think of him, the more I do and I won't be able to get through the year if this keeps up.

"I can't believe..." Jenn says and then stops when Mike comes to grab his sandwich out of her bag. "Jamie said Danny is in your drama class. Can you believe he's hanging out in the quad?" What? I hadn't seen him, but as soon as I look outside our group, sure enough, there he sits ...staring at me.

"What's wrong?" Josh asks, pushing his hips in between my knees.

"I'm just sad we don't have any classes together," I lie and wrap my arms around his neck trying to be as convincing as possible. That promise I made to stay away from Danny is going to be harder than I thought.

"Don't worry! I'll talk to your dad about getting to come to practices and hopefully your mom will let me start coming over to your place. Any word on getting your license?" Josh leans into me and rests his hands on my legs.

"I took the classes over summer, but mom hasn't made the appointment yet. Besides, I don't really think they are going to get me a car. I'll have to get a job and . . ."

"Dude, did you see that?" Mike slaps Josh on the back and our conversation is over. After the beach yesterday, we've barely talked. He claimed Crystal is the sister he never had. I guess she is like this BFF that I never knew about. They live on the same block, went to the same daycare, preschool, elementary school and junior high. Why I never heard of this friendship before yesterday is beyond me. But I'm determined not to rock the boat. Next year, Josh will be at college and risking making him mad now would be stupid, juvenile, and my jealousy coming out over nothing. If either of us should be jealous, it should be he after all the confusion Danny brought on last year. I'm surprised Josh even stayed with me.

The bell rings and everyone scatters to their classes, including Josh, without saying goodbye. It stings a little, but I know he's got a lot on his mind.

"Hey, how have you been?" I jump when Sara starts talking to me at my locker. I hadn't talked to her at all over summer, so to say I'm surprised she's standing just a few feet from me is an understatement.

"I'm good. How have you been?"

"I'm good." There's a brief silence that feels more like hours. "So, you're still with Josh?" Sara disapproves, but so does Danny, I'm sure.

"Yup." I pull out my afternoon books and toss my morning ones carelessly into my locker.

"The fight, them hitting you, none of it made any difference to you? You still don't realize what he's like?"

"No. He's not like that anymore." A lie, but there's certainly no way I'm talking to her about it. "We are fully committed to each other. We are working things out." Then I let my jealousy over the blonde kick in. "What does it matter? Danny seems really happy."

"He is." She folds her arms across her chest. "Jackie is a really good girl and he's never been happier. He's totally in love. She's convinced him to make an effort in school and has him right on track to graduate this year."

He's never been happier. He's totally in love.

I stumble over my words trying hard not to be resentful. "That's good. I'm really happy for him."

She steps close to me. "Doesn't it hurt to see him with someone else?"

"No, it doesn't." I reply too quickly to make it believable. So I add, "I'm really happy for him and it's good he's turned his life around."

The corners of Sara's mouth slightly turn up; she knows I lied. Her blue eyes penetrate my skin and bore into my heart for every deep, dark secret. "Well, I guess I'll see you around then." Just as quickly as she appeared, she disappears into the crowd, leaving me more than a little dumbfounded by our exchange. So much for avoiding Danny and his whole group of friends.

I want to jump for joy when the final bell rings. Jamie, Jenn and I meet Josh, Ben and Mike at our lockers after school. Unfortunately, Josh and Mike have to stay tonight for football practice. I really want to stay with him, but it already looks as though he has the weight of the world on his shoulders, so I don't dare gripe now.

"Is everything ok?" I ask and wrap my arms tight around him, trying to take any stress off of him that I can. But he shrugs out of my arms and pulls away from me. It makes me worry that my talk with Sara got back to him.

"Yeah, just stressed about practice and a few games; don't worry about it. It'll be fine," Josh says, but it seems he is trying to convince himself, because I really have no idea what he's talking about. I'm coming in on the fourth quarter with only two minutes left in the game and no time outs. It probably has something to do with the Homecoming game against Hillview, but who knows since he's not offering any further information and seems annoyed that I even asked in the first place.

"Okay," I say, sounding quiet lame, which seems to only irritate him more.

"I'll see you later." He turns and walks away without saying goodbye again. Jenn and I both stare after him and Mike. This is really not how I wanted my first day back to go.

"What is up with them?" she finally asks as we're almost at the parking lot. Danny and Sara are at the benches. Sara is nose to nose with Danny, yelling at him for something— probably over Jackie or Drama or Brandon. Maybe it's true he's hanging out at the benches again. Who knows? I can't worry about their issues with Josh acting weird.

"I don't know," I finally say after I realize she is staring at me for not answering.

"So, who was the girl he was with? Mandi said Sara came to your locker." Jenn is the only one who knows most of what happened between Danny and I. I can't lie to her about my confusion over Josh's attitude and Danny's reappearance; she'd see right through me.

"She did. Sara said her name is Jackie and she got him to focus on school and stuff."

"How hard was it having him in Drama with you?" She looks at me sympathetically.

"It was ok. I guess. I didn't expect him to be with someone already."

"It's been several months." She half laughs making me realize how dumb I sounded. Most boys wouldn't have waited a week, let alone a few months. I guess I didn't think I'd see him so... in love.

I try to shrug it off. "I know. But ... it's hard."

"Have you ever thought you made the wrong choice? I mean..." I stop her before she can justify her totally misplaced question.

"No. I never belonged with Danny."

"But ..."

"No. No buts. I'm supposed to be with Josh. I love Josh and he's my future." That's my final word on the subject. I refuse to have another repeat of last year. Plus, I need her to support my relationship with Josh, not to encourage one with the enemy. I decided to turn her question around to show her how crazy she sounds. "What about you? Have you ever thought you weren't supposed to be with Mike?"

"No. Why would you ask that?"

"Because sometimes it's just easier to point the finger at someone else," I say realizing she didn't get my point at all.

"Speak for yourself." We both look back at Danny and Sara, still arguing at the benches.

"I'll see you later." I leave Jenn standing there and head to Mandi's BMW. I managed not to talk to Danny all day, even after he was in my class and at the quad with us. Without a doubt, I wouldn't start now.

"How was your first day?" Mom asks, setting the table for dinner. We would be on our own again for dinner tonight since Dad was at the school.

"It was good. A little confusing. I have play auditions this weekend and I have to put in two hours a week after school for choir."

"That seems like an awful lot for electives. What about fees for costumes or anything? Do we need to pay anything now?"

"Yea," I dig into my book bag. "I have pamphlets. We have to rent two outfits. Ms. Anya said they went with a cheaper company this year to keep students from dropping out of choir."

"Did anything else happen today?" she asks with her back to me. It's obvious what she is getting at.

"Well, if you are referring to Danny, he's in my drama class." I lower my voice, not really wanting to tell her the rest, because I'm not okay with it yet.

"Oh really? Did you tell him hi and ask him how he's been doing?" Mom turns and stares me down, ready to detect any lie I plan on feeding her. So I tell the truth.

"No, he was busy with his new girlfriend." Involuntarily, my lip pouts.

"Oh, do I sense some jealousy?" The corner of her mouth sneaks into a smirk and it really annoys me.

"No, it's not that. It seems they are really happy. I'm happy for him." I am jealous and uncomfortable with the whole idea of him dating someone, but can I really expect him not to?

"Did you really think that he'd wait around for you to figure out what you wanted?" My mom half laughs, more than likely because she thinks she is right about Josh and me.

"I don't really want to talk about this."

She laughs and continues making dinner. I sulk all the way to my room, shuffling my feet the whole way. No, I didn't expect him to wait for me, but I didn't think he'd fall in love with someone else so fast. Seeing it on the first day of school... well, it sucked.

<u>D a n n y</u>

Sara caught Crystal and Josh making out next to the gym between lunch and fifth period. I'm not sure what she expects me to do with this information as we watch Jenn and Lauren heading up the sidewalk after school. Lauren stares at us, but she doesn't stop or give me any chance to call her over. She's in Mandi's car and leaves before I can even process what Sara is saying.

"What's going on?" Jackie asks walking up to us looking absolutely thrilled over her first day. She loves Mountain View. She can't believe she never knew regular high school could be this way. Sara and Alexis helped her find her classes today and at lunch she couldn't stop talking about how cool it is that we have fast food restaurants catering in our lunch room. She's not used to having anything less than a five-star chef preparing her school lunches. Who would've thought Taco Bell is a treat?

"Nothing," I grit my teeth and nudge Sara slightly away from me. If she stays in my face, Jackie will think differently. And right now, it doesn't seem as though Jackie heard even one nasty rumor about me today.

"Great, let's go to Vince's. This girl I met today invited us."

We pull into Vince's parking lot and my truck sticks out like a sore thumb next to all the BMW's and Acura's. It never really dawned on me that the benches kids hang out at DJ's, so the quad ones go to Vince's.

"Uh- I don't know about this." Mandi's BMW is in the parking lot and considering I saw her pull out of the lot with Lauren after school...

"Come on. It'll be fun," Jackie says pulling me towards the door. I give Sara a fearful look. She knows what I'm thinking when her eyes lock onto Mandi's car.

The entire corner of the restaurant is full of teenage girls in blue and gray cheerleader outfits. Surprisingly, none of them is Lauren. Mandi, Melinda, Crystal and her best friend Lindsay are laughing at one of the end tables.

"Hey girl! Come sit with us!" Tammy, one of the cheerleaders calls out to Jackie, until she realizes Jackie's with me. "Uh…" Everyone at the table stops breathing. Most of these girls used to be Sara's friends, before she went to the dark side with piercings and multi-colored hair.

"Jackie…" I yank back on her arm. "We can't go over there." It annoys me that Jackie doesn't know Sara's past either. She just expects us to go over there and sit with these girls that turned their back on Sara when she needed them most. I won't stand for it. I'm not sitting with them and we aren't staying much longer. Maybe long enough to get a pizza and then we are out of here.

"It's fine. I'll introduce you." Jackie gives me a wide smile. She's completely oblivious to the fact that Sara's already inching towards the door.

"No, it's not." I pull my hand from hers.

"This isn't fair. We always hang out with the people you want to and go to the places you want to go. But you can't just hang out for a few minutes with my friends?"

"I guarantee those people aren't your friends."

"You're being ridiculous," she quips and folds her arms across her chest. Sara has already exited Vince's. Jackie turns and heads to the tables. I go to the counter, weighing my options. Sara is standing next to my truck with her back to me. I unlock the door with the remote so that she can climb in.

"Could I have a supreme?" I ask the cashier and look at Sara sitting alone in the backseat of the truck. "To go." I wait at the counter and look at Jackie laughing with the cheerleaders and their wannabe's. I wonder if Melinda will tell Jackie she's slept with me. I'm not sure that she will though, since that would hurt her precious reputation.

"Danny?" The girl behind the counter brings up my boxed pizza.

I glance back at Jackie laughing with the other self-absorbed cheerleaders before I walk out the door leaving her. It's her fault she didn't listen to me. Not mine. She can find her own way home.

"I won again," Sara announces and bounces onto her knees on the bed. After seeing her new friend embrace all of her old ones, I decided a night of beating her big brother at monopoly was exactly what she needed.

Bev comes into my room with the phone, "Jackie's on the phone for you." She holds out the house phone. I turned my cell phone off hours ago, not willing to listen to her complain about being left at Vince's tonight. It's her own damn fault for not listening.

"Danny?" Jackie sniffles when I put the phone up to my ear.

"What do you want?" I say harsher than I intend. Sara curls up with my pillow and turns the TV to cartoons. She knows I left Jackie at the pizza place, but she hasn't said a word about it all night and hasn't responded to any of Jackie's texts, either.

"This is not fair Danny. I'm new. I didn't know that Sara doesn't get along with them. Neither of you told me what I was getting into when I agreed to come to Mountain View."

"No one asked you to come to our school. You could've stayed at your school."

"I thought you wanted me to be with you for our senior year . . ." she pouts. I never told her that and never implied it and never intended us to stay together this long as it is. Senior year would be easier with her as a distraction, but it's really not worth it.

"Jackie, I think it's best you go back to your old school. Mountain View is not the place for you."

"What? You don't want me to be with you? With Sara? She's my best friend and I love you," she sobs. I hate when girls cry.

"Jackie, this isn't fair to any of us right now. I can't undo our history at school. I can't miraculously turn myself into the popular kid for you to date." If I could've, I certainly wouldn't do it for

Jackie.

"That's not what I want. I just want you."

"I don't think that's a good idea. You shouldn't change what you want. If you want to be popular and hang out with the cheerleaders, then more power to you."

"That's not fair Danny," she huffs. "Why can't you just tell me you love me? Why can't you tell me it'll be ok and you'll try to help me get used to being at school with you because you want me there?"

I don't tell her, because I can't. I don't truly want her at Mountain View. "I can't," I say and hang up on her.

The next morning she's at my house before I'm even done showering for school. She's sitting on my bed when I walk out in my towel. "Danny, what is going on with us? I mean, people at school are saying things about you and you were acting weird all day yesterday. Then, you leave me at Vince's and hang up on me when I try to figure out what's up." She wipes a tear from her cheek and I can't look directly at her. This isn't fair to her. I can't let this go on.

I walk back into the bathroom to start getting ready for school, but she follows me. This isn't going to happen right now. "Look, I have to get ready for school. We'll talk about this later," I say and usher her out of the bathroom door. But in true Jackie fashion, she folds her arms, sits on the bed again and pouts trying to get her way. I slide into a new pair of jeans and pull a clean shirt from my closet while she mumbles and snickers behind me. What she's saying really doesn't matter because she's irritating me more than anything right now. If she weren't a girl, I'd throw her out of my room, down the stairs and out the front door. But, I can't do that. Even raising my voice will make her cry. Mr. Hyde has to stay in check right now. She may have heard the rumors about him, but she can't come face to face with him first hand.

"Look, I can't change anything I've done. Nor can I do anything about what the jerks at school say about me. Sara and I both warned you about coming to Mountain View."

She sighs, "I thought you guys really wanted me to come; you just didn't want to ask me."

"No, I usually say exactly what I mean."

Jackie pushes her curls off her shoulders and straightens, "tell me you love me then."

I turn, not willing to lie to her. I've never told her I love her. *Ever.* "I can't tell you that."

"Why not?" she pleas.

"Because that's not a word you just throw around. We've only been together a month. And I told you when we started dating that we were going to take it slow. I'm not interested in all this right now."

"You're not interested in talking or you're not interested in me?"

"I need to stay focused on school, Jackie. I can't keep fighting with you over things like this."

"We fight because you don't talk to me." She stands from the bed and grabs my hand before I can reach for the knob. If we continue to argue, we will be late for school and that's not good as the year has only just begun.

"Look, we have to get going. Let's just get through this week and we'll talk about things this weekend."

"Okay," Jackie purrs and pulls at my arms until they are wrapped around her back and her Eau de Toilette is stinging my nose and eyes. She sees this as a victory, but it's not. It's just prolonging the inevitable.

"Come on." I yank back and pull the door open, thankful to have dodged this bullet for now, but I know this is a conversation we are going to have soon.

L a u r e n

Jamie's mom drops us off on Saturday morning for the play tryouts. I'm not feeling very well today, and seeing Danny's truck in the parking lot makes it that much worse. Josh is already mad that I missed all of his practices this week because of choir; if he knew that Danny came today, it would be an all out war. I grip my playbook tight to my chest and squeeze Jamie's hand in mine as I walk towards the theater. The play is something Ms. Nelson wrote about a teenage love triangle between two boys and a girl trapped in the middle... talk about irony! All I want is to get the credit for showing up for the tryouts, and if I end up with a part, hopefully it's a tree or a bush.

"Wow. I can't believe he showed," Jamie says pointing to Danny's truck. Now I wish Jenn came with us; she'd be a little more tactful.

"Yeah," I say and keep pulling at her arm to get this over with: the sooner, the better.

Jamie and I settle into our regular spots and more students, some in drama, some not, start filling in the seats around us. Danny, Sara, Jackie, Alexis and a few others are sitting across the aisle and in several rows back from us. Sara and I lock eyes and I look away before my face betrays me and shows her exactly what I'm thinking. Hopefully Ms. Nelson won't call on me to actually audition, but I highly doubt I could be that lucky.

"Okay everyone. I'm assuming you've each done your homework and reviewed the playbooks?" She waives one in the air, "as you know, Julia is our lead female who is dating Michael but she's in love with Joseph and the story goes on from there. Now, I want each of you to put everything you can into these parts and read the lines as if it is really your life." That's not such a long shot from me, but there is no way I'm going to play Julia.

The teacher obviously doesn't agree with me. "Mrs. McIntosh, will you grace the stage for Julia? Mr. Jones, please come and read for Michael. And that leaves Joseph, the love of Julia's life. Who can we get to play him?" Several male students raise their hands and I glance at Danny as I climb the stairs to the hangman's noose. Just as I think I'm safe, "Mr. Cummings, please join us on stage and show us your version of Joseph." *Crap.*

"Okay. So this is act three, scene two. Julia finally admits her love for Joseph and Michael interrupts them. Got it? It is on page 75. Do you all have it? Remember to read from your heart. Imagine this is you; this is the love of your life standing in front of you and you've finally realized it and you are relieved and regretful all at the same time." I shake my head; this is ridiculous. I already feel the crimson taking over my face. My legs and arms won't cooperate and getting my lips to utter a word is practically impossible.

"Lauren? Your line is first." The teacher motions for me to read the lines.

I glance towards her and the dozens of students in the auditorium. Danny is sharing the spotlight with me, staring at me, and the urge to run away twitches my feet. Tremors spread through my body like personal earthquakes and my eyes start to betray me with moisture building in the corners. I clench my jaw trying to stop the nervous breakdown that's coming on. I've practically read the full play and it hits entirely too close to home. Now, I have to face my regrets head on—something I never planned on doing in a million years and it feels as if spontaneous combustion is totally a viable option.

Danny raises his eyebrow and looks towards the playbook. I slowly read, "I'm sorry that this has happened. I wish I had..." I stutter, swallow hard and look at Danny. I wish the teacher hadn't picked this scene; it mirrors our life. My heart is going to burst out of my chest if I don't get out of doing this stupid play. He motions to keep going, "I wish I had realized sooner how much I *loved* you," my voice cracks, "I'm so sorry for the heartache I have caused you. I'm afraid that it's too… late for us." My voice is trembling and my knees are shaking . . . all these people are about to see me pass out. Ms. Nelson is leaning on the stage taking in the spectacle, oblivious to the fact she'll have to call the paramedics soon. My voice gets quieter as I read the lines, trying hard not to burst into tears from the pressure, but a lone tear escapes and rolls down my cheek. Thankfully, only Danny can see it, but that's bad enough.

Danny doesn't look at the playbook as he starts talking, "You know that I love you more than life itself. I would let you hurt me every day for the rest of our lives if that is what you want." Danny's voice is calm and smooth, unlike mine; and weird . . . it's weird, being so close to him after being away for so long. He doesn't take his eyes off me as he continues with unrelenting confidence, "I'm sorry that I have allowed you to be torn apart. I wish I could take back every nasty thing that I've said to Michael and let you take the time to figure things out for yourself." Danny steps closer to me and takes my hand easily in his. His fingers feel rough—but gentle—clasped around mine. Lost in his eyes, I wonder if these lines are even in the script, but Ms. Nelson hasn't stopped him yet, so I have to assume they are. Danny seems so at home on stage and when I look deep into his eyes I see no sign of fear and no terror like I'm feeling.

Christian interrupts our stare with Michael's lines, "I can't believe you've done this! How dare you choose that loser over me!" There is a long pause. My hand is sweating and shaky in Danny's, but his thumb is slow and comforting as it rubs back and forth on my palm bringing back the memories of being at Jess's house and waking up so close to him.

"Lauren… it's your line…" Ms. Nelson says impatiently; her

head is cradled in her hands as she stares at us from the edge of the stage.

I look at her briefly, "oh- I'm sorry." I take my hand back from Danny and fumble with the playbook to find my place in the scene. I almost forgot we had an audience until I could hear someone shifting in their chair. "Michael, you don't understand. I tried to love you, but it just wasn't right. I have a deeper love with Joseph than I can ever have with you. I'm so sorry." These words come easier as my heart finally slows and air makes its way back to my lungs. Danny did it again; he calmed me down and single-handedly stopped a panic attack. *Damn him.*

Danny starts again, "Michael, neither of us meant to hurt you. Just accept that she has made her choice. She *loves* me." His lip curls uncomfortably over the word *love*. Admittedly, it's hard to hear a word like that coming from his mouth.

"I'll never accept that! She doesn't love you. You've confused her and played upon her weaknesses. She will see through your lies soon enough!" Christian says the words with so much emphasis that it's as if he's screaming into the audience. The crowd laughs, but neither Danny nor I move.

It's my turn again and the words come easier, "I don't know how I let it get this far, but I know what I want now, and it's not you." Reluctantly, I turn and look at Christian as he storms melodramatically off the stage. When I look back to Danny, his swimming pool blue eyes hypnotize me; it feels as though I could drown in them as he comes closer.

"I'm sorry for the pain I've caused you with my confusion." This feels like words I really should be saying to him, but I never will. Unless I get this stupid part ... then I'll have to say them to him over and over again in front of a crowd of people for three matinees and two night performances. *Ugh. I think I'm going to be sick.*

"You have the rest of your life to make it up to me." Danny

reaches out and rests his palm on my cheek and sweeps his thumb across the trail my tear left. We stand there—locked in this stare for several moments, not wanting to move for fear my body would fall apart, one useless piece at a time. Then, without warning, a loud whistling and clapping erupts from the audience, forcing me back into reality.

Ms. Nelson brakes through the noise and I quickly take a step back from Danny. "Excellent! I'm so glad the two of you really got into these characters! You both did a great job in these roles. It was so realistic; as if you really felt the pain the characters were going through! I'm really impressed!" Ms. Nelson claps her hands. I feel frozen on the stage with his eyes still on me and the new distance between us. I can't move, or maybe I don't want to. It's too easy to be this close to him, but it shouldn't be; I'm supposed to be avoiding him like the plague.

"Go Danny!" A girl shouts from the audience making Danny look away from me and into the audience. Freed from his trance, I turn and rush down the stairs, off the stage and back to my seat next to Jamie. I slide as far down into the chair as I could as Ms. Nelson calls several more students onto the stage to embarrass them. I paid my dues; if she calls on me, I'll claim illness before I'd get up there again.

"What was that?" Jamie asks.

"I don't know..." I start to say when Ms. Nelson calls on Jamie to read for another part. I'm thankful to have missed the inquisition for now, although, I'm pretty sure the rumors of Danny and I will be rampant on Monday.

By the end of the afternoon Jamie, Danny, Sara, Jackie and all the other students had read multiple times, but I excused myself to the bathroom each time she looked for a new volunteer.

"The cast list will be hung up on the doors of the theater on Monday morning. I want to thank all of you for coming and auditioning today! You all did wonderfully." Ms. Nelson was completely clueless as to the high school drama she actually caused with her little play. I seriously hope she doesn't pick me for a part... not even a tree.

Jamie and I pick up our things and wait for the precession of students to file out of the theater. Danny stares at us when we walk past the aisle he's in. His eyes are serious and menacing again, not comforting as earlier. Jackie is glaring at me, so I examine the carpet and wait my turn to be free of the theater doors.

Jamie wants to go to the mall after the tryouts, but that doesn't interest me in the slightest, so her mom drops me back off at home. I rush through making lunch and head to my room to check my emails and get homework done, taking full advantage of mom and dad being out of the house and occupied with errands. I can't wallow in what happened at try outs, or my fear of the rumors that will get back to Josh about today. So, to save my sanity, I boot up my ancient computer and pick the crust off my sandwich. I have several emails in my inbox when I finally get onto the Internet. The first is from Jenn. I knew it wouldn't take long for the rumors to start.

Hey girl- heard you had a good time at tryouts? What happened between you and Danny? I heard the play is a modern version of Romeo & Juliet? How weird is that? Can't you just do something normal? Anyway- we are all going to dress shopping tomorrow? You in? Let me know- k?
Muay~ J

I write her back letting her know we are on for tomorrow. Homecoming game and the dance are in just a few weeks. I need to get a new pair of jeans for the rally and a dress for homecoming. I don't mention the tryouts in my response; that would have to wait until we are face to face. I mean really, how would I explain it anyway? I still don't even know what happened.

The next email is from my sister, Lynn. Her timing is always ironic.

Hey sis- how are things going with your classes this year? How did your auditions go? I broke up with Mike yesterday. He was too clingy. Anyway- Love you!

Lynn

Another boy? She's already dated more than twenty since she got to college. She's in her sophomore year and still has no idea what she wants to do when she grows up. I haven't decided what college I want to go to, let alone a career I want either, so I guess I really can't say anything.

The third email is from a sender I don't recognize. I figure it's just spam until I open it . . .

Lauren,

I figured it would be better if I emailed. I'm not sure you would talk to me even if I got you on the phone. I'm really sorry for today. I had no idea the teacher would call on me and I'm trying hard to get my act together this year. I didn't want to tell her no. Anyway- I'll try harder to stay away from you. I'm going to try to get my elective switched so that you won't feel uncomfortable. I'm sorry. If you don't respond, I'll understand.

Danny

So much for avoiding him and the whole stressful crap from the day! I read and re-read the email more than a dozen times. I don't know if I really should email him back or not. I don't want him to switch his class because of me, but it would be easier if he weren't there every day. I walk away from the computer for a while and watch some TV trying to numb my mind and quiet the voices telling me things they shouldn't. It's past ten o'clock by the time I can talk myself into attempting to email him back.

Danny,

I'm surprised you have my email. No hard feelings for today. Don't worry about it...

No. Not that. I erase the email and start again.

Danny,

How did you get my email? I didn't notice anything wrong today-what are you talking about?

Nope, that's not it either. I've tried that route with him before, and it didn't turn out so well. Maybe I'll just go with the truth.

Danny,

I'm assuming you got my email from Sara? It's no big deal if you did. I will admit that today was uncomfortable. I'm sorry if I embarrassed you. I didn't mean to start crying. You know how I am with being in the spotlight like that. Anyway, I'm not uncomfortable being in the same class with you. I was just surprised to see you. I'm glad that you are happy and that you are getting into school. I'm sure things will get easier.

L~

I hope he won't be mad at my response. I am happy for him, but I'm not that happy myself. My mom's right. Why did I think that he wouldn't start dating someone? I'm happy with my decision, but seeing Danny with Jackie has brought back painful memories from last year. I walk away from the computer; I can't look at it again for now. I distract myself by helping my mom bring in groceries from the car instead.

"You remember I'm going tomorrow with Jenn and Jamie dress shopping right?" I have to get my mind off of Danny.

"Yes, the money is in the envelope on the counter. Don't forget what I said about the dress; nothing too tight or revealing; something… tasteful." *Yea, I know.* "Your hair appointment is between the game and the dance, so you can't hang out afterwards. Don't forget…" She goes on, but I tune her out by letting my mind drift back to Danny; today definitely violated my agreement with Josh. How am I going to explain this to him?

Danny

Jackie is in my face the minute we walk out of the theater doors. Sara and Alexis are walking far ahead of us as she drones on and on about why I took Lauren's hand, touched her face, and why she seemed so upset when she left the stage. I guess the rumors over Lauren's birthday didn't get to Jackie ...yet.

"Are you going to answer me or just keep tuning me out?"

"What do you want me to tell you?" I say, looking around to see if Lauren or Jamie is in the parking lot. Sara and Alexis are almost through the fence and will see them first, I'm sure. I hope Sara behaves herself. Alexis told me that Sara went to Lauren's locker and confronted her about being with Josh still. I've told her to back off. Lauren couldn't have made any other choice after her birthday. She had to stay with Josh after what happened. I'm sure her dad has heard all the rumors about me, so there's no way he'll let me near her again. Lauren's not the type of girl who would go against their wishes or sneak around to be with me.

"I want you to talk to me." Jackie jerks at my arm. "Stop, tell me what the hell is going on. Is she an ex? Did you date her?" Her eyes beg me to say no, and that's the appropriate answer. Technically, I wouldn't be lying because we never did date. But, again, that's just a technicality and not disclosing my feelings is lying.

"We never dated, but I wanted to."

That's not what she wants to hear. Jackie's hand slips from mine, and I look longingly at Sara climbing into Alexis's car. She's abandoning me. Now I'm on my own to deal with Jackie. See if I let her beat me at monopoly again.

"So, why didn't you guys date?" She pouts and moisture forms at the corner of her eyes as she starts a conversation I don't want to have. "I mean, it's obvious from all the rumors that you've not been shy about pursuing girls in and out of school."

I straighten and step back from her. "You're right. I haven't, but again, you knew I wasn't an angel when you met me. Hell, most kids here don't even know I was in rehab last year, but you do because Sara told you."

"I don't care that you went to rehab," she growls, "I just don't like hearing that my boyfriend has slept with half the student body."

"I haven't slept with half the student body." I glance at the parking lot again, wishing Sara hadn't deserted me. This isn't a situation I'm comfortable with. Jackie is not a girl I would normally date: juvie or no juvie. She is too high maintenance, clingy and controlling.

"Look, I can't undo what I've done and if you want out, then that's cool with me. I'm not stopping you from breaking up with me and chasing the life you want."

"What? No!" She grabs my hand. "I don't want to break up. Why is that so easy for you to just toss out there? Why is that your resolution to everything?"

I step back again and release her hand, "I can't do this right now. I shouldn't have started dating. This was a mistake." It hurts to say those words, considering Lauren told me exactly the same thing in her bedroom last year when I kissed her: that kissing me was a *mistake*.

"What? A…" her lips quiver. "You can't mean that. You don't mean that. All our times together? We can't break up."

"Just because we've been together over a month doesn't mean that we are meant to be together forever." Yeah, I said it. She is not my future and this affirms it for her.

"Danny, I thought you were going to get a place next year and…"

I glare at her. "And what? You thought you were moving in with me?" She looks at me with her hopeful eyes. No, that's definitely not happening. "No, you aren't moving in with me. You are going to college next year and you'll be away from here and me."

She cries, "I don't want to be away from you. We are supposed to be together."

That's ludicrous. She doesn't even know me. "Let's go." I grab her hand and head to the parking lot.

"Are we..." she pants, "are we ov-ov-over?"

"I'm going to take you home. I won't leave you here like I did at Vince's."

Jackie cries louder. It's as if she's going through her terrible-two's and she's throwing a tantrum for a new toy. This probably works on her parents wonderfully, but right now, it's backfiring.

I open the door to the truck and help her in and then rush to my side. We drive in silence, she quietly sobbing the whole time, until we pull in front of her house. Then we sit in silence again and she doesn't climb from the truck, so I shut the engine off. If she were a nameless one, I'd tell her to get the hell out of my truck, but she's hung around too long and she's Sara's best friend. Damn it, why did I let myself get talked into this?

"Danny, I know you love me even though you won't say it. I see it in your eyes when you look at me." She brushes her polished nails down the back of my hand. "I feel it when you touch me. I was stupid today. That girl, whatever she was, she is the past now and we'll just move on. It's nothing, she's nothing, and you're with me now and I shouldn't have been jealous." It hurts when she says Lauren is nothing, because I'm sure that's what she told Josh I am. Jackie puts her fingers under my chin to make me look at her. Her mascara is smeared across her cheeks from her wiping her tears away. I pull out a napkin from the center console of the truck and hand it to her knowing that breaking up is harder on her than it will ever be on me. Losing her won't hurt me.

"Look, I'm not saying we are breaking up, but right now, I just need some time to get things straight. Last year was a hard year for me, not only in my family, but at school, too. I need to adjust to all the changes still."

"I know," she bites her bottom lip, "and I want to help you but I feel you shut me out half the time and the only real reason I'm around is because I'm a warm body."

That's not why she's around. I don't want to hurt her feelings or Sara's. And really, I'm afraid when we break up, she'll dump Sara too and that's happened one too many times already. Alexis is Sara's only other girlfriend at this point and she's not the best influence. "That's not it," I say and take my hand back from her to strangle my steering wheel again. "Can we talk about this later?"

"Sure." Jackie's eyes don't leave my white knuckles. I don't know if she sensed she's in danger, but it motivates her to reach for the door handle. "Will you call me later?"

"Yeah, whatever," I say, mainly just to get her out of my truck.

She mumbles something about how easily I run away from things, jumps from the truck and rushes towards the house. On the second step she drops her book bag and papers scatter everywhere. I don't climb from the truck to help her; that's what she gets for calling me a runner.

"So, a great big thanks for ditching me today," I say to Sara as I walk onto the patio.

"Sorry, I figured you were going to break up with her after I saw you on stage with Lauren. You are going to try to get Lauren away from Josh again, aren't you?"

"I didn't break up with Jackie. Did she tell you she planned on moving in with me when I get my apartment?" I stare her down, ready to detect even the smallest of fibs.

"Yeah, um… she mentioned it but I told her you were getting a one bedroom place and it seemed to make her even more excited. Sorry I didn't tell you." Sara's fingers twist up and down over a long piece of her purple hair. "I just didn't want to upset her because she seems so happy and she is my best friend."

"I know that." My teeth grind together. "That's why I didn't want to date her."

"Okay guys, food's ready!" Bev calls from the kitchen and starts carrying out dishes to the patio. Just a few more months and eating outside won't be feasible because of the weather. I guess I should enjoy it while we can, but when I get a place, a patio is a must.

"We'll talk about this later," I say under my breath to Sara. The last thing I need is Bev getting wind that Jackie wants to be a long term thing.

After lunch, I turn on my laptop and despite Sara's protests, I email Lauren to apologize to her and let her know I'll change classes so that she doesn't have to. Watching her shake on stage today was more than I could handle; forget the extra credit I need to graduate. I don't know if her nervousness was from being on stage or being near me, but either way, it's going to be miserable watching her fall further in love with Josh and farther away from me. Jackie is not my future, but it is obvious Lauren isn't either. I look at the apartment and house brochures on my desk and leave the computer on for a response from her, but nothing comes—not that I'm surprised. She probably won't answer anything from me, anyway.

An hour later, I've finished my homework, reorganized the desk, scanned some of the brochures and hit the refresh button on my email more than a hundred times. Who am I kidding? She hasn't even gotten my email yet; she probably went to Vince's with Josh after practice. Josh. The jerk that's getting to live the life I should've had. I guess it's my own fault anyway. The effort I made to win Lauren was too little, and too late. The four months in rehab put me behind the eight ball, not ahead of it. She still doesn't even know I went to rehab, let alone that I went so that I could have a shot with her and a future.

By nine o'clock I'm bored out of my mind and end up at Jess's place hanging out with Jeremy. By nine-thirty, I'm checking my email on my phone hoping she's read it and she's at least considering responding. I want her to talk to me. I want to ask her if she's okay and if she forgives me for ruining her party. But she still hasn't answered. I've gotten more than twenty emails and text messages from Jackie telling me how sorry she is and how she didn't mean anything she said in the truck or at the school. It's past ten by the time Lauren emails me back and it's just as rambling and indecisive as all of Jackie's have been. It makes me mad to compare the two of them. They are polar opposites, even though I thought Jackie could've been like Lauren in the beginning, and deep down, that was really the reason I started dating her. I email Lauren back almost right away.

Lauren,

I will change my class if you want me to. Just say the word. I have been doing better than I was doing. Jess says hi. I'm at her place right now. If you get a chance, you should come by and see her. Just let her know in advance so that I'll know not to be here. Anyway, see you.

Danny

As soon as I hit send, I want to take it back. The email is too laid back and doesn't really convey what I want. I thought mentioning Jess would get her talking and get her to email me back, but by midnight, she hasn't responded and it's safe to assume that bringing up Jess and her house has brought back some very bad memories for Lauren, memories that I'm sure she's more than anxious to forget. I don't blame her. The things that happened last year were disastrous for both of us.

With the news droning in the background, I put my phone on silent after clearing what has to be the eightieth text message from Jackie and get comfortable on Jess's couch. Her apartment is nice and all, but it's filled with a lot of bad memories that I'd like to forget. I'll have to find another place. I have to let everything from the past go… including Lauren. Being here reminds me of her too much.

The rambling thoughts of my future and my past keep me up past two a.m. I check my email one last time to find nothing from her. I clench the phone tight in my hand until the hinge and screen cracks and breaks apart. After I get off work tomorrow, I'll have to buy a new one. But this isn't the first time I've broken something over my green-eyed captor. She is going to drive me insane.

L a u r e n

The next morning my mom wakes me at eight. I didn't sleep well. Dreams of being on the stage with Danny haunted me. My mind kept replaying the one tear I let escape and the look on his face, his hand in mine, his touch on my face. *Damn it*. I want to scream at myself. Aren't I happy? Isn't he happy? I run down the hallway to the kitchen and grab the stack of dress magazines that mom bought and plop down at the table. I seriously need a diversion right now. I graze most of the magazines and point out a few dresses to mom while she makes breakfast. She likes a few, but hates some of the others. The one I really want is a black knee length halter dress with soft chiffon ruffles. Luckily, she gives the dress her seal of approval.

Jamie and Jenn show up just as I finish loading the dishes from breakfast into the dishwasher. The plan is to go to Glamour Girl first, but as we walk closer to the store lead starts collecting in the soles of my shoes, making it impossible to get any closer to the store. After the fiasco there last year, I don't want to jinx the dance by trying on dresses there again. None of us could really afford to buy from there anyway, so we head to the other three dress stores in the mall and avert the pending disaster of running into Sara, or worse, Danny again.

Two hours and two dress stores later, we still haven't found anything and we are starting to seriously doubt that we will. As we walk up to the final dress store, Sara and Jackie both walk out carrying dress bags. Sara smiles, but doesn't say anything. Jackie scowls and keeps walking with her nose in the air. By now, she's probably discovered my history with Danny, but thankfully he's not with her to make this moment more awkward. Plus, it would be my luck a mysterious dress would show up in my room again. *Note to self: only wear the dress that you buy today! Regardless of what Glamour Girl dress appears in your room. Damn him.*

Jenn and I try on several dresses until she finally pulls on a perfect black spaghetti strapped dress. Jamie returns to the dressing room with a crystal blue knee length halter dress that is very close to the dress I wanted. I strut from the dressing room to the floor-length mirrors. It's not my first choice of colors, but mom would approve since it's not too revealing or slutty.

As soon as I walk in the door to the house, mom is asking to see the dress and tells me to put it on as soon as she sees it on the hanger. Dad and mom both wait at the kitchen table while I rush to my room to put on the dress, shoes and earrings. Luckily, they both think the dress is suitable and mom snaps a few pictures so that I can send them to Lynn. The whole experience turns out easier than I thought it would be; usually they would pick apart my choice and criticize how I look.

I take the camera and head to the computer in less than a minute to upload the photos and connect to the Internet. I have another email from Danny. I should've known he wouldn't like the fact that I didn't respond to his email about Jess. She's always been nice to me, but it's really hard to think of being friends with her or even going to her apartment.

> *Lauren,*
> *I'm not sure you got my last email, so I'm sending you another. Do you want me to change my class? I'll be online the rest of the night. Please let me know— yes or no. Sara said she saw you dress shopping. Are you going to homecoming with Josh?*
> *Danny-*

I don't hesitate to email him back.

> *Danny,*
> *I don't want you to change your classes because of me. If you want to change your class I will be fine with that. It's up to you. Yes, I'm going with*

Josh. Are you taking Jackie?
  L.

He emails back in less than two minutes.

> *Lauren,*
> *I don't mind changing my class for you. I hope that you have a good time at the dance. Jackie talked me into it, but I don't want to ruin your night. I'll tell Jackie we aren't going.*
> *Danny*

I don't want him to do that either. That would be selfish of me and Jackie deserves to be happy and have the perfect night like I'll have with Josh. I can't let Danny not take her because of me.

> *Danny,*
> *Please don't do that. I don't want to ruin Jackie's time either. That would be very selfish of me.*
> *Lauren*

I drum my fingers on the desk. I know he's going to email me right back and I know talking to Danny is really off limits, but I can't help myself. Curiosity is killing me. Less than a minute passes and the computer dings that I have a new email.
Can I call you? This would be easier.

> *Umm ...not a good idea ... but.*
> *Ok.*

Less than a second later my phone rings. I hesitate and take several deep breaths, not sure I'm ready to have this conversation, but the alternative would be talking to him at school, so the phone is probably easier and less messy.
  "Hello?"
  "Lauren?"

"Yeah."

"Umm… it's Danny."

"I know." Ok… awkward.

"Umm… ok- so- do you want me to change my classes or not?" he says sounding impatient and slightly annoyed.

"No. I don't care if you change or not. Only change if you want to." My thoughts jumble in my head along with my words. Regardless of his annoyance, this isn't a decision he can force me to make for him.

"Lauren, please just tell me."

"Danny, I'm serious. I don't care if you want to switch or not. I don't want you to change for me." It would be easier if he changed, but the fact is Sara said he's finally on track with school, so I don't want to be the reason he gives up on his future. I don't want that on my head, too.

"Have you forgiven me yet? Does seeing me bother you?" He pauses and my heart skips a beat hearing him ask me for forgiveness. Then he asks, "do you hate me?"

Dead silence. I say nothing. I don't want to answer and now I wish we had kept this to email. "No"

"No?" he says quickly, "to which one?"

"No. I don't mind seeing you. It's just hard." I lay back on my bed staring at my ceiling and then glance at the pictures of Josh and I on my bulletin board. I'm skating too close to the edge of oblivion being on the phone with Danny, but how do you turn your back on someone you still care about? And worse, how can you care about someone that you swore you would avoid?

"Do you want me to stay in Drama?" he asks directly with the annoyance in his tone growing, and a loud tapping vibrates through the phone from his end. "I want you to tell me. I need your answer."

I pause, realizing he is basically asking me to choose again; it feels like the same crap from last year: stuck between two hard headed boys who want things their way—or no way… "I don't care," I say passively.

"Lauren," he says agitated, "just answer me damn it. I want to know if you want to be rid of me or not."

So I answer the best I can. "It would be easier if you weren't in my class, but since you still go to the same school I'm still going to see you anyway, so it won't matter."

"That is so frustrating. Can't you make up your freaking mind?" He's getting more and more aggravated with me. The phone is silent for a long time before he finally speaks again. "Do you want to see me or not?"

How can I tell him that I want to stay with Josh and I don't mind seeing him as long as it's not with a girl? How is that fair? This must be how he feels seeing me with Josh, or, at least how he used to feel.

"No, I don't mind you being in class with me. Is that enough of an answer for you?" I'm annoyed that he's backed me into a corner and made me admit that it's not *unpleasant* seeing him. In fact, if he wasn't on stage with me at tryouts, I never would've made it through them and gotten an F for the day.

"Ok then. I'll stay in the class for now. If things change, you'll tell me, right?"

"Yeah," I say without truly thinking through the implications of having to deal with Danny everyday... having him so close to smell, to touch.

"So... how are things with Josh?"

"Fine." I don't want to talk to him about Josh. In fact, I know I've made a mistake by telling Danny it was okay to stay in class with me. All I've done is complicate my life further—trying to save his feelings and holding onto hope that we could all peacefully co-exist. That's never going to happen. Ultimately, the best thing for all of us would be for Danny to switch schools, altogether.

"Have things been okay?"

"You know, I have to go. It's late and if my mom catches me on here, I'll be in trouble." He may have been nice to me during the auditions and I've told him it's okay to stay in class—but that is where our niceness needs to end. We can't be friends. All I have to do is get through this year without completely losing my mind.

"Okay... I'll see you tomorrow."

I hang up without saying goodbye. I'm sure I'll be haunted by dreams of him again tonight and I'll be dragging through my classes tomorrow. Fantastic. Hopefully he won't see this as an opportunity to make me have breakfast with him again or see that my niceness is a clue for him to try to start a relationship. Sure I'm jealous that he's with someone else, but I can't focus on that.

It feels as if I haven't slept in days. My dreams were haunted by every encounter I've ever had with Danny. You know those types of dreams that seem to be a near-death experience and your life just flashes before your eyes? Well, that's the kind of night I had. I've had another brush with death and my own personal Hades. That's what I get for trying to be nice and trying to make everyone happy.

Mom drives me to school since I'll be staying after for Josh's practice and riding home with dad. She doesn't like the idea, but she agrees since she has her own work stuff to deal with. I ask her a few questions about going to the DMV for my license, but it seems she's not even hearing me, so I turn up the radio and stare out the window. If she didn't let me get more drive time in soon, I'd forget everything I learned over summer and right now my license would come in handy for finding a job. Mandi said Vince's is hiring, but I'm not sure I want to work there considering I'd be serving all the cheerleaders instead of being one of them. Having a license would give me more freedom to get a job farther from home and farther from having to serve pizza to people I don't want to.

Josh is standing in his normal spot by the gate when we pull up. I rush to give him a kiss, but he turns to look at Mike and my lips plant firmly on his cheek instead. Mark and Ben join the three of us —and yet another football story from summer camp distracts Josh. Jenn and I stand there as they bump shoulders and slap each other's backs heading into campus.

"What is up with them? They PMS worse than us! This is

seriously getting old…" Jenn says exactly what I'm thinking.

"I have no idea. Maybe they're stressed over the game?"

"Yeah, Mike's being a real jerk about the game. He wants me to ride with him to the warm up and then wait the whole game out and let him drive me home. If I do, I won't have enough time to get ready and he says I'm not being supportive."

"Josh said the same thing. He wants me to ride with him and stay the whole time too." Which I know isn't happening, considering mom already warned me about missing my hair appointment.

The quad is a flurry of students rushing to and from lockers. A bunch of kids are in front of the theater doors and it reminds me of the stupid auditions this weekend.

"Might as well get it over with," I mumble to Jenn and head across the grass to the theater doors. It's bad enough to be in class with him; I seriously hope Ms. Nelson doesn't make things any worse for me.

As we get closer, we see Danny and Jackie working their way back through the mob of students. He mouths *I'm sorry* and walks quickly past us. That can't be good. Then I see my fate. I'm Julia… and he's Joseph. Oh my God. This can't be happening.

"Oh shit," Jenn says as she stares at my death warrant hanging there for the world to see. Josh is going to be furious.

D a n n y

Jackie's nails are digging into my wrist. My patience is wearing thin with her acting like this. I can't do anything about the play although I saw it coming. After Lauren's stellar performance—and my need to fix her on stage—we were pretty much destined for the roles. If I go to Ms. Nelson and tell her what's going on, it'd probably just fuel the fire more. Jackie yanks my arm again towards the lockers and I pull back.

"I think that's enough," I say and turn in the opposite direction. The fight from yesterday is still unresolved, and the fact that I will kiss Lauren in the play won't help things either. I have to get out of this relationship before it destroys everything I've worked so hard for the last few months. I head straight to the parking lot and pull out my phone to call Jeremy. A climb will do me good right now, but I don't want to go alone. If he's off today, we could be there in a little over an hour.

"Danny, stop," Jackie rushes behind me with her sweater half off her shoulders and her book bag weighing her down. "Please, stop. We need to talk about things." I'm almost at the gate and the safety of my truck is in sight.

"I told you we'd talk this weekend."

"What happened? Where are you going?"

"I'm going up to Molden with Jeremy. I'll be back this afternoon." I don't add that I'm only coming back because of the rehearsals tonight with Lauren, because truly, that is going to be the highlight of my day and breaking up with Jackie will be the low. But it will be done today. I've decided. There is nothing she can say to make me feel any different.

I walk to the driver's side of my truck and she scurries to get to the passenger side before I can turn the ignition. But then her screams pierce the truck's windows and I fly out of the driver's seat to her side to see what is wrong. The words *You're a Deadman* are spray painted in red down the side of my truck. Jackie's book bag and all its contents are scattered on the ground and she is huddled against the car next to us covering her face. The words don't scare me in the slightest, and she's really overreacting, but, then again, she's never known that life or about the death threats I used to get pretty much weekly. Looping my arm around her shoulders, I pull her into my chest. She's sobbing and shaking and mumbling something about how horrible and why would someone do that. I won't answer, but the possibilities are endless. It could be Robert for what Uncle John did to him or it could be my cousins for me abandoning them or it could be any of the countless people I collected from. Being a collector is not like doing a group sport; you can't just wake up and say *Hey, I don't feel like doing that anymore.* No, not at all. The demons of your past can creep up and attack you when you least expect it and no one would call a penalty flag for you.

Then again, I always knew getting clean wouldn't be so easy, but I just didn't know when it would rear its ugly head. I guess it has and now I'll have to deal with it. I'll step up my efforts to get my own place and put a safe distance between my family and me. They shouldn't have to pay for my stupid mistakes.

"Come on," I say and start picking up Jackie's things once she's stable again.

"Who would do this? Do you think it's someone at school?"

"No. It's not."

"Then who?" she asks as we walk through the gate onto the safety of the campus. Aaron and Matt wouldn't dare come here and Robert's thugs aren't that stupid. Things with Josh haven't been an issue lately; then again, I was cast as his girlfriend's lover this morning although I don't think he could've known that when this was done.

"Let's just get you to your first class. You'll need to catch a ride home tonight with Sara," I tell her trying to get her to shut up so that I could figure things out. But she refuses to let it rest.

"Danny," she yanks away. "You have to tell me what is going on."

"I don't have to tell you anything." I point out, and then add, "I had a life before you, and that is part of it."

"People threatening your *life* is part of it?" Her voice goes to that squeaky girl level that sounds like nails on a chalkboard. All of the hair on the back of my neck stand up when she continues, "So what? Now I'm in danger because you did awful things to someone?"

"You aren't in danger," I say confidently. I highly doubt they would use her to get to me—they know my track record with girls. And thankfully, Brandon is the only one who knows how important Lauren is and he wouldn't be dumb enough to mention her to anyone. He knows I'll kill him if something happens to her.

"How do you know that?" she asks and yanks at my arm as I start to walk again.

"I just do. They aren't like that."

"How do you know? Did you know they would come and damage your truck like that?"

If I hear one more word out of her I'm going to scream. "Look," I put my finger in her face before adding, "I'm lucky that's ALL they've done so far." She jerks her head back as though I've touched her, but I haven't and it aggravates me to think she assumes I would. "Yes, I knew they would come for me. Yes, I knew they would retaliate. That is the way these things go. No, you are not in danger. I guarantee that." I take her hand in mine again and pull her stiff body farther away from the parking lot as the bell rings. She's quiet the entire time as I drag her to her first class, determined she will get there in one piece. Not just because of the crap on my truck, but mostly because she's gotten under my skin and our relationship is a time bomb just waiting to go off.

And then she lights the fuse, "this is about Lauren, isn't it?"

"You know. We're done. This isn't working out. I'll have Sara drive you to our place tonight. You can get your things. Don't call me or come to my house again," I say with my fists tightly closed not wanting to punch the door, the wall, or the row of lockers next to the classroom. I don't yell, but she starts wailing as if I did. I turn on my heels and walk away before she can say anything else. I didn't want to hurt her, but this is for the best because Mr. Hyde is about to come out and play again, and if she can't handle a little spray paint, she definitely can't handle him or his evil ways.

I don't want to, but I flip open my phone and dial Brandon's cell number. It's been at least a month since I've seen or talked to him. Last I heard he was working for Uncle John again and I don't want to be sucked back into that life, but I have no choice at this point. If someone is coming after me, I'm going to need his help.

"Brandon?" I say when I hear the phone answer and the clicking echoing into the receiver. No one responds. "Brandon?" I ask again and still nothing. It's not even nine yet; he's probably taken the phone off the hook. Quickly, I dial Jeremy's number. Molden Rock is out for today, so I'm hoping he's at work to get the spray paint off the side of my truck. I'll have to deal with whoever did it later.

Dad and Captain Reyes are standing in the front yard when I pull up to our house from Jeremy's garage. Most of the paint is gone, but it needs a serious wash and buffing still. Hopefully they won't notice anything; I park on the street just in case.

It never dawned on me that I'm supposed to be at school still. "Son, what are you doing home so soon?" dad asks. I climb from the truck and make a show of grabbing my book bag from the back seat.

"They didn't need me in tech today. I have to go back for rehearsals in an hour though." If they call to confirm, they'll find out I'm lying, about the tech part at least.

"Good, that's just enough time," he says and they lead me up the stairs into the house. Something's definitely up. "Captain Reyes wants to talk to you about a few things." Dad pulls out several sodas from the fridge and we gather around the table on the patio.

"So, what's going on?" I ask when they've shared a few glances and start examining me. "Did I forget to pay a parking ticket or something?" They both laugh; that would be a minor infraction compared to the things I used to do.

"No, nothing like that. Your dad said you've been working for him doing private security."

"Yup, for the last few months." I take a sip of my soda and watch the grin growing on my dad's face.

"Well, is it your plan to guard the rest of your life?" Uh-oh. It becomes painfully obvious where this conversation is going. "Rosa said you withdrew your application to the explorer program."

Suddenly, I can feel every lump in the patio chair and the steel rods that make the chair's seat. "Yeah... I did."

"Why didn't you tell me?" dad asks.

He knows why. "I knew what you'd say."

"What would I say?" he asks.

"You'd say I'm giving up on my future."

"Yeah, that sounds like me," Dad says, "and that is what I'm thinking now."

"I know," I mumble and thump the top of my soda can.

"Danny, you'll be nineteen soon. You can go into the academy next year and you'll be behind if you don't go into the explorer program in January."

Dad walks into the kitchen and returns with the applications for Mountain View Police Department, the apartment brochures I had on my desk and a new home guide for Summit Estates, a new community catering specifically to police officers, teachers and hospital personnel. I already knew about it, because that's all he's talked about since I got the acceptance letter to the program. *It's an investment in your future*, he says almost daily.

"Don't you think we need to start thinking about what happens when this year is over? When you're not in high school anymore?"

"I'm going to get an apartment and keep working for you," I say, knowing that's not really what he wants to hear. He wants me to become a cop and be on the force and have a house... I want that too, or at least, I used to.

"That is not what you want for the future."

"Don't you think a house is a lot of responsibility for a teenager?"

"And you don't think an apartment is?"

"Not as much as a house is," I answer and watch Reyes shift in his chair. He was my dad's boss for over fifteen years, and I do respect him, but this isn't really a topic that I want to discuss with him.

"Danny, I don't think Clint is trying to force you into anything. I think he is trying to get you to focus on the things you want instead of just milling along without any clear objective."

Then it's silent. I glance sideways at Reyes and dad. Both men are waiting for me to give in and fill out the applications and buy the house and have a future they can be proud of. "Does a decision have to be made right now? I do have to get back to school."

"No, but we want you to seriously consider it since the deadline for January is in a few weeks."

"Thanks for coming by Paul." Dad shakes his hand and shows him to the door. When he returns, he taps on my first choice apartment brochure, "wouldn't you rather invest in your future than paying for someone else's?" The house and police department brochures are fanned out all over the table like a road map to my future. There are smiling faces on both, families on the house ones and young cadets on the other. In a few short weeks, my future will call; what will happen if I don't answer?

Lauren and Josh are arguing by the gym when I climb from my truck before rehearsals. Her face is crimson and streaked with long silken lines of tears flawing her perfect face. The two curved petals of her lips are twitching and pouting. Josh's eyes are looking everywhere other than at her, the same look he gave to Sara the last time she begged him to take her back.

Maybe...

Just maybe.

Maybe they are over.

Maybe I'm getting ahead of myself again.

Yeah. Probably.

The sidewalk to the theater has gotten longer, or I'm fighting every step that is drawing me farther from Lauren and the danger and hurt that awaits her. I can't bring myself to pull open the theater door, so I wait.

Impatiently.

Very impatiently.

The tips of my fingers drum the side of the building and I shift back and forth on my heels. Not knowing what is going on is aggravating. He wouldn't touch her, but the emotional pain she's about to go through is disheartening. There's no way to stop it though; she must see it for herself, must see him as he truly is, in order for her to let him go once and for all. That is her destiny, her future. Because there is no doubt he hasn't changed.

"Hey," I say jumping as she walks around the corner with her arms folded across her chest. "Are you okay?" She almost forgets to stop walking and is swaying mere inches from me. Then, she's sobbing into my chest. I'm not entirely sure she meant to be there, or if she wanted my arms to loop around her back, but they end up there. She's soft and vulnerable, and in this light, she looks like an angel surrounded by a halo.

Shhhhh . . . She sucks in several breaths and then lets them stagger back out.

"What happened?" I ask and mindlessly rub her back until my fingers end up in her hair. My chin and cheek sit perfectly on the top of her head until the smell of her shampoo starts to intoxicate me more than the best bottle of rum ever could have. I can't concentrate on the murmur of her heart against my chest, causing mine to speed tenfold. And I wonder if she realizes the increase with her face pressed against me.

"He's mad that I'm in the play," she says. My arms won't listen to my head to let her go, and she's not really pulling away either. She's perfectly fine where she is right now; in fact, I'd give everything I own for her to stay there forever. She's going through unnecessary pain staying with Josh and she doesn't realize that he's not her future and I really can give her the world—if she'd only give me the chance.

"Because of me?" I brush hair away from her cheek to see her emerald eyes giving way to more moisture.

"No..." she sniffles, "not really. He's mad that I'm not going to his practice."

Typical, self-centered ... "It's not your fault Ms. Nelson chose us."

"I'm going to try to get out of it."

"No, you can't." If she's not in the play, then there is no point in me doing it. She can't drop out. "Don't let him force you into anything. He's just worried you'll become more popular than he is." I half laugh and she does too. It's hard to be upset when you're laughing. "See? It will be fine. We'll get through this thing together." It would be easy to tell her about Crystal right now, about what a lying jackass Josh is, but somehow, that doesn't seem to be fighting fair. And if she chooses me, it has to be because she wants me, the real me. Not because of Josh or anything else. I refuse to have her in my life that way—always wondering if I have been the runner-up choice. So I'll keep my mouth shut.

L a u r e n

Ms. Nelson is setting up chairs on stage when Danny and I finally walk into the theater after I made a stop in the bathroom to fix my hair and make-up. Josh has been so mean to me lately that things might be better once the Homecoming game is over. It has to get better. Mom never said dad's games ever stressed him out this bad; in fact, I don't remember James ever being this big of a jerk either.

"Good, I'm glad you are both on time," Ms. Nelson announces. A quick glance to my watch shows we are actually ten minutes late, but she probably doesn't even realize what time it is. She's in her own little world up on stage with the amber, blue and red lights shining down on her. "We are going to do some basic character development tonight and talk about how you two are going to bring these characters to life for your audience."

Having to rehearse for two hours seemed like such a chore, but it's over before I can even blink. Danny and I laugh and joke through most of the scene and character development. He teases me about having to kiss at the end of the play and Ms. Nelson says technically it's not cheating, it's only acting. Either way, Josh and Jackie are not going to like it.

"Tomorrow night we will have Christian stay and we'll start running scene one. Thank you so much for coming tonight. I think the play will be a smashing success." Ms. Nelson smiles and we say our goodbyes after she makes Danny promise to walk me to the parking lot since it is dark outside.

"I'm sorry for earlier," Danny says as we get halfway to the parking lot. "It's hard seeing him with you." Mom's minivan is already parked at the curb, so I grab his arm to stop his pace.

"Danny, I don't get you. I've been so…" I stall, afraid to bring up the subject I've tried so hard to avoid, "mean to you. I basically pushed you aside to be with Josh. I don't get why you keep trying."

Danny stands there, no more than eight inches from my pounding heart, staring at me as if he's searching for the answer to the world's toughest trivia question. "I just want what is best for you," his voice strains, "and if you tell me it's him you want, then it's him you want. But I can't stand to see you miserable and I know he's doing that to you." He glances at mom's mini-van, while I scramble for a response. But he continues before my head can grab a hold of any of the thoughts speeding by. "I guess I'm just waiting for you to realize you've made the wrong choice." He half laughs, but the pain in his eyes tells the truth.

"Danny, I don't know if that is going to happen...."

He interrupts me, "do you have feelings for me?" I suck in a breath and wish I hadn't. It sits in my lungs like a caged bird waiting to be freed. "Just wait. Take your time; think about it."

My mind races away from me as though the bird has finally earned his freedom but relocated to my head. The thoughts flap around helplessly trying to find an escape. All I come up with is, "I don't know." *Yeah. Idiot.*

"What do you mean you don't know? How can you not know?"

"I don't..." I try to find a good way to explain the shattered feelings in my heart, but he won't let me think for a minute. He's already asking more questions before I can even understand the last answer I gave.

"Lauren, when I'm near you, my heart instantly speeds up. I search for things to say to you, to do with you. I want to touch you." He runs the tips of his fingers down my cheek, and I think I might explode. "I just want you to be as close as possible, to talk to you, to be with you." He moves closer and my mind tells me to step back, but I don't. "Well?"

Danny is waiting for my answer, one answer I want to give and one answer I should give. Yes, I wonder what it would be like to be with him. Yes, it hurts to see him with Jackie. And yes, I dream of him being this close to me. But this still isn't right. If Josh and I could just get past homecoming, we'd be fine.

"Yes, but…"

"Well, at least I know you have feelings for me other than hate and distain. That's a good thing." He chuckles and his eyes dance in the moonlight to this little victory, or as he sees it, a victory. That simple three-letter word probably just fueled the flame for him all over again. Leading him on is not fair. But, confusion is a weakness. One that is consuming me and there is no twelve-step program for it.

"No, wait, I have those same feelings for Josh. My heart races, my mind goes fuzzy and I can't find the right words to say. So, how am I supposed to know the difference between those feelings?" I glare at him. He always seems to have the answers; it's time for him try to figure it out. But he tosses it back onto me.

"That's up to you. Only you can make that decision. Can you live without him? Do you want to live without me?" And he touches my cheek again with the palm of his hand; it's balmy and chilled and perfect against my flushed skin. It doesn't take long and I'm lost again in those eyes, his smell, his lips…

"I don't know. Please don't ask me to choose again. I'm so tired of this. I'm tired of getting pulled in two different directions." I back up. "Does it have to be all or nothing?" My frustration came through loud and clear in my tone. I'm exhausting being the rag doll.

"No, I'm here as long as you want me to be, even if you just want me here as a friend." He smiles, but my heart is breaking. His friendship is not something I deserve from him. Plus, this isn't what he wants. He wants more of me and it's not something I can give without giving up all I've ever wanted.

"Do you really mean that? Would you be satisfied by only being my friend?"

Danny glances over my head, as though he didn't expect me to ask him that. "Yes, I'll be anything you want me to be. If you'll be my friend, I'll be thankful to have at least that." His arms are back around me again, curling me into his chest and my arms naturally slide around his waist. He pulls me closer as my fingers intertwine around each other.

"I don't think Josh is going to like this," I think out loud when reality sets in. Josh isn't going to like this … and I like it entirely too much. It doesn't make sense that he'd allow me to have the best of both worlds.

"Well, lucky for us it's not his decision." He loosens his grip and starts rubbing the curve of my spine sending chills up my back and neck. "You okay now?"

"Yeah. I'm fine. Just, um… confused," I add looking up into eyes that appear to be getting closer to my face in an invitation that I'm certain I'm giving him right now.

Danny pulls back as though he knows the terrifying thoughts rushing through my head. "Well, that makes two of us." He grabs my hand instead and starts pulling me towards the parking lot, his thumb rubbing over my knuckles bringing back memories of the first night we hung out at Jess's apartment. My mom is staring at our hands as we get to the van. I should've released his hand a long time ago. When her eyes bulge, I know what she is thinking, but she is wrong. Or at least, half wrong. I'm still with Josh, and I have no idea what just happened.

"Hi Danny! Long time no see!" Excitement drips off her every word.

"Hi Mrs. McIntosh, how are you?" Danny gives my mom a wide smile and squeezes my hand tighter when I start to pull it away from his.

"We are doing fantastic. When can you come for dinner again?" She asks, in a way nowhere near subtle.

"Hopefully soon," he says with another squeeze. "Sara and I had a fantastic time at your place. Sorry we haven't been back; we've been really busy."

"Well, you have to eat right?" Did she forget that I'm with Josh?

"Mom, Danny has a girlfriend now. Her name is Jackie… she's really nice." Thoughts of Jackie in Danny's arms invade my head with every swoop of his thumb on my hand. Either the circles are to calm him, or to calm me, but I don't think it's working for either of us.

"Well then…" She looks at our hands again. "She can come too. I'm sure she is wonderful."

Danny leans in and whispers, "we broke up." Just as quick as he leans in, he leans back and smiles at my mom. I'm dumbfounded. The conversation we just had on the sidewalk makes no sense. If he's not with Jackie, why would he be okay just being friends? Why wouldn't he tell me they aren't together and he wants me to be with him? *Ugh. That's not what I want.*

"Lauren?" mom asks. "Did you hear me?"

Shaking my fingers from Danny's, I grab the straps of my book bag and inch away from him. "What?"

"How did Josh's practice go?" She doesn't realize I hadn't stayed for the practice tonight. In fact, she doesn't even know I got a part in the play yet.

"I don't know. Actually, I didn't stay for practice."

"You didn't?" she asks suspiciously and examines the growing gap between Danny and me.

"Lauren and I actually got parts in the school play. We have rehearsals three nights a week together. So, if you ever want me to give Lauren a ride home I can." *Oh no…*

"That would be great. Maybe sometime you can drop her off this week and stay for pizza." Mom gives him a huge grin, as if that is what she has wanted all along.

Danny glances at me and backs off of the topic. "I'd love to, but I have the rehearsals and I have to work this week."

Mom keeps digging, "are you going to homecoming?"

Danny looks down at me and my teeth dig at my bottom lip. "No, I'm not. I actually have to work that weekend."

"That's a shame. I'm sure you'd look dashing in a tux. Well, we better get going. It's great seeing you again Danny."

"Thanks Mrs. McIntosh, you too." Just as I think I've escaped, he grabs my hand and pulls me back into his chest to hug me. I didn't mind hugging him before, but this is going to set off the inquisition when I get in the van.

"Call me," he says. "Do you have my number?"

"Yeah." I respond with no intention of calling him tonight.

"So what is that all about?" Mom says grinning from ear to ear as we pull away from the school.

"Nothing, Danny and I just decided to try to be friends. He's going to help me get through this whole play thing. I don't know where it's going from there. We are taking things slowly." Hopefully she'll leave it at that, but of course, she doesn't.

"What is going on with Josh," her voice rises. "Did you break up?"

"No mom. We are still together. Just, Danny and I are trying to get along without there being so much drama. As I said, we are taking things slowly right now."

"Well, I'm glad to see you are trying to be friends with people outside of Josh and his minions. If you want him to come over anytime you let me know."

I don't like the fact that she's so pro-Danny and so adamantly against Josh. It's unfair. She's trying to take away my right to choose for myself. She probably doesn't want me to succeed where she's failed although, technically, I'm failing too by allowing thoughts of being with Danny sneak in.

"I'm still trying to work things out."

"Are you still confused?"

"Yes, very." I don't want to say that to her, but it's true. I am confused again. Danny understands everything I've gone through and remains a powerful force in my heart. But Josh is everything I've always wanted—he's perfect, smart, honorable, athletic and forgiving. I get cold chills when he holds me and can't wait to be near him. The way he kisses me leaves me weak in the knees and I don't know how to explain it, but Josh just feels like the right choice. But, where does Danny fit into my life? Does he really fit there at all? If he weren't in my life, would it leave a permanent hole?

Danny

Lauren climbs into her mom's van and I watch them pull away. It would have been simple for me to say yes to her mother's invitation. My truck could be headed to their house by now, but it's not. It's on the way to my house to finish the conversation I started with my dad and Reyes earlier today. House and apartment brochures litter every available space on the floor of the truck, reminding me of the choice they want me to make. Unfortunately, the baseball bats that Brandon and I are fond of are lying on top of the brochures in the back seat and I find it ironic—a mixture of my old life and my future all colliding in one centralized location for my enjoyment.

No one is home when I pull into the driveway; well, at least none of my family is. A familiar red mustang is parked in my sister's spot, and my fingers loop around my old friend in the backseat as I climb from the truck. If Brandon wants a fight, he will get one. Getting closer to the door, I find the lights are off in the house and the air feels as though it's getting heavier with every step. It's not that I'm scared to fight him, but who knows how many guys he's brought with him or if they are armed.

"Brandon?" I ask wishing my eyes would get adjusted to the dark porch. My feet slip on the stairs to the house and I realize that it is blood, and a lot of it. Crimson red is smeared across the stairs and it looks as if it's all over the front door, but in the darkness, I can't be certain.

"I messed up man," Brandon says drawing my attention to the patio chairs. With the little light there is, I can see he's got blood on his face and more is dripping from his mouth, as I get closer.

"What happened?" I ask and help him into the house. His blood coats my shirt and arms, but it's not the first time I've seen him bloody, but every other time I've been next to him, backing him up. "Are you alone?" The baseball bat is still in my hand, but with the condition he's in, he couldn't help me fend anyone off and I highly doubt only one guy did this to him.

Brandon settles onto one of the barstools in the kitchen and I grab towels from the cabinet to soak up the crimson droplets that look like breadcrumbs leading to the front door. Bev will be pissed if she comes home to the mess. And I know she won't really be happy I'm using her kitchen towels for this.

"What happened?" I ask again and hand him a towel for his face and the blood that he's coughing up. This is the worst I've ever seen him and it would probably be best if I took him to the hospital, but he'll just refuse to go if I even suggest it.

"I went to Vince's to collect for John," he spits out more blood, "and I waited until the guy came out and when I got out of the car, I got jumped."

"Do you know who did it?"

"All I saw was Aaron..."

"What?" Did I just hear him right? "You think Uncle John set you up?" That makes no sense.

"They've been pressuring me to set you up or talk you into coming back. I told them it wouldn't work."

He didn't sell me out. Then again, we've been best friends since I got out of juvie, so I didn't really think he would.

"Was Matt there too?"

He coughs again and his body lurches, "nah man. I didn't see him."

"Maybe we should take you to the hospital," I suggest, but he protests by waving his hand and walks down the hallway to the bathroom.

"Can I take a shower?" he asks, but he's already pulling a bath towel from the cabinet. He knows it's okay. He knows if he gets clean he could move back in here and my dad would give him a job. But, I'm cautious because he's disappointed me before by promising to go to rehab and this could be a set up to go along with my truck tonight. Although, deep down I don't want to believe he'd set me up at my own house.

Thankfully nothing happens while he's showering and Dad and Bev show up before Sara does. At least I can explain to them what is going on before she gets home and goes ballistic over Brandon's shattered face and missing teeth. He complains when dad insists on calling Jess, but when Bev puts her foot down, he begrudgingly agrees.

It takes less than five minutes to determine he has several broken ribs and needs more than forty stitches to close up a gash below his eye and on his neck all of which took her less than an hour to clean and sew up.

"What's going on?" dad asks pulling me from the room and Bev's prying ears. He knows I won't tell him the truth, well, not to the extent he expects.

"He said some guys jumped him at Vince's." I try to keep a sneer off my face, but fail miserably. I won't jump to conclusions until I get more information. Dad's first reaction was to call the police, but he didn't. He probably knows this has something to do with Uncle John.

"Does he have any idea who it was?" he tries to bait me.

"He didn't say."

"Well, did he tell you anything else?"

"Not really…"

"I'd feel better if we at least called Reyes and file a report."

"You know Brandon won't talk to the cops."

"Well, do you think he's on drugs right now?"

"I'm not really sure." I hope not, because Sara's already going to be heartbroken when she gets home. If he's incoherent when she gets here, it will make it so much worse. "Can he stay the night at least?" I ask, thinking of how much he's been there for me. Tonight holds so many mysteries, and letting him back out into the world would be a mistake. And not one I want to make. I'll go stay at a motel if dad won't let him stay.

"Do you really think Bev will let me kick him out, even if he is high?"

We both laugh for a second as there would be no way. "Yeah, I guess not."

"I'll have Bev get blankets and the air bed for him." He pats me on the shoulder and heads back into the kitchen.

I click open the phone and call Jeremy. There's no way the writing on my truck and Brandon's attack are a coincidence. I'm almost done explaining when Sara's shrill voice fills the hallway.

"What happened? What's going on? Oh my God! Who did this? Brandon, tell me what happened to you."

Bev tries to calm her mile-a-minute voice. "Sara, why don't you let Clint talk to Brandon for a bit and you can help me make the boys some dinner."

"Danny?" Sara begs for my guidance, my saving. "What happened to him?"

Jess interrupts as she comes back in from cleaning her kit, "Sara, he's going to be fine. Go help your mom."

"Come on," I say to Brandon and sling my arm around his shoulder, to comfort, but also to sense, sense whether he is on drugs or alcohol or both right now. He refused to go to rehab and dad won't let him stay longer than tonight if he has any of that stuff on him now. "Hey, you're not carrying, are you?"

"Nah, I don't have anything on me ... oh um, I have my flask. No drugs though. There's a 9mm in the trunk of my car."

Damn. "Whose is it?"

"I don't know. Aaron had it in his car last week and you know what an idiot he can be, so I took it."

"Okay." What the heck could Aaron have needed a gun for? Maybe Robert had threatened them, or maybe without my watchful eye they were getting careless.

"I'm so sorry, Danny," he says and groans sitting on my bed. The air mattress unfolds and puffs as the first air reaches the ends and it starts taking shape. We've both had to sleep in our cars before, so this is a step-up, especially if he is on the outs with John—he has nowhere to go back to.

"We'll figure it out," I say. "You've got to get clean. You can't keep living this way. You can't go home and you can't stay here if you're using."

"I know, I know," he says and rakes his fingers through his hair. The blood is gone, but it's replaced with bruising under his eyes, his cheeks and his forehead. The stitches Jess did zig zag his neck and under his right eye. He's shaking and straining to breathe, more than likely from the pressure of the broken ribs. I don't envy him; that was me just last year and I didn't go to the hospital either.

"I'm going to get a place in a few weeks … you can move in with me and start working for dad like I am."

Brandon stares at me, "you don't have to do that. I'll figure out what I'm going to do in the morning."

"What? You can't trust them anymore. They did this to you. They are going to be out for you."

"I know…" he smashes his hands together, "…I know how hard it was on you to get clean. Man, I don't have the motivation you do. There's nothing for me."

I don't want to tell him there is nothing for me now either. Lauren is lost to me—the reason I got clean—and he partly ruined it. But, I can't blame him; he hung onto that life as much as he could and she threatened it. "Look, all we have is what we make of the future. We can turn things around." I sit next to him on the bed and put my arm around his shoulder. "It's not easy. Getting clean is not easy and I'm not going to pretend it is. But you can have better than what you've had … and I'll help you."

"You mean it?" he asks as if he didn't believe what I said. He's my best friend after all, and he was the only one that understood what I went through in juvenile hall, considering when we met he had just gotten out for his own indiscretion at school. His parents never let him back into the house.

"Yeah, I'm here for you." The second time tonight those words have left my lips, one not more important than the other. Both times to people that mean the world to me, and could fill my future. I'm just not sure where the two of them will end up fitting into my life.

Four hours later, I realize Lauren hasn't called. With the events of the night, I'm not sure I would've been able to really talk to her anyway. Now the evening has calmed down and I can smell her on my clothes again. Brandon is out cold on the air mattress. He's going to rehab next week and meeting with Renee, the substance counselor, tomorrow. This is just the beginning of his struggles. He thinks what he's already gone through is bad; he has absolutely no idea how hard the next four months will be on him.

My own talk about the future was put on hold for Dad to talk Brandon into getting his life together. Hearing him talk to Brandon tonight gave me chills—it hit entirely too close to home. The words were so ... familiar. I've already been through it and Brandon will have me to lean on.

My phone says it's 12:01am, too late to call Jeremy back to see if he found anything out and really too late to call Lauren. Tomorrow, I'll have to figure out what I'm going to do with my life now that I've signed on to support both of them and their futures. How can they really lean on me when I have no clue what I'm doing?

L a u r e n

Danny seems aloof the rest of the week. Maybe he regrets telling me he'd be my friend? Maybe he worked things out with Jackie and she told him to stay away from me? Who knows and I can't really ask him directly without stirring up a heap of trouble. Josh is still being a jerk and with the homecoming pep rally tonight, I seriously hope he stops taking things out on me. It's not my fault that practice hasn't been going well, his teachers are giving him extra homework, or the fact that he and Mark are fighting about something—but he won't tell me what.

Jenn and I ride to my place to get ready for the rally together. Mike's been crazy all week too and we can't wait to get this game and the dance over with already.

"Did you see what Crystal was wearing today? I swear she got her cheer skirt shortened by three inches or so."

"I know, and it's not as though she has the best legs." It's not as though I do either and really, it's just jealousy talking now considering she's hanging out with us every day and she gets to go on the bus to away games with Josh. Something about her mom being the organizer for transportation or some crap like that. She's the only cheerleader that gets to go on the boy's bus and it's really not fair.

"And what is up with the Lindsay chick? I mean, did you see her rubbing Mike's leg? I wanted to strangle her."

"Did you ask him about that?" I say and twirl my hair over my index finger. The streets fly by until we are at my house and neither of us wants to talk about the boys anymore or their stupid game. I really want to skip the rally tonight, but considering Crystal and Lindsay are both going to be there, we aren't going to miss it.

We pull on our jerseys and decorate our faces with blue and

gray stars on our cheeks and sparkled curls in our hair. "Ready?" she asks and there's no way that I am, but we can't stop time, so off we go.

Josh and Mike are waiting at the gate when we pull into school. "Hey Babe!" His face holds a wide grin for me, the first I've seen from him in what feels like weeks. He wraps his arms firmly around my back and lifts me off the ground as Mike does the same to Jenn. Talk about what a difference a day can make; at school today he pretty much ignored me. "I have something for you," he pulls out a necklace with a number nineteen charm on it and a card. "You can't open the card until you're alone. Okay?" Curiosity is going to kill me, but I agree as he turns and runs with Mike back to the field. Jenn has her own necklace with Mike's number on it. Is there anything they don't coordinate?

Josh, Mike, Mark, and Ben act as if nothing is wrong and there is no rift as they hoot and holler their way through the battle calls to the cheers of the student body. With the note burning a hole in my pocket and the necklace searing my neck, the rally doesn't end soon enough.

After the rally, Jenn and I climb into her car, and with the note carefully unfolded, I read and re-read his words over and over again, searching for something, anything, to justify the past few weeks, but it's just filled with promises... promises that I need, that I want, and words that make my heart melt. But he still gives me no answers.

To my dearest Lauren,

I know these past few weeks have been hard. I want you to know that I love you with all my heart. It is impossible for anyone to have ever loved anyone more than I love you. I know why I was put on this earth. I will spend the rest of my life making you happy if you'll let me. I am so sorry for everything I've taken out on you. I never meant to upset you or worry you. I'm looking forward to the dance and just having you alone with me. I'm always thinking of you. I love you- always.

Josh

Vince's is a flurry of football players, cheerleaders, parents and other students getting pizzas and rallying for the upcoming game against Hillview, our school's rival. Why the schools are rivals? I have no idea. All I know is they are one town away from us and last year they stole the football league championship trophy from our stadium. But, actually it is just a plastic trophy with a fake gold eagle on top. Why go to war over that? It's like you can't walk into the local trophy store, buy another one and stick a nameplate on it to say whatever you want.

Josh and Mike claim a huge corner booth that was reserved for them by Tim and Allen, Josh's elder brothers. Their entire football team came tonight to support Josh and Mike against West Gate. The booth fills up quickly with Josh, Tim, Allen, Mike, Mark and Ben all crammed into it. Jenn and I end up on Mike and Josh's laps instead of having our own seats, but that's okay. Josh rubs my legs and back while he talks casually with his brothers about the game. Jenn and I exchange looks and head to the counter to get pizzas and drinks. I've had enough football for one night, but when Crystal struts through the door, I find it in myself to stay while Josh commiserates with his brothers and their friends and parents and students and other customers. It's a steady line of visitors to our table for the next two hours, long after the pizza and drinks are gone and half the students have left. But they are still going strong with stories by ten and I have to be home in half an hour—it's a school night, and Jenn is my ride unless Josh takes me; I doubt if that will happen.

I lean in to whisper to Josh that I need to go home and he nuzzles his face into my neck. Next thing I know, he nibbles at my neck. I never expected him to do something like that and jump in response—he laughs, so does Mike. "Geez Babe," Josh says, "what's gotten into you?"

Ummm… maybe the fact you just bit me in front of all these people? "Nothing," I say instead. "It's getting late. I have to go home."

He looks at everyone at the table, all still laughing and goading each other about past games. "Okay," Josh says downhearted. This is really his night and his rally and I'm ruining it with my stupid curfew. If I could get my license already, maybe they'd let me stay out a little later. Scratch that ...

"Never mind, I'll have Jenn take me home," I say sliding from his lap, not wanting to leave yet, but not wanting to ruin his time either.

"No, it's okay. I'll take you home."

Then Jenn yawns, "I'm really ready to go," she says and starts getting up too.

"Are you sure?" Josh asks her as she pulls out her keys.

"Yeah, I'm going anyway. I'll take her home."

The table continues to clap and laugh as we walk out to Jenn's car. My eyes feel as though they have two toothpicks holding them open as she drives me home and I'm wondering if leaving isn't the biggest mistake.

Mom is in the kitchen when I come in and it doesn't take long for her to disappear to her bedroom. She has to work tomorrow and since she didn't say anything to me, she's probably annoyed that I walked in the door so close to curfew. I sort of regret it too —I'll be dragging tomorrow and probably catch hell for leaving Josh on such an important night.

The alarm goes off at five a.m. Sliding into my running shoes, I slip out the front door as the coffee brews in the kitchen. Mom is already at the counter with her nose in the paper and Dad's still in bed. Typical. I take my regular route around our neighborhood, past the park and back up around the opposite way from our house. I'm dripping with sweat by the time the run is over even though it is cool outside. Dad is slumped over the sports section and a cup of coffee at the table. He stayed at the high school last night later than I was at Vince's.

"Good morning, eggs and bacon?" Mom asks flipping two eggs over in a pan.

I grab an apple from the counter and head back to my room.

"No thanks. I've got to get ready." I shower and take bites of the apple in between washing my hair and shaving. School the day before a big game is always laid back—even the teachers don't care if you are late or talk in class, so today will be awesome. Last year, on rally days, Josh walked me to all my classes since he could be late to his, and I'm really hoping he does that again this year.

I slide into a pair of jeans and my jersey, blow-dry my hair straight and head out to the curb to meet Mandi and Jamie. Both have ribbons in their hair and blue and gray stars on their faces, and in my rush, I forgot mine. I'd have to go without today because neither brought extra. The two of them talk the whole way to school about *all* the girls in Homecoming court getting ready tomorrow at Crystal's house. Obviously, Jenn and I hadn't been invited. If we had made the squad we would've been obligated to go to her place; maybe that's an added bonus of not making it onto the squad.

"What do you think?" Jamie asks. I grab my book bag and climb from the back seat of the car.

"About what?" I ask blatantly; they hadn't included me in the conversation all the way to school, so why start now? Besides, I tuned them out five minutes ago.

"Dinner tomorrow? Are you guys going with us?"

"I think so ... Josh planned it out with Mike." Like everything else.

"Hey, I'll catch you later," I say annoyed. They are back to talking about how cool it is that Crystal's mom is having a hair stylist and manicurist come to their house to get all the cheerleaders and court ready for the dance. As if I really want to hear that—go ahead, remind me how I'm still not really part of the in-crowd even though I'm dating the captain of the football team. *Ugh.*

Jenn hasn't gotten to school yet, so I pull my backpack tighter and head straight down the long walk way to my first class. Sara and Danny are sitting on the benches and I wave to both, unsure if Mandi and Jamie are following or not. If they are, I know they saw it because I didn't even try to hide it. Danny said he would be my friend, and that is what we will be although Josh doesn't know yet and he'll be pissed when he finds out.

"Hey, want company?" Sara jogs to my side. Her first class is in the same building as mine.

"Sure," I say and expect Danny to join us, but he doesn't. We round the building to the main quad and he's still firmly planted at the benches. "Um... is something up with Danny?"

Sara looks over her shoulder at Danny watching us go. "No. He's okay. We just have a lot going on at home right now. He's trying to figure out what he's going to do next year and he's been working for his dad every night after school."

"And he's doing the play and school full time too?"

"Yeah, so he's a bit stressed out right now. Actually, he's a lot stressed out right now. I'm worried there is too much going on." Yeah, me too.

By lunch, I still haven't seen Josh. He didn't come to any of my morning classes. Rumors were already swirling on campus that he'd gone to Mike and Crystal's classes all morning. Not to mention the fact that the rumors of the football team going to Crystal's house last night after Vince's is plaguing me. One girl even claimed that the whole group of varsity cheerleaders and players have ditched the whole day to hang out at the stadium. I don't doubt it; the seniors did that last year before the game.

I toss my morning books into my locker and head towards our normal table in the quad. The afternoon sky is looming with clouds and hanging out alone in a downpour is not my idea of fun. It'll probably pour all day tomorrow and unfortunately the stadium is completely uncovered. I'll probably be sick for the dance tomorrow night after sitting in this crappy weather at the game. I pass the coffee cart and think of how awesome that warm caramel goodness would be right now; in fact, Danny's mom's coffee from last year sounds awesome. I pull my wallet out for cash and end up not only buying one, but two. And do something stupid... Josh isn't at the tables, neither are any of my other friends. I don't want the coffee to go to waste. I head to the benches. Oh. My. God. Someone stop me. What the hell has gotten into me? *Stop.* You can go back now. You can still save yourself from this. This is a mistake. This is a...

The benches come into view. There is no going back now. Two steaming cups of coffee warm my hands. Danny is sitting by himself on one of the tables at the end. Determined, I lock my elbows to keep my arms from shaking with the coffee in each hand.

Danny looks at me as if I'm lost. I am, kind of. I stay my course and quicken my pace, hoping to build some confidence, and head straight toward him. He leans forward and the smile on his face grows along with the curve in his eyebrow. He looks happy to see me. I seriously hope I'm not crossing any boundaries in our new *friendship* by abruptly invading his territory.

"What's going on?" he asks and I hold out one of the coffees to him.

"It's a cold day. I can't bring my friend a coffee?" I ask and climb onto the table next to him. It was chilly in main quad, but with the trees overhanging the benches, it's freezing and all I have on is a tank top under my jersey—standard football girlfriend gear. Ridges of goose bumps rush down my arms and I wrap both of my hands around my coffee cup, mostly to steady my nerves, but it's warming me slightly too. Some boys and girls snicker at me sitting next to Danny. I'm in enemy territory with this #19 jersey on. But no one would dare say anything with Danny next to me—one thing I've learned is most of the people here are scared of him, no matter how hard they look or act.

"Oh, no." He sips the coffee. "I'm not complaining in the least." Silence fills the void between us and I shiver from the chills running across my arms. The coffee helps, but it's no match for the wind that is drafting through the branches. "Here, take my jacket." Danny slips out of his jacket, and then stops. Last time we were at the benches with coffee, well... it didn't end so well.

"Thank you," I say and lean into him, allowing the jacket around me. I came here to be friends after all and to refuse his jacket would be repeating history. I won't do that to him again. He slides the jacket completely around my shoulders and pulls away instead of lingering like last time. *Friends.* That's what we are now. There is no spark between us because we are just friends, sharing coffee, on the benches, at school, in view of everyone, that is anyone. *Friends.* The oddest of friends.

This. Was. A. Bad. Idea. At least now the glaring #19 is blocked from view; everyone knows it's still there though.

"Do you want to run lines or something?" he asks and looks around the crowd. Some of them were there the night he saved me at DJ's, others were at Jess's house, all are staring at the unlikely matching of Danny and me warming up with our coffee together.

"No, I don't want to talk about the play. How's Jess doing?"

Sara bounces up behind me and throws her arms around my neck, "it's about time you started hanging out with the cool kids." She laughs. "What's going on?"

"Not much. Just thought I'd bring your bro a pick-me-up." I point to the coffee and add, "it's nowhere near as good as your mom's though."

"I won't disagree with you there."

"Did Danny tell you he got a new place?" She takes a seat on one of the chairs near us and pulls out a sandwich. "I can't wait to move in after next year. Danny promised I could stay with him while I'm in school." My eyes won't leave Danny and he won't look at me. He hadn't told me he was getting a place—then again, I guess I didn't give him the chance to. The only thing we talk about during rehearsals is running lines, nothing else. I guess we weren't at that part of our relationship where we are sharing our deepest, darkest secrets. Getting an apartment is probably not as dark as his secrets come, though.

"You got your own place?"

"Yup. Believe it or not. Some of my stuff's already there."

"I'm going over on Saturday morning to help unpack things for him and decorate before the dance."

"How cool!" I say, but really I'm in shock. "Congrats!" I bump his shoulder with mine. "You should've said something, I could've helped you pack or something." He grins and lets out a small laugh.

"Most of the stuff is brand new; it's not like I had to actually pack anything."

"Oh," I say feeling a little foolish, "well, congrats anyway."

The lunch bell rings and there are a few moments that pass before I start to move. "Thanks for letting me use this," I say shrugging out of his jacket. His arms are ghostly white and he has his own collection of geese competing for space on his forearms. "Sorry," I say and run my fingers down his ice-cold arm. If my fingers were wet, I would've been stuck to him for the rest of the day. I shouldn't have touched him anyway.

"Don't worry about it," he says after a very long uncomfortable silence.

"So, you're going to the dance?" I ask Sara and start walking to my next class trying to distract myself from Danny's hypnotizing blue eyes and the curiosity over what type of place Danny is moving into.

"Yup. I couldn't sucker Danny into going. He has to work, so Jeremy is taking me."

With Danny still gathering his stuff at the tables, I ask, "what about Brandon?"

Sara looks back at Danny walking towards us. "I don't want to talk about him right now."

"I'll walk you guys to class," he says and Sara squints as if talking about Brandon is off limits right now. I don't want her in trouble, so I don't say a word. It's already been a strange afternoon, and right now, I'm not sure how I'll explain not showing up in the quad for lunch. I'm sure word already got around where I was anyway. I don't need a crystal ball to see a huge fight in my near future. But that's what Josh gets for ditching me all day.

D a n n y

I never thought I'd see the day that Lauren McIntosh would hang out for an entire lunch period at the benches. Never in a million years. But, she did, and she actually weathered pretty well considering every single one of Brenda's hoes gave her dirty looks from the minute she got there until the bell rings. I walk Sara and her to class, trying to figure out if her appearance at lunch has to do with Josh hanging with cheerleaders all day, or if it's her finally realizing what is up … Maybe she is just trying to be nice and take me up on my friend offer. I'm not sure, but whatever it is, I'm going to enjoy every last minute of it. Even if it doesn't last, it's a small victory.

We drop Sara off at her class and walk down the hallway until we get to Lauren's classroom. I'm going to be late to my class, but that doesn't matter. I'd be late to every one of mine if it meant I could walk with her to hers. "So you're working tomorrow huh?"

"Yeah, I'm picking up as many extras as I can to get my place." That's a lie, but I don't want to tell her I'm only working to keep my mind off what she'll be doing tomorrow night.

"That's so cool. I'm excited for you. I can't believe you are getting your own place."

"Yeah, it's time I get my crap together."

"Me too. I'm looking at this house in Summit Estates," she says and giggles.

"Dad tried to get me to buy a place in there." She looks at me as though she doesn't believe me; then again, she probably didn't think I'd ever amount to anything. In fact, I know that's what she is thinking.

"Why didn't you?" she asks as if it's the most obvious thing ever. If I could buy a house, why didn't I?

Ummm ... I want to smack myself in the face right now because the look she's giving me is pretty much the equivalent. "I just thought a house would be too much right now."

Lauren looks past me down the hallway—the football team is heading our way with Mike at the head of the pack. I don't want to fight right now, and I'm sure she's thinking that's the last thing she wants too. "I'll see you later," I say ending our friendship for now and leaving her to deal with the life she's chosen. Eventually, we will get the chance to finish this conversation. Overall, I'd say we are making progress, even just as friends. Getting the condo is probably one of the best ideas I've ever had—it'll show her I'm not a reckless loser without ambition.

Sara climbs into the truck after school to head to my new condo. She unpacks towels and dishes that Bev got for me and loads the dishwasher, but we can't run it since electricity won't be turned on until tomorrow. We take turns removing the plastic on the new furniture I bought. Luckily, the furniture store delivered and set up everything, but I'm not entirely sure why they didn't unwrap it all. The couch looked as though a 1950's housewife got a hold of it with their vinyl covering; all that was missing was the plastic floor runners.

"Do you know why Lauren came to the benches today?" I toss some of my clothes into one of the drawers. "Did she say anything to you?"

"No. I didn't even know she was there until I heard girls talking about it at the snack bar." Sara picks up another box full of junk. Stuff I probably should just get rid of since it's been in Dad's garage for years and I haven't missed whatever it is yet.

"Josh was with Crystal all day, wasn't he?" I ask, but I know the answer.

"Yup," she says indifferently. "I think Lauren's starting to realize something's up." Sara pulls my baby blanket from one of the boxes she is poking through. "awwww... further proof you were once a cute baby!"

"Give me that," I snatch it away and the box dumps out into the floor. Black and white photos cascade to the ground of a woman in her twenties holding a baby. That baby is me. The woman ... well ... she doesn't matter. She left me a long time ago.

Sara scrambles to pick them all up and shove them back into the box before I say anything. But the damage is already done. I hadn't seen the pictures in years and really thought Dad disposed of them. Obviously, I was wrong. Now I've tainted my new place with them and bad memories of how she left us.

"Never mind," I say and throw the entire box into the closet. "Enough unpacking for one night. Let's go. It's going to be dark soon and I have to meet up with Dad."

"Don't you want me to make your bed? You're staying here tomorrow night."

"Nah- leave it. It can wait until tomorrow." I toss the unopened sheets onto the bed and walk back into the living room. A two-bedroom is overkill considering it's only me, but if Brandon moves in after rehab, it will be just right. The only problem is Sara wants to move in next year when she is ready for college. We'll have to figure out the logistics of the sleeping arrangements later.

The next morning Sara is droning on and on about homecoming and how excited she is that Jeremy is taking her. I almost called Lauren last night, but I know she's going tonight with *him* and I just want to numb myself from it all instead of thinking about it. Dad's right. I have to focus on my future and figure out what the hell I'm doing already. Brandon in rehab right now makes things precarious with Lauren. If Josh and the team come after me for her little stunt yesterday, they are going to kill me.

Bev puts breakfast onto the kitchen table and Sara starts putting all the paperwork for the academy and sheriff's department into a pile on the bar. "Think you'll fill those out today?" Bev asks.

"I don't know yet."

"You know you're going to," Sara chimes in and drops several forks onto the table in one loud clink.

"Can I get used to being in my own place first? I do kind of have a lot going on right now." A new place, a best friend in rehab, a girl I'm in love with about to be ruined by a guy I hate more than Mr. Hyde, and a deadline to the proverbial "fork in the road" fast approaching. Not to mention the red paint on my truck and Brandon being beaten up.

"Okay guys, he's thrown in the towel for now," Dad says and takes his seat to eat breakfast, possibly the last breakfast we'll have together at their house after I'm settled in at my own.

By two, I've finished packing everything in my room, including my Gibson and old football trophies. Sara is dancing around the hallway in her princess pink dress, clip in multi-colored hair and black and pink tights. "Sure you don't want to go?"

"Positive," I respond tossing my computer cords into another box.

"It could be fun," she tries again, and then adds, "you aren't the least bit curious?"

"No, not at all. I have to get ready for work." I say and usher her out of the room in her frilly dress. I'm sure she will have an awesome time tonight and I'll have to hear all about it tomorrow when we go up to Molden Rock with the group. I've been looking forward to this trip all week and I don't have time to focus on going to that dance or trying to stop the inevitable. Lauren said she can't go on being confused, but she seems perfectly fine letting me live in that confusion, pining for her and my own happy ending.

"Ready?" Dad knocks on the door to head to the airport. There are ten of us going tonight—seriously overkill for a Union meeting —but I think he knows I need to keep my mind off things. A life is slowly forming in front of me, one that I'm not sure I've accepted or wanted, but it's too late to back out now. The future is here, regardless of if I want it or not. There's no room for me to second-guess my decisions. My main priority is to keep my family safe and keep the demons from my past at bay. Eventually, I'll have to pay the price for the things I've done, but thankfully, that day is not today.

L a u r e n

Of course we go to dinner with the other football players and cheerleaders. Josh looks smashing in his tux and I feel like a princess on his arm tonight. I just wish we didn't have so many friends with us. I was hoping for a super romantic night, with just the two of us, but he doesn't seem interested in anything other than the fact that they won the big game today. Boring. Seriously. There really is more to life, I swear.

The Hilton ballroom is a fantasy wonderland of twinkle lights and shimmering diamonds flashing against the walls and huge vaulted ceilings. Couples are twirling and dancing on the dance floor to the best music. There are huge ice sculptures on the dessert and punch tables. We just stepped through the doors into Cinderella's ball and we are the honored guests.

Unfortunately, dinner ran over, so soon after we arrive the Coach takes over the microphone and starts calling the Homecoming court to stage, including Josh and Mike. Jenn and I stay arm in arm along the fringes of the dance floor, waiting for our men to get their duty over with. And I'm okay with that, until Josh is named King. I squeal and yell and jump up and down on my strappy heels, almost falling over and breaking my neck, but Jenn catches me and we squeal again. The celebrating is short lived when Crystal is announced Queen and they take the dance floor for the obligatory King and Queen dance. I fall into the nearest chair to wait.

And wait.

And wait.

Five songs later they are still on the dance floor. Mike is with Lindsay, one of the queen's court. I keep reminding myself that Josh and Crystal are just really good friends, but with how good she looks tonight, it's hard to believe that nothing has ever happened between them. And if things couldn't get any worse, Sara and Jeremy are two tables away, witnessing it all.

"Can I have a dance?" Jeremy asks Jenn and I'm more than a little surprised when Sara joins me at the table with two cups of punch. Jenn links her arm around Jeremy's and they head to the dance floor. *That should be me out there with him.*

"He shouldn't be hurting you like that," Sara says and points to Crystal and Josh slow dancing.

"He's obligated," I say trying to justify the spiteful feelings churning in my throat.

"No, he's not," she replies, pointing out exactly what I'm really thinking.

Josh twirls Crystal away from him and pulls her back into his arms. If he holds her any tighter, they'll be doing the deed on the dance floor. I pull my eyes back to Sara—I can't watch him with her. I can't watch her laughing and smiling and resting her head on his shoulder. I haven't gotten to dance with him yet and she's had him the entire time we've been here, or at least, it feels like it.

"I'm going to get some more punch. Want something," Sara asks.

I don't want her to leave me here alone, but she can't stay with me all night either. "No, thank you," I say and turn to watch Jenn dancing with Jeremy. If Mike saw them together, he'd be ticked. But he is on the other side of the dance floor with Lindsay swaying to the music. Then an evil thought invades my mind, if Danny were here, I'd be on the dance floor with him right now dealing out my own healthy dose of jealousy on a plate for Josh to chow down on.

Sara is by the punchbowl with her cell phone to her ear; there's no doubt in my mind that she is calling Danny. Secretly, I hope she is. Then again, that would be selfish and possibly put Danny in danger without Brandon here to back him up. Then again, Jeremy is quiet imposing too—and getting even closer to Jenn on the dance floor.

"Here you go. I brought you some anyway."

"You weren't talking to Danny, were you?" My mouth runs away from me and I slip saying exactly what I'm thinking.

"No, why?" She sips her punch and smiles as Jeremy dips Jenn.

"Never mind," I say and focus back on Josh on the dance floor. The song is coming to an end and couples are exiting the dance floor. Jeremy leads Jenn back to our table; she's beaming and I can't help but wonder if she doesn't realize the mess she'll be in like I've been with Josh and Danny.

Jeremy pulls Sara out to the dance floor and I stare at Jenn, "okay, so you want to tell me what that was about?"

She grins as though she just ate a two-pound whole box of candy by herself. "Nothing. Why?"

"Yeah, whatever." I glare back at Josh. The dancing is over, but now the King and Queen's court are surrounding them on the dance floor. Jenn and I should be over there in the middle of it, not sitting at a table like complete outcasts. "Come on."

With Jenn's hand firmly interlocked with mine, I pull her toward our group and through the crowd of squealing cheerleaders and various athletes. We stop just outside the inner circle next to Mandi and her flavor of the week. She barely notices we are there; nor do Josh or Mike. We just hang out there like the biggest losers in dance history. And we stay that way for what feels like three hours, before Josh and Mike finally stop talking about the game, the football camp and whatever other sports stuff they always talk about. I stop listening when they start talking about the game winning play, again, for the billionth time. The dance, so far, has just been a repeat of last night at Vince's. You'd think they'd get bored talking about themselves.

"Wanna go get some air?" Jenn asks. Every part of my body is sweating under the layers of fabric; it feels like a sauna surrounded by everyone.

"Yeah," I answer, but she already has my hand and is heading out of the crowd towards the ballroom doors.

"You'd think they'd get tired of that," Jenn says and we both start laughing. "I mean, seriously. I've never met anyone so full of themselves in my whole life."That's an understatement.

"Can you believe they brought up that play again?"

"I know! Didn't we cover that twenty times last night? Ugh, and what about the offside kick? I mean, seriously, do they think that no one saw it coming?"

"We were there; we saw the game. I'd understand if we missed it and they wanted to recap it for us ... but hello, I saw it live."

"Yeah, but it wasn't much better than the recap." Jenn laughs and we both giggle again. Josh would be upset if he heard us talking this way, and I know this is really just our jealousy and disappointment over tonight being sucky so far. Once he's done with all the obligatory festivities, he'll be mine again and we'll get on with our evening. Then again, with Jenn and me heading outside, I wonder how long it will take for him to realize I'm gone.

D a n n y

Governor Allen is already an hour into his visit to the Union when my cell rings. There are so many of us that it looks like we are guarding the President himself. So it's no big deal when I slip out into the hallway to find out what's up. She's supposed to be at the dance and I almost drop the phone, worried that something has happened.

"Danny, can you get out of work?"

"What's wrong?" My voice betrays my authority. There's no way I'm staying at work if she says she needs me, or worse, Lauren needs me. The red paint on my truck comes to mind, and Jeremy is at the dance with Sara alone. Jeremy knows the history I have with the football team, so I know he hasn't started anything but that doesn't mean the football team hasn't started something with him; or the fact that Matt or Aaron may have shown up.

Sara doesn't answer soon enough and I raise my voice, "Sara! Tell me what's going on."

"I have this really bad feeling that something's going to happen. Josh is out on the dance floor with Crystal and ... I just feel something's up."

"So, no one's hurt?" My heart finally starts to slow down; every muscle in my body starts to loosen from the rush of blood that just ran through me.

"No," she says. "But, I would feel better if you were here." I look back at the doors and at the phone.

"If you feel something is wrong, why don't you leave? Do you think someone is going to start something with Jeremy?"

"No, nothing like that. I can't explain it."

"I'm on my way," I respond and hang up the phone. So much for thinking I wouldn't get sucked into this damn dance; but if Sara thinks I need to be there, then I'm going.

"Hey, can I cut out?"

Clint examines the tense muscles in my jaw line, my clinched lips and my squinted eyes. "What's going on?"

"Sara wants me to come to the dance. She said she has a bad feeling."

He looks at me with both understanding and confusion in his eyes. "I hate when women say that—especially one of my women. When Bev says she has a bad feeling, someone usually gets hurt." That's what I'm worried about—Sara has the same talent as her mother.

"Yup, that's what I was thinking."

"Go ahead and get going then. We can handle it. Are you going back to your place tonight or are you coming home?"

"My condo is home now ... remember?"

He laughs and slaps me on the back. "Guess I have to get used to that."

"I'll come by after the climb tomorrow."

"Be safe. If Sara wants to stay at your place, that's okay. Just text me. I'll tell Bev. It'll be nice to have the house to ourselves tonight." He winks.

I grab my jacket and head straight to the truck. The baseball bats on the floorboard comfort me as I pull onto the freeway heading back to Mountain View. If I park in the front, we could get away easily, but we'd also risk being seen. Parking in the back would be better. I'd only have to drive over two curbs to be on the main street. A quiet, somewhat inconvenient getaway would be better than everyone seeing us. Hopefully I can get in and out before being attacked by paper mache flowers and disco balls.

Pausing before pulling open the doors, I check my reflection. My black sports coat and black uniform makes it look as though I intended on coming to the dance all along. I push my hair back off my brow and stare at myself another moment before gripping the door handle and pulling it open. In and out—I repeat to myself making double time across the ivory marble floors, past the check in desk, and to the banquet rooms. Sara better be ready to go when I find her. The last time I came to a dance, it didn't end well and I don't want to linger just in case.

"Hey," Jeremy says. He's standing near the punch table; Sara's nowhere around. "What's going on?"

"I don't know. Sara called and said she had a funny feeling."

"She didn't say anything to me," Jeremy says and looks around. "Do you know where she is?"

"Restroom. She's been gone a while though." Glancing around, I find that she's not at the tables or the dance floor—nor is Lauren or Josh.

"Go check the restrooms. I'll check the lobby and front desk."

Fifteen minutes later, still no Sara, no Lauren, and no Josh. I end up at the check in desk, "Can you tell me if you have a reservation for Miller?"

"What's the first name sir?" the girl behind the computer asks.

"Josh or maybe Tim?"

"No, there is no room booked for either name. I'm sorry."

Jeremy walks up and he's had no luck finding them either. I dial Sara's cell phone again and it's still off. Damn her for making me come here and panic like this. We head back to the ballroom to look again; we've had to have missed her.

"Danny!" Sara shouts as she exits the elevator.

"Sara, what the hell is going on?" I'm relieved and frustrated to see her getting off the elevator... alone.

"Josh got a room; he pulled Lauren away from the dance floor and I couldn't find Jeremy. I tried to follow, but I lost them."

My heart sinks. Sara was right—if I had been here earlier, something bad may not have happened to Lauren. Although, I can't guarantee she didn't go with him willingly ... but I'm sure she's not expecting what he has planned. The douche bag obviously hasn't changed his ways. I can't stand the idea that Lauren will go through the heartbreak that Sara did.

"Do you know what floor they're on?"

"No," she says deflated. The look on her face tells me how

disappointed she is in herself. I'm not blaming her for what is probably happening to Lauren right now—but the fact is, once tonight happens, Lauren will never be the same. It will either strengthen their bond, or taint her. Tomorrow she will be a nameless to him with her innocence being his victim.

We head back to the check in counter to try every name we can think of. If they got on the elevator, then their room is definitely here. Sara heads back into the ballroom to ask a few people if they'd heard Josh bragging about tonight, where they were going or what the plans are. After more than fifteen names, the desk clerk is growing tired of my game of go-fish and she tells me she can't be of any further assistance. I'm dead in the water.

"I know you don't want to hear this ... but maybe Lauren is ready to go there with Josh. Maybe he won't do the same thing he did to Sara." He lowers his voice. "Look man, I know how much she means to you, but I don't think there's anything we can do."

"Don't you worry about Jenn being in a hotel room with Mike right now?" I ask, using his obsession against him. He can't stand the fact that Jenn came to the dance with Mike—even after he told her he would take her himself to keep her from going with Mike.

"Yeah. I hate it. But she wanted to come with Mike. I tried to stop her, just as you tried to stop Lauren and it didn't work. I want to be with Jenn and I hope that Mike doesn't hurt her, but I'm not going to fight her over her choice. I'm not going to make her hate me over it."

Lauren hated me for a portion of last year, so I can see his point. But I refuse to believe that every encounter I've ever had with her doesn't matter. It has to. Or maybe that is just my stubbornness kicking in. I refuse to believe that she might not have true feelings for me, even if she's confused and trying to deny them.

L a u r e n

We walk down the long hallway, heading further away from the comfort of the dance. Mike and Jenn are just feet behind us. Josh pulls me to a large ornate door and slides the key card into the lock. The bedroom suite is huge, with big French double doors that separate the bedrooms from the living room and a formal dining room. Like I said, huge.

Mike grabs Jenn's hand and pulls her to the doors on the right. He is laughing and saying something to her. My heartbeat is pounding in my ears drowning out everything. Josh is pulling my hand towards the other bedroom. Jenn and I share panicked glances as the doors shut, sealing our fate.

Josh turns on the radio and twirls me around. "Take off your shoes," he says and bends to slip them off my feet before I can object. His arms are back around me and he's holding me so tight that I can feel his hips against my stomach. He starts to hum into my hair and the room seems to be sinking on me. I can't breathe; I'm drowning and gasping for air.

"Wasn't tonight wonderful?" he asks but doesn't let me answer. "I can't believe I was crowned and the game! Today couldn't be more perfect."

He wants to dance with me now, but he didn't approach me on the dance floor once. "It could've been …" I mumble what I didn't want to admit. Tonight sucks.

"What's wrong?" he asks.

"Why didn't you dance with me downstairs?"

"What?" he says, but he didn't really want an answer. He dips me and twirls me wide and back to his chest. He starts humming again as though he's none-the-wiser over why I'm aggravated.

I'm about to ask about Crystal, further destroying this perfect night, when he leans in and kisses me hard, harder than he ever has before. He's strangling me. I can barely catch my breath as his lips seer my face, lips, and neck. Josh's hands roam to the back of my dress and I'm about to stop him when he stops himself.

"I have a surprise for you!" He runs into the bathroom. "Close your eyes," he announces before he comes back from the bathroom and I comply wondering what he has planned. "Okay," he says, his voice much closer than before. When I open them, he is kneeling in front of me, with a small black box in the palm of his hand. A simple platinum band with small diamonds on it rests inside. Now I know I've stopped breathing. *Holy Shit!* I stare at him confused."

"Lauren, you are the love of my life. I can't live without you," he is crooning. "I can't imagine what my life would be without you. This past year has been hard on us both, and it's a good indicator what a strong relationship we have. I want you in my life. I want you to be my wife, to be by my side. I want to spend the rest of my life making you happy. I'll be at USC next year, and this is a promise for the future ... our future."

The pounding in my ears doubled and tripled until it sounds like a herd of elephants trampling through my head. This is what I've always wanted, I've always seen for myself, my future, and he's asking, kneeling before me, offering me my fairytale ending, offering me everything my mom and sister never had.

"Josh, I ..."

"I know this ring is not much. But, this is just the beginning. It's a promise. When it comes time to ask you to marry me, I guarantee I'll buy you a huge ring." He stands and pushes stray hair out of my eyes. I look at him perplexed—so, he's not asking now? "Please promise me that you will love me, and only me, for the rest of your life," he says and pushes the ring onto my ring finger without my answer. "We can have everything we've talked about. We'll buy a little house; have a little boy and a little girl. You can have everything you want... it'll be perfect." It takes me back to all the quiet moments we've had, the times that were just us. Everything he has promised me before, he's offering wholeheartedly now and I can't believe it, but it sounds perfect and he is perfect and this moment is the great moment I've dreamed of all my life.

I press my lips to his, pushing out every doubt from the corners of my mind. My dream is within reach—the house, family and the perfect man in my life.

"I take that as a yes?" he pants when he pulls back.

"Yes," I repeat over and over. The delicate ring spins on my finger up and down, symbolizing how crazy and chaotic this night has gone. First, I doubted every part of our relationship, and now, I'm in a huge suite with a promise ring on my finger and Josh in my arms. It may have had a rocky start, but it would turn out to be a perfect night after all.

"I'm going to get us some champagne to celebrate," Josh says and goes back out the doors to the living room.

I stare at myself in the bathroom mirror for a long time—looking for a change in me. Had I matured in just a few minutes? I can't take my eyes off my new fashion accessory. The ring is beautiful, but what would he replace it with? Maybe just a round solitaire on a platinum band ... maybe this ring can be my wedding ring? Maybe he would buy me a huge ring instead with a lot of diamonds that would shine brightly in the light showing me how much he loved me? Anything he picks out would be fine. Maybe we'd plan our wedding on the beach at sunset...*Lauren Miller*... OMG!

Josh is lying on the bed when I emerge from the restroom. His face lights up when I walk back into the room and he pats the bed next to him. I hesitate for a minute realizing we are alone in a hotel room together and I just promised him forever ... what would he expect from me in return for the sparkly bangle now occupying my ring finger. Maybe I sold my soul to the devil for this.

I walk over to the bed and claim the spot next to him. He's propped up on a few pillows and puts his arm behind my shoulders to pull me closer to him. I half lie on his shoulder and half on the bed. We stay that way for a long time, at least until my skin stops tingling and my heart slows. A comedy show comes on the TV and we both laugh at the jokes until my sides hurt. Josh rubs my shoulders and my arms and traces the lines of my face with his fingers until he follows the curve of the beading on my halter-top. My hand roams over his chest and the light dances off the precious stones in the ring. It's the most beautiful thing ever. Lynn is going to be pissed that I'm engaged before she is. Then again, I'm not technically engaged … yet.

"Do you like it?" He rubs his thumb over the ring.

"I love it," I respond easily even though I know I'm going to have to hide it from my mom and dad for a while. Neither will be happy about it, and admittedly it came a lot sooner than I thought it would—but nothing ever goes the exact way you plan, right? So what if we are young?

"Are you sure? I know it's not much." He twirls the ring around my finger, solidifying the future with every turn. "Does it make you nervous?"

"No. It's perfect. I couldn't have picked out a better one for myself." I smile wide and pull myself up to his face to kiss him. He kisses me long and passionately again like he did when we came into the room. I pull back for a moment but his face is back at mine quickly. I pull back again, thrown off by his sudden forcefulness.

"What's wrong?" he asks.

I hesitate to answer. I don't want to ruin the day. "Nothing. Why?"

"You seem tense…" he nuzzles his face into my neck and his tongue presses hard against my rapid pulse. "Just relax," he whispers. The door to the main room opens and closes, vibrating the door to our room. Several people start talking and laughing in the living room. Music turns on and someone starts singing along.

Josh pulls at the halter of my dress again and I shift away. "What's wrong with you tonight?" What's wrong is, this feels forced. He's trying too hard to make this happen. Doesn't he care that all of our friends are in the other room? "Don't you love me? I thought you wanted to."

"Josh, I do love you, but I'm not ready. Just, not like this."

He leans up onto his elbow. "What? What do you mean not like this? We've just had the most romantic night of our lives. I gave you that ring to show you how serious I am about being with you. I've promised myself to you forever."

He's making me feel like a total ass. But, it doesn't change the fact that I'm uncomfortable. "I know, I love you too and I promise you forever. I want to do this with you ..." He doesn't let me finish. He's back on top of me on the bed and pulling roughly at the halter on my dress; the weight of his body presses me harder into the mattress.

My dress is ruined, half ripped and torn off my body. He's working at the clasp of my bra and I'm telling him to stop in a panicked voice. The music in the other room is so loud that no one can hear me. I'm trying not to scream; this is just a mistake, a misunderstanding ...

"Josh, please stop," I beg and he finally listens.

"What the hell is wrong with you?" He sits up and rakes his hands through his hair. I try to pull my dress back together and cover my bare skin. I don't know how I'm going to explain my ruined dress to my parents but I definitely can't tell them the truth.

"You don't love me," he whispers and gets off the bed.

"What? No. I do love you." I reach for him, but he is already almost to the door.

"You don't mean that."

"Yes, I do. I love you, but this isn't how I thought my first time would be. All of our friends are in the next room. You want them knowing that we're in here doing it?"

"I don't care who knows what we are doing! Why do you care so much what other people think?"

"I don't."

"You're a tease," he growls. "This whole night was about making things special for you ... making them right for your first time. You didn't even appreciate everything I've done for you ... that I've given up for you."

"I do appreciate you and what you've done. This just isn't right." Tears are rolling down my cheeks. How did this night go so terribly wrong?

"I should've listened to the guys. I never should've done all this for you and bent over backwards to give you everything. You're so selfish."

I dart off the bed, out the door and down the hallway before I can stop to think of how horrible I look or what everyone is going to think. My dress won't close and I have no shoes. I'm sure I look homeless with my hair messed up and my make up smeared all over my face. How am I going to get home now? And worse, how do I explain how bad I look to my mother? She's going to take one look at my frazzled, unnerved appearance and assume something more happened. Tonight is one big misunderstanding ... it has to be. How can he call me selfish?

I can't worry about what went wrong now—there are other things to worry about. Maybe I can rent a hotel room for the night, even that would be better than going home.

D a n n y

Jeremy almost has me convinced to leave ... almost. I don't like giving in so easily. But, he's right. Lauren may have gone to the room willingly and all of her dreams are coming true. Damn it. That thought has to go. I can't think of his lips on her, his hands going around her waist and him getting to sleep in a bed next to her although he's not interested in the sleeping part; the part of being vulnerable enough to trust someone enough to lie with them —be with them—with no expectation of receiving anything in return except the opportunity to dream next to them. *Shit.*

"Let's go," I say crunching my keys under my fingertips. The keys' jagged edges dig into my palm taking my mind off of how lucky Josh is right now, especially if he has changed and Lauren is special to him.

"Sara," Jeremy calls to her, "we're going."

"But, Danny ..." she starts but stops abruptly. She's standing in front of the open elevator door, no more than twenty feet from me. The look on Sara's face shifts and for several seconds it feels as if I'm trapped in slow motion. Lauren comes stumbling out of the elevator and straight into Sara's arms, taking both of them to the ground. The soles of my shoes slip on the marble floor in my haste to get to them. Jeremy is to her before I'm even halfway there. No one else comes off the elevator. Her shoes are missing and her dress looks as though it's torn in a few places. My blood is cooking all of my internal organs as I fight not to overreact. Josh is lucky he's not on that elevator right now.

"What happened? Lauren, are you hurt? What happened to your dress?" Sara is asking Lauren a thousand questions. I just want to ask one: where the hell is the soon-to-be-deceased Josh Miller?

"It was a mistake, a misunderstanding," Lauren is shaking her head as if she's trying to believe her own words. Sara pushes back Lauren's hair and tries to fix the clasp on her dress. I'm resisting the temptation to touch her. If I touch her, I'll come unglued because she'll probably push me away.

"Danny," Sara shifts. "I need to find a pin to fix her dress. I'll be right back," she says and rushes towards the concierge desk. I pull off my jacket and cover Lauren's splotched pink and red skin. She's sobbing and crying and hurt. He hurt her, as I knew he would. And here I am, not willing to touch her, but wanting to fix it for her all over again. She stretches her arms through my too-long for her jacket sleeves and wipes a few stray clouded black tears from her eyes.

"Do you know what happened?" I ask her still preventing my hand from grabbing hers. "Where are your shoes?"

Lauren's bloodshot eyes finally lock with mine and she lets out a raspy breath and sobs again. "No- I ..." she stutters, "my shoes ... I left them in the room."

"What room? Where is he?"

She stops blinking and several tears race down her cheeks. "I don't remember ... I don't know."

I glare at her, but she swallows hard and I can't be mad at her. I'm doing everything I can to make this right for her, and she's doing everything she can to save me from the demon that is screaming to come out.

"You don't remember?" I gulp, not wanting to ask, but then the question erupts from me, "what did he do to you? Did he hurt you?"

"No, he didn't." She brushes hair off her neck and tucks her legs under her on the floor. Sara returns from the lobby and we help her to her feet.

"We'll be right back," Sara says and ushers Lauren towards the restroom. Jeremy and I pace the hallway waiting for them to return.

"You don't think he raped her, do you?" Jeremy asks the question that has been torturing my mind since Lauren tumbled out of the elevator. No. Josh would never stoop that low, but if Lauren is in this condition it makes me wonder where the hell Jenn is and if we need to stay to bail her out of something too. I'm sure Jeremy has already wondered about that himself.

"No, I don't." I then ask, "what about Jenn?" and watch his whole body go rigid. He already said he was okay with Jenn's decision, but I guarantee he wouldn't be so composed right now if he saw Jenn looking like Lauren did.

"I've already tried her phone," he admits. "It's off." I slap him on the shoulder.

"It'll be okay. Hopefully she's fine. Mike is a jerk, but he doesn't have the track record Josh has for this."

"Yeah," Jeremy says, digging the heel of his shoe into the ground. Impatience overtakes him and he opens his phone to dial her again.

"Ready?" Sara has pulled Lauren's hair into a low ponytail and she's taken all of her make-up off. The slight ruffles of her crystal blue dress peak just below the bottom of my oversized jacket.

"Is she okay?" I ask Sara, wanting to hear Lauren respond, but she doesn't. She doesn't even look at me, and it hurts, more than I can even consider. The fact is, I'm putting myself out there just by being here right now, and she'll never realize or probably even appreciate it.

"Yeah, she's just a little ..."

Jeremy clicks off his phone thrilled with his victory. "She's coming down." He paces in front of the elevator for a few minutes until it finally dings and Jenn rushes off the elevator and into Jeremy's waiting arms.

Lauren is still sobbing and curled into Sara's side. Seeing Jenn so thankful to have Jeremy makes me wish that would've been how Lauren reacted to seeing me. But after what just happened to her, I didn't really expect it.

"Now we're ready," Jeremy announces triumphantly with his tux jacket over Jenn's shoulders. She is crying too, but not nearly as bad as Lauren. She grabs Lauren's hand and they hug before we start heading out the doors to the truck. Seeing both of them comfort each other is more than I'm willing to accept.

I stop before we get to the doors, "What room are they in?" I ask Jenn. I'd drop them off at home and come back to finish what I should've done a long time ago.

Jenn, Sara, and Lauren all look at each other. Sara slightly shakes her head in protest.

Jenn answers anyway with venom seeping through each number, "1022."

"We will take them home and come back," I say to Jeremy and he's already agreeing. Without knowing how many people are up there, we will have to get some friends to come back with us. "Where's your car?" I ask Jeremy as my truck comes into view. I don't trust leaving it here, especially if any of the football players saw us rescuing Jenn and Lauren.

"It's over there." He points two rows over from my truck.

"Okay, I'll take Lauren home and you take Jenn. I'll meet you back at my place." If we can get Justin and Ricky to come back, that will be enough. We'll bring my truck so that we can make a fast getaway if things go bad.

"Danny," Lauren has broken away from Sara and Jenn, "you can't come back here. I don't want you getting in trouble or hurt." I keep walking to my truck, trying not to listen to her. "Danny," she grabs my arm and rushes in front of me, stopping me in the dark parking lot. The slight glow of the fluorescent lights illuminates her blood shot eyes. "Don't be stupid." I look away from her. Sara, Jenn, and Jeremy are already at my truck. I push the unlock button for them to climb in, but Sara stays next to the truck staring at Lauren and I.

"Danny?" Lauren touches my forearm and every muscle in my arm twitches under her chilled, trembling fingers. "Please. Don't."

"Are you worried I'll hurt him or that I'll get in trouble?" Please let her say it's the first.

She chews at her bottom lip like she did the first night at Jess's house. I can't think about that. I can't think about those lips, or the splinters I had to pull out of my knuckles after that night or the broken ribs that never healed from the first time I saved her.

"He's not worth it," she says staring at me with a certain ease in her tone that makes me think I imagined every last word.

"What?" I ask.

"He's not. I don't want you in trouble over him. He's messed up your life, and mine, enough."

Happiness is not something I'm used to having, so when I hear those words from her lips, I'm not sure how to respond. So finally I say, "That's what I've been waiting to hear." Maybe I'm reading more out of what she said, but right now I'm thankful she is leaving the dance with me and not rushing back in to patch things up with Josh.

"Do you promise you aren't coming back here tonight?"

"I promise," I say. I'm shocked when she takes my hand in hers and squeezes.

I help her into the passenger seat of my truck and walk with Sara to the opposite side. "What did you say to her?" I ask Sara while we are alone.

She gives me a sly smile, "I told her you loved her."

"You did what?" I grab Sara's arms and spin her around.

"You know it's true. You'd never tell her yourself." She's right, and I'm not admitting it. I open the door to the truck for her to get in. Maybe Lauren, hearing I love her from someone else, has changed her mind? Is that why she suddenly decided I couldn't come back here? Has she realized what I've done for her and what I'd continue to do for her?

I start the truck and turn down the radio. Sara, sitting in the back seat, rubs Lauren's arm. Her hand is sitting less than six inches from mine on the center console of my truck. Her fingers are calling to mine like the singing sirens themselves, but that would be dancing in dangerous waters right now. I'm sure she wouldn't be okay with me hitting on her, considering what Josh did tonight.

We pull onto the main street to head for her house and she

says, "I can't go home."

"What?" Sara and I both say.

"If my mom sees me like this, she'll know something happened." Lauren sniffles. What the hell am I going to do with her? "Can you take me to a hotel or something? Maybe I could stay at Jenn's place?"

Then Sara says the one thing that I'm thinking, but don't want to consider as a viable option. "We could go back to your place." Yeah, MY place. My new place. Crap.

Lauren objects as I knew she would. "No, I can't ask you to do that. I'll call Jenn. She'll probably be cool with it." She opens her phone and dials Jenn's number. We're sitting at the red light at the corner of the street that goes to my house. All I'd have to do is turn right and we'd be at my place in less than two minutes. That would be so much easier, but she'd get into serious trouble, I'm sure but I'm praying Jenn says it's a no-go.

"Jenn said she doesn't want to go home either," Lauren says and closes her phone. Jeremy calls on my line.

"What do you want to do?" Jeremy asks, as the light turns green.

"Pull into the bank parking lot," I say and turn right and then right again into the parking lot to come up with a game plan.

Sara and Lauren stay in the truck while Jenn stays in Jeremy's car. "What do you want to do?" Jeremy asks and lights a cigarette. We look at both the cars and the girls depending on us to figure out a plan. We can go back to my place, but Lauren's parents won't like that, and she's a minor. Both girls are minors. Jeremy and I would be in deep shit if they called the cops on us.

Jenn climbs from the car with her cell phone in hand. "I called my mom. I told her I'm staying at Sara's tonight. She's cool with it." Jeremy lets out a sigh of relief. Jenn is solved. Now, Lauren.

"I bet Lauren's mom would let her stay at Sara's ..." Jenn says and waves for Lauren to get out of the truck before I can stop her. Lauren climbs out with my jacket pulled tight around her and the ruffles of her dress swishing against her legs. Even though she's shoeless and frazzled, she's the most beautiful thing.

"Do you think your mom will let you stay at Sara's?" Jenn asks Lauren, so I don't have to.

Lauren looks at me, unsure how to respond. "I don't know. I can call her." She pulls out her cell phone and walks away from the group to talk to her mom. She comes back and grabs Sara's hand. Technically, she isn't lying about staying at Sara's house—next year my place will be Sara's place. That's just a minor detail I'm sure she left out.

Lauren seems surprised when her mom agrees—once she talks to Sara on the phone. I'm a little surprised myself, because two seconds later we are heading to my condo.

The group follow me up the sidewalk to the door and tremors are rushing through my fingers as I try to get the key into the lock. Lauren is going to see the new me that she helped mold and create. It's after eleven and I'm wide-awake when we walk inside. Luckily, I have electricity now. Sara goes straight to the dishwasher and washing machine and starts both. Lauren and Jenn both take off our coats and drape them on the back of the couch.

"Is it cool I stay the night?" Jeremy asks looking at Jenn. He sees this as his chance and it probably is.

"Yea, it's cool," I say and pull some waters from the fridge.

"What do you guys want to do? Hungry?" Sara asks and pulls out chips from the cabinet.

"No, thank you," Lauren says. She's standing there looking around the living room, judging every inch of my existence. I'd kill to read her mind, see how she feels about being here with me.

Sara turns on the TV and settles onto the wrap-around couch. "I'll be right back." I head to the bedroom to get out of my uniform. Then I realize that Sara, Lauren, and Jenn are still in their dresses and probably uncomfortable. I grab shirts and shorts for each of them. Sara will be fine sleeping in my clothes, but Lauren and Jenn may not be. We may end up making a run to Dad's place to pick up some of Sara's clothes for them. And I guess tomorrow's out now, too. Jeremy and I will have to postpone our trip to

Molden.

"Um…" I hold out the clothes to the girls, "sorry I don't have anything else."

Sara jumps from the couch and takes the whole stack of clothes from me. "These are perfect! Thank you." She doesn't give the other girls a chance to object, "Come on." Then she calls out as she heads upstairs to my bedroom, "I ordered pizza. Hope you have cash." I guess we are making it an all nighter? Now I know tomorrow is definitely out: a sleepy climber is a dead one.

Lauren comes halfway down the stairs about five minutes later. She's still in her dress. "Is it cool if I take a shower?" I shake off the image of my lucky bar of soap getting to slide against her naked body in my new shower. I haven't even showered in there yet. She'll be the first. And, the first girl I've let stay the night, in my clothes no less. Even Superman had kryptonite, and I'm definitely not made of steel.

"Of course," I say and my voice cracks. "There are some towels in the cabinet. Do you need anything?" My feet shuffle the full way closing the distance between the bottom stair and me.

"No, I just think I'll feel better with a shower," she says and comes down one more step. And I take one step up; we are just three steps apart now. She appears as if the weight of the world is off her shoulders being here. She's not tense or reserved as she had been. She's breathing easier and I am too, until she steps down another step, closing the gap even more.

Then I say something stupid, really stupid, "I'm sorry about tonight. If I could've stopped it from happening, I would've." Open mouth, insert entire shoe store.

"Uh, yeah. I know," she says, and this intimate moment is ruined. She lets out a deep breath and I want to take back every word I just said.

"I'm sorry, I didn't mean to …" I say closing the gap even more and taking another step up. Showing her this is what I want, she is what I want, and I'm offering her everything I have, everything I am—the good, the bad … and the stupid.

"It's okay," she mumbles and shoots me down when she takes a step back. "I better go shower." The ease behind her eyes is gone and I want to kick myself.

"Okay, have a good shower," I say like a complete moron. I'm such a fool. I watch her trudge back up the stairs and want to go with her. But I don't.

Jeremy and the pizza guy show up about the same time. Sara and Jenn are on the couch curled under one of the new blankets Bev bought. Lauren still hasn't come down, so I try to talk Sara into going to get her, but she refuses. I climb the stairs to my bedroom, my feet getting heavier with each step. The bathroom door is shut, but the shower is not on. I knock, "Lauren?"

"Yeah, I'll be right out," she answers and I stand there—looking at my new bedroom furniture and the sheets waiting in the package—I pull them open to make the bed while I wait. Actually, it's wasting time. I'm scrambling for something to say the minute she opens that door. But the fact is, nothing could prepare me for the sight of her in my shirt and shorts rolled up at the waist. I lose control of the stretchy corner of the mattress cover and it snaps across the bed. She laughs instantly lightening the mood and I'm thankful her stress seems to have been washed down the drain.

"Need help?" she asks and grabs the mattress cover on the opposite side of the bed. We finish pulling the cover on, lay out the sheet, and then cover it with the new comforter Bev picked out. I look at Lauren a few times, and each time she catches me, I smile. This is heaven; I don't care that we are doing chores.

"Hey, did you forget the pizza's here?" Sara asks leaning against the bedroom door, ruining this perfect moment of marital normalcy.

"No," I say trying not to blame her. Would it be rude if I walked over and shut the door in her face?

"We'll be right down," Lauren answers and grins at me. She's dismissing her. She wants this to continue or at least I hope that is what she's thinking.

As soon as Sara leaves and we finish the bed, she sits and I join her. Her on the right side and I on the left. "Are you okay?" I ask, not bringing up Josh, but wanting to let her know that I care about what she went through and I care about her.

"Yeah, I feel better."

"You look better." I slip. "I mean, you look relaxed."

"Thank you," she says and her eyes get moist. She could stay here; she's perfect here. This could be our reality. I hate that the door has just thrown itself back open and those damn applications are lying behind her on the dresser. Shit. This is my future. There is no doubt ... at least for me.

I scoot further to the middle of the bed to wrap my arm around her and she pulls herself into me. She stays there, letting me hold her until it feels as though she is a part of me—the best part. She smells like me, and I, like her. Fantastic. Even though I want to stay like this, Sara comes to the door again and coaxes us downstairs. Jenn and Sara smile as I slide pizza onto a plate for Lauren first, then myself, and offer her a soda.

By two a.m. we've eaten pizza and watched a movie. Jeremy and I are sitting on the floor and all the girls are asleep curled around each other on the couch. "Guess we aren't going tomorrow?" Jeremy asks.

"Guess not," I say looking at the girls. There is no way we are going anywhere tomorrow. "Ready for bed?"

Jeremy taps Jenn on the shoulder and she wraps herself into his arms to go to the second bedroom. Now I'm glad I bought a spare bedroom set. I hadn't planned on it originally, but figured Brandon would need one.

Sara is curled onto the lounger part of the couch. I cover her with the blanket and look at Lauren. She helped me make the bed, so that's where she'll go. I pick her up and she stirs. I wait for her to object, but she doesn't. Her sleepy eyes flutter open and she folds her arms around me and snuggles her face into my neck. I'm in trouble. Collecting for Uncle John was hard, but leaving her in my bed is excruciating, especially with how crazy every touch of her skin is making me. "Someday, it'll be my turn to save you," she whispers against my neck, half asleep. I carefully climb the stairs to my room with her safely in my arms.

"You already have," I say and lay her gently on the bed and cover her. I've never had such a strong connection with a girl, or thought one looked so irresistibly sexy, in my entire life.

I grab my pillow and a spare blanket and lay on the floor next to her. There's plenty of room on the couch, but I can't bring myself to leave her and climbing in bed next to her is out of the question. It's a queen-sized bed, but she'd probably freak out. I don't want the rumors she's heard about me make her doubt why I brought her here.

L a u r e n

Nightmares of Josh pushing me onto the bed and tearing my dress shock me awake. The room is dark, but I know where I am. Danny saved me, again. I reach to the opposite side of his bed, and he's not there. I slide my legs off the bed to go find him. It doesn't take long to realize that he's fast asleep on the floor next to me and I fall across him. It startles him awake and he jerks up from the floor, grabbing me in the process.

"Are you okay?" he asks holding me tight.

"Yeah," I say, forcing the words from my mouth, "sorry. I didn't mean to wake you."

He lets me go and scoots back, relaxing against his nightstand. "It's okay, I wasn't really asleep. It's kind of weird being on the floor."

"How come you slept on the floor?" I ask, and I'm glad the dark is hiding the blush that's burning my skin. Then he turns on the light and I blush even more; he only has a pair of shorts on and I'm staring at every well-defined ripple in his arms and chest. Oh man. My mind just went into a dozen places, all of which are cumulating into bright red beacons on my face.

"I didn't think you'd be okay if…"

I try to blow it off as though it is no big deal. "I wouldn't have minded. I sleep with my girlfriends all the time. And we're friends, right?"

"Yeah," he answers and grins with his dimple that makes warmth spread through me and brings a five-alarm fire raging beneath my skin.

"Okay then," I say, trying to quell the fire and my nerves. "It's settled." I grab his hand and stand from the floor to pull him toward the bed. I swear his skin is turning just as red as mine. What am I doing? I seriously hope the rumors about him weren't *all* true. Otherwise, walking away from Josh tonight may have been futile. Because I'm sure being with someone I haven't even dated wouldn't be perfect for my first time either. "You don't have to sleep on the floor." I reassure myself this is the right thing to do, that Danny knows I'm only inviting him into the bed as a friend, nothing more … he won't try anything.

I settle back into bed and watch him stride easily to the other side looking completely unaffected. That is, until he hesitates pulling back the covers and looks at me again. He finally eases onto the bed and covers his legs.

"You ready?" I ask and he nods. Turning off the light causes the mood in the room to change quickly. Heat from his body is radiating under the sheet against my side and my leg. I swear the bed just got a whole lot smaller. I roll the opposite way to face away from him—hoping it calms my nerves—but it doesn't and I find myself flopping towards him.

"I can go back to the floor," he says and the bed shifts.

"No." I reach for him through the darkness.

"Lauren," he comes closer to me on the bed. He's just inches away, but I can't see his face. "I know what happened tonight. I promise nothing will happen, but I don't want to make you uncomfortable." He's talking barely above a whisper, saying just the right thing, at the right time. "I can sleep on the floor, it's no big deal. Really."

But it is a big deal, a big deal for me. I want to ask him what he was doing at the dance tonight. I want to ask him if he knew what Josh had planned and I want to know what is going to happen between us—if anything, because right now it seems something will … or maybe I want something to happen. He said we are friends, does that mean he doesn't want anymore? Does it mean that he doesn't feel anything since I went to the dance with Josh? Do I really want him to feel something? That would be playing with fire, and I don't like being burned, especially since everyone was very judgmental at the benches when we were hanging out. Do I really want to put myself out there like that? I'd never fit into his world … nor he in mine. Our friends won't allow it, and neither would my parents if they heard any of the rumors about Danny.

"Danny," I sigh, trying to calm every frantic thought racing through my head. And his breath on my face is not making things better, bringing back memories of being in his arms and kissing him in my kitchen last year.

"Lauren," he whispers breathlessly. "I'll sleep on the floor," he repeats as though he's trying to convince himself it's what he should do. The bed creaks and he's gone.

"No, please don't," I say. "I'll sleep on the floor. This is your first night here and this is your new bed."

"That wouldn't be very chivalrous of me," he laughs. I don't.

"It's okay," I start to move, but he stops me by reaching across the bed and grasping my forearm.

"Okay, we'll both stay in the bed. But, if you get uncomfortable, I'm hitting the floor. Deal?"

"Deal," I say convinced that I can calm myself and be mature enough to make it through this. I wait until he settles back into his pillow before I huddle down into the covers and try to steady my nerves. This is really no big deal. I sleep with my girlfriends all the time after all. This isn't any different, right?

When the sun starts coming through the windows three hours later, I want to throw a pillow at it. I've never slept so sound in my entire life. Danny's chest is slightly rising and falling beneath my face; my arm is draped across his bare stomach. His skin is just like his personality: hot and addictive. I want to stay here the rest of the day. But girlfriends don't usually cuddle with each other. I roll the opposite way, hoping he doesn't catch me lying on him. His eyes are closed, but the corner of his mouth pulls up. He's already awake and I can't help but wonder how long he's known I was there.

"I wondered if you were awake." He covers his face with his hands and rubs his eyes before rolling over to face me. "Did you sleep okay?"

Something tells me he's been awake for a while, but didn't move because I was lying on him. *Embarrassing.*

"Yeah, but I'm not ready to be awake yet," I say, but it comes out like a whine.

"Okay," he slides out of bed and pulls the curtains shut. Then walks to the bathroom and closes the door the room goes dark again. He opens the bedroom door as if he's leaving, but he looks up and down the hall and shuts the door again. He climbs back into bed and I watch him carefully and wait. He settles back onto his pillow, fluffing it and adjusting it until it's perfect. "What's wrong?"

"Nothing," I answer and lie there uncomfortably. The bed suddenly isn't as easy to be in as it was before. He notices.

"Something's missing," he says and lifts up the sheets and holds out his arm. I'm shocked that he picked up on what I craved, but didn't want to ask for. Then again, having girls share his bed isn't a new thing. I don't say anything. I just move closer and put my head on his arm. He shifts his shoulder and my face ends up on his chest. "You weren't shy before. It's not like you didn't sleep there all night, already." He laughs and his arm tightens across my shoulder when I start to move away. He holds me against him, ending my feeble attempt at getting away.

Finally, his eyes close and he's breathing easy. Testing the water, I ease my hand onto his ribs at first, and then rest my forearm there. It's not until I'm sure he's back to sleep and he has relaxed his grip on my shoulder that I lay my arm completely across him. My hand presses into his side and I hold him, not wanting the day to come, not wanting this moment to end and not wanting to face Josh yet to find out what the hell he was thinking, and where we go from here. Being in bed with Danny can't help that situation, I'm sure.

Danny's cell phone rings a few hours later. I'm still curled into his side with my face hovering close to the nape of his neck, drifting in and out of consciousness. He moves as little as possible to get the phone from the nightstand. "Hello?" he quietly answers and his fingers run the length of my spine. Then he kisses the top of my head and I seriously stop breathing. Friends definitely don't kiss … in bed … half naked. I start to pull away and he tightens his grip again. I look up at him on the phone, "sorry," he mouths.

"I don't think we're going. I'll have to call you back." He disconnects and stares at me, carrying the weight of the world. "I know I just crossed the line. I'm sorry, I wasn't thinking."

My regret from waking up with him the night at Jess's comes to mind and I relax. I won't continue to live with regret. "It's okay," I say. And it feels he's not breathing anymore. He's waiting to see what his little show of affection will do to this precarious situation we are in. He may be used to this, but its really uncharted territory to me. I've never shared a bed with anyone other than my girlfriends and family. I don't tell him that although he probably already knows.

"Are you ready for breakfast?" he asks to break the ice and I'm not sure that I am. In fact, I'm not sure where today is going after the feeling of his skin under my palm and him kissing the top of my head. Overall, his whole attitude seems to have changed literally overnight. And now, seeing his place and hearing he is working makes things even stranger. Danny told me before he can't change his life and he didn't see a house or have a direction—but that is exactly what's going on. He woke up and decided to be everything I've always wanted, except the football part. There are trophies from middle school in a box next to the bed, but they look as if he's throwing them out.

"Yeah," I finally say when I've stalled long enough, wondering if I really want to climb out of bed. Life has to start again sometime, and it's almost 10am as it is. My mother will expect a call from me soon, or expect me home. I'm going to be grilled over the dance and why I ended up at Sara's house when I went to the dance with Josh. Mom knows Josh and Danny hate each other, and there shouldn't have been any reason for me to hang out with her at the dance, or at least, no reason that I'm willing to tell my mom. I'll have to come up with a plan before I head home and an acceptable pair of clothes to wear.

D a n n y

I mess up and kiss the top of her head. She tenses against me and her heartbeat quickens against my side. *Crap.* I hold her tight and apologize immediately, but the damage is already done. Friends don't leisurely kiss their friends while cuddling in bed. I'd like to pretend it never happened, but it did and she's going to jump out of bed any minute in response. After what Josh did, I'm surprised she even climbed in bed with me at all. She trusted me and with one stupid gesture, she's shutting me out again, probably assuming that I'm looking for a lot more than just lying here. But nothing can be farther from the truth!

Evan called to remind me of our climb and find out when we are meeting up but I tell him I don't think it is happening. I still have to get Lauren home and if she's willing to spend the day with me, Molden can wait. I ask her about breakfast to see if she's willing to at least hang around here after spending the night with me. It is hard thinking tonight she won't be in my bed and my new place will be completely empty for me to share with my demons.

She agrees to have breakfast and I watch her pull herself off of the bed—still looking amazing in my clothes. I'm staring at her perfect legs and jealous that my shirt gets to hold her body like that. I remind myself to behave and start pulling on a shirt when I notice she is watching my every move. It didn't dawn on me that she's probably never slept over with a guy and it's thrilling to think that I may hold that honor. Maybe. I'm not sure how close she and Josh got over the summer. "Do you like pancakes?" I ask and she jumps and looks to the floor as if she's looking for something that's obviously not there.

"Yeah, they're okay," she stutters, still feeling uncomfortable. She's staring at the bed; she's probably worried what people will say about her leaving the dance with me last night and wondering what Jenn will tell her friends about us being in bed together and sleeping in so late.

Lauren is anxious and dazing off, and I want to reassure her that everything will be fine, but that's not for certain. Tomorrow we will be back at school and I can't control the rumors that she'll face or how she'll handle them. All I have is last night and right now. And time is fleeting. The plan for the day needs to be laid out soon before she can change her mind.

I cross to her side and watch her carefully. Does she already regret staying here? Is she going to call this a mistake? I'm going to scream if she does. Don't ruin this. Don't destroy this memory for me. "Are you okay?"

Lauren looks at me as though she didn't realize I walked over to her. Our bodies are definitely closer than I'd be comfortable with if she were anyone else. She shivers and slightly shakes. "Are you okay?" I ask again. My question goes unanswered. She's not okay, and it's probably the regret she's already feeling over sharing something so personal, so intimate, with me. What she doesn't realize is, last night was a first for me too; I've never let anyone stay in my bed overnight before. Never. Because that means they are important, and my old life didn't involve attachment to anything that could be risked.

With my fingers under her chin, I pull her eyes up to me and a stray tear breaks free of her lashes and rushes down her face. "What's wrong?" I ask the one thing that I don't truly want to know. Doubt is building in my stomach and I hate that I've put myself out there to let my heart get trampled again.

"I'm tired," she whispers.

"Do you want to go back to bed?" I ask and pull the comforter back for her to climb in. Maybe the look of disappointment on her face isn't disappointment at all? "You can go back to sleep if you want," I say, being mindful not to imply I'd stay with her. She can stay here permanently and I'd sleep on the floor if that would make her happy.

"No, I can't go back to sleep. My mother is going to be mad if I don't go home soon." And she escapes back to her safe life. But not before I can ask, "Can we talk about last night?" My lungs can't stretch any further than the amount of air I just pulled in. I want to ask her where we go now and what happened with Josh specifically. Mostly because I want to hear her say they are over for good.

"I don't," she sucks in a deep, ragged breath and I can't help it. My arms close around her and pull her so close to me that her faint breathing is working its way through my t-shirt. I'm an ass for trying to push this now and it's upset her again. I have permanent foot-in-mouth syndrome. I let the subject drop and she stays in my arms. I won't bring it up again. I won't risk this being the last time she is willing to come here. I have to watch what I say, because this is really thin ice I'm skating on and there's definitely a risk of drowning.

"Hey, you up?" Jeremy knocks at the door.

"Yeah," I say with Lauren still in my arms. I start to step back and her arms snake around my waist showing me she isn't ready for me to let go yet. "What's going on?"

"Evan called, said he can meet up at noon if we can." I look at the clock, it is ten-thirty and really, noon is doable, depending on Lauren. If she says yes to going today, we'd have time to get some breakfast and go. But if she says no, then it's going to become more involved—plus, I'm not sure I'd want to go anyway. I've already decided I'm never washing the clothes she's wearing and I'm debating how long her smell will stay on the sheets.

"Go where?" she asks without taking her face from my chest.

"Molden Rock. We were supposed to go for a climb today."

"Go ahead and go. I'll call my mom." *Damn.*

"No. I told him we couldn't go this morning when he called. I want to make sure you get home and stuff."

"I don't want you to change your plans." She releases my back and pulls the bottom of her shirt straight as though she's going back to business as usual. "You should go. I'm sure you'll have a blast."

"Why don't you and Jenn go with us?" I ask and silently beg for her to say yes.

She weighs her options by looking at the bed, then to me and to her dress hanging on a hanger in the open closet. If she says yes, it is going to be the best day of my life. If she says yes, that means everything from last year is undone and we are starting new. If she says yes, that means Josh is a thing of the past and I'll have her to myself for the first time since we've met. If she says yes. And she knows I'm waiting, patiently watching every breath leaving her perfect lips. "We can go to my dad's place and pick up clothes for you guys. We'd be back by dark. It's only about an hour long drive." I add, hoping to entice her in any way possible.

Two hours later, we meet Evan, Ricky, Alexis, Justin, Jess, and a few other people in the grocery store parking lot at the base of the mountain. Lauren, Jenn and Sara are in the backseat of my truck, laughing and giggling. Mr. Hyde must have done something right during his stay in hell, because this is paradise. Lauren will get to see me in a new light today doing something I love and something I'm dying to share with her.

Josh Miller and Mr. Hyde can go back to hell, never to be seen or heard from again; now that Lauren is at my side and letting me in, nothing can go wrong. All I have to do is get her to see the real me and get her through the miserable week of rumors ahead. My application to the explorer program will be completed as soon as I get home and I may even fill out the application for Summit Estates. Yes, the future is looking bright and Lauren is the sun.

L a u r e n

My mother is going to be furious. I call and leave her a message on her cell phone, knowing I'll get bad reception until we get closer to home. When she gets the message that I'm not coming home until late, I know I'll be in deep trouble. I'll be grounded for another month at least although, if rumors over what happened at the dance get back to my dad, they'll probably throw me into a convent. At least Danny isn't on the football team, and I highly doubt Jenn will tell anyone I slept in the same room with him last night. She has too much to risk considering she slept with Jeremy. Nothing happened between any of us, but it can be implied.

We stop at the grocery store for sodas and snacks before taking a really long, steep road up the mountain to a huge clearing with rock cliffs on one side and a dense, tree-lined shoulder on the other. Danny climbs out and starts pulling on heavy-duty boots as Jenn, Jeremy and Sara cross the road into the trees. I stay by the truck with Danny, concerned that the borrowed tennis shoes I have on are one size too big and not enough for what he has planned.

"Don't worry; you won't need anything heavier than that. We'll be doing the real climbing today." He smiles and I want to stay lost in his eyes forever, that is, until he pulls off his shirt to show his perfect washboard abs that I can still feel under my finger tips. He's beautiful, he knows it ... and that terrifies me. Guys like Danny don't stay with girls for too long, even the girls at school confirmed that about him and I doubt I can hold his interest. He grins and pulls another shirt on and a sweatshirt while I try not to think about what everyone has said about him.

Danny grabs my hand and pulls me across the road into the trees down a path that I can't see too well, but he seems to know exactly where we're going. Up and down we go through the dense forest, surrounded by evergreens at least ten times taller than me until we come to a huge rock clearing. People I recognize from Jess's house and some I don't are already winding their way up the large white boulders next to a perfect stream. There's no way I'm going up those; each of the rocks is at least two times taller than I am. Danny pulls on my hand and we are over the first set of rocks before I can blink. It's easier than it looked with Danny holding onto my hand and gently guiding me up the easiest path.

"Just one more," he says, but it's the largest rock so far. He slides his hand between the crevices made by two rocks pushed against each other. With his boots pressed hard against the face, he maneuvers up the steep facing. The veins and muscles in his arms twist and contort until his entire weight is at the top. Last year I would've sworn those arms were from fighting; obviously, I was wrong since it seems he is a pro.

"Give me your hand," he says leaning down as far as he can. "Put your foot there," he points to a rut in the rock. I comply, but I'm not stable when he starts to pull me up. My foot slips and my chest hits hard onto the side of the rock knocking the wind out of me. Sharp pains radiate through my ribs as I gasp. My ears are ringing from the pain. Danny tightens his grip on my hand and wraps his other hand around my forearm to gently ease me back into a heap on the ground.

"Can you breathe?" he asks climbing from his perch and kneeling beside me.

I'm not sure how to answer other than to cough. Several of the guys heard Danny yell when I slipped and they start climbing back down to us. This is really awkward. He'll never want to bring me again, I'm sure. "Here, sit up," Danny wraps his arms around me and pulls me towards him until I'm sitting with my head cradled into his neck. His cologne, or maybe his deodorant, is drifting from his skin and I lean into him to get a deeper smell of it.

"Is she okay?" Jeremy asks from above us. Neither of us moves. Danny's arms stay around me, enveloping me in his safety and his warmth.

Danny presses his face close to my ear, "You can stay there all day if you want, but you have to tell me if you are hurt first."

A grin spreads across my face, "I'm okay." I resist laughing at myself.

"She's fine," he says to Jeremy and I hear footsteps heading away. "Are you sure?" Danny leans in and asks again. Leaning back, I stare at the fear behind his eyes. He looks terrified, but he's struggling to keep it together.

"Are you okay?" I ask and sit up on my own. "Danny?" He glances away and up towards the top of the rocks.

"You ready to try again?" He avoids the question and stands to turn away from me.

"Danny," I grab his hand and pull myself off the ground. I wedge myself between him and the crevice. "What's wrong?"

"Nothing," he says, but he won't look at me and he's starting to remind me of the day in the parking lot at school when he started crying for no reason. I hope he doesn't cry or take off on me.

"Why won't you look at me?"

So he does; but he looks down at me, keeping his head tilted so that the moisture doesn't escape. I've upset him. He's probably disappointed that I didn't crawl up the rocks as though it was no big deal. Sara and Jenn both did it so easily; it can't be as hard as it seems. "I'll try harder. I'm sorry I almost pulled you off the rock. I'll be more careful. I promise."

Danny furrows his brow. He didn't like the lack of sincerity I put into my words, so I repeat, "I'm sorry. I didn't mean to fall." I put emphasis on my apology but he rakes his fingers harshly through his hair and steps back. So much for today being awesome and figuring out what's going on between us. He is just as judgmental as Josh is ... errors are not an option. I can't get into that type of relationship again.

The truck is not far, and the rocks below us are not as treacherous. When he doesn't respond and his frustration with me is growing, I slide out from between him and the rock and start heading back down the way we came. I turn around to lie on my stomach to ease down the first set of rocks; Danny has his hand over his eyes and he's shaking his head. I'm going to apologize again when he finally looks at what I'm doing.

"Stop ..." Danny comes towards me, "you'll hurt your stomach if you do that." He grabs my hands and pulls me back up next to him. "Sometimes I don't get you ..." he says staring at me through his blurry eyes. "Why are you apologizing? You did that at Jess's house too and I don't understand that. You have nothing to be sorry for."

"I didn't want you to think I wasn't trying ..." I'm careful with my words; I don't want to piss him off and get left here. I heard the rumors about him leaving Jackie at Vince's, so I'm not taking my chances. "I don't want you to think that I don't want to be here."

He laughs. "If you didn't want to be here, I assumed you'd just tell me. I know you're scared to do this, but I didn't think you intentionally slipped or tried to hurt yourself."

"What were you upset about?" He swallows hard and then stiffens like a statue—cold and lifeless.

Reluctant to answer, he finally looks me in the eye; all color has drained from his face. "Because, I've watched you pull off in an ambulance before and I can't stand the idea of that ever happening again." A lone tear escapes his lashes; he blinks hard and swipes it away like a toxic poison. The fight at my house still looms in his mind, but to me, that's old news.

"You didn't mean for me to get hurt that night; it wasn't your fault." I say, voice shaky. "They hurt me, you didn't." It feels as though he is denying me air when he won't look at me; he tilts his head back with his eyes closed. "Danny ..." I whisper, craving those ice blue pools to look at me. "What happened to me isn't your fault. That fight, my injuries, none of it. I've never blamed you. It was Josh's fault." He finally opens his eyes and several more tears race down his cheek faster than my heart is beating. He may blame himself, but I've blamed my mother and her meddling since that night.

"Watching you pull away in that ambulance ..." He takes a deep breath trying to stop more tears from coming. "That was the most awful day of my life. Just letting you go, not knowing if you were okay. When you slipped just now, I panicked. I don't know what I'd do if you got hurt again because of me."

I wrap my arms around him and his body shakes. The sun is peaking above the trees into the valley and it's starting to warm my arms behind his back. His heartbeat sounds like a full high school drum line pounding deep in his chest. "After today, I don't want you to think of that night ever again." I stand below his eyes and squint at him with the sun glaring down on us. Our group is yelling and clapping on top of the rocks and the sound of people splashing in the creek is echoing through the valley. It's too chilly to get into the water, so I hope that's not what Danny has in mind; then again, after this I'm not sure he'll want to stay. I'd hate to think this could ruin our day, but it can.

"It's hard not to ..." he finally says and rests his forehead to mine. The tenderness in his eyes and in his arms makes me feel like the only girl in the world and brings back the thousands of thoughts I've had about him. That very first day I walked into Mountain View High School I was so focused on my future and finding my football hunk that I completely overlooked him. But that doesn't matter now. There's always been something missing with Josh that has always been there with Danny, even through the confusion and the heartbreak. Deep down, I know he only came to the dance last night because he knew I was in trouble. He knew it even before I did, I'm sure. He would've killed Josh if I gave him the chance. The absurd ring Josh gave me is burning a hole in my pocket and it will go back to him tomorrow, along with any feelings I've ever had for him. He was out of line trying to trick me into having sex with him. Danny had me half dressed next to him all night and was happy simply lying with me and comforting me with no expectation of anything in return. I've been stupid chasing Josh all this time, when I've had someone like Danny standing right in front of me. God, I hate when my mom is right.

"I don't want you blaming yourself anymore." My palm slides

easily up his chest to his cheek and around his neck. I hesitate and let out the air trapped in my lungs, trying to gain the courage for what I'm trying to do. I've never made the first move with a guy, but if I don't try, I may never know what might have been.

Danny's right hand comes up to rest at the base of my neck as he tilts his head down to me. My shaky hand moves to his jaw line and I lick my lips just seconds before his meet mine. Electricity pierces through every part of my body. If he feels half of what I do … this has to be love. Love? A four-letter word I never would've thought I'd use in the same sentence as Danny. But right now, he consumes every inch of my being. How did this happen? How did my dream life change after one night? I must be insane, or maybe it's all the fresh air. Either way, it's blissful being wrapped in his arm in this beautiful place. Perfect. Absolutely perfect.

D a n n y

Lauren pulls me down to her lips and presses her entire body against me. The raw emotions racing through me burns every part of my body stronger than any shot of alcohol I've ever taken. She is my new drug, my new addiction, but then again, she has always been. My heart threatens to explode out of my chest. If I don't calm down and regain control we are going to be in trouble, but it is thrilling and refreshing to have her crave me for once. There are worse ways to die than to be lost in her kiss.

With her back resting against the large rock, she pulls me in tighter and I have to stop to catch my breath. Her growing smile, the twinkle of the afternoon sun in her eyes, and her perfectly smooth lips are making me want to ditch my friends and go home to the comfort of my bed for the rest of the afternoon. If she kissed me like this last night, I never would've slept next to her; a cold shower and the couch would have been my best friends. In fact, I'll need to breathe steadier and stop thinking of her in my t-shirt … then she whispers my name before my lips claim hers, sending my body into overdrive.

Lauren has to know what she's doing to me and how much I love it. We can't stay down here the whole day; my friends will start goading me soon and I'm sure that will embarrass her. None of my friends have seen me with a girl like Lauren, so I'm already going to catch hell for her coming today. This kiss, and her not so innocent touch, is worth it. She has awakened parts of my soul that Mr. Hyde had locked away deep inside.

My body curses when I pull back from her passionate lips. Part of her still lingers deep inside me, but this isn't why I'm with her, and I refuse to have her compare me to Josh ever again. I won't hurt her or betray her trust. "Do you want to try again?" I ask, and wait for her head to catch up to the rest of her body. I press my fingers to her heart wanting to feel a part of me has relocated to her. I'm hoping she's let me in and decided that what I'm offering her is all she's ever wanted and more.

"Can you give me a few minutes?" She relaxes against the rock and basks in the sun as though we are at the beach. It is getting warm, or my temperature has risen by at least ten degrees. I pull my sweatshirt over my head and watch her yank hers off, revealing a paper-thin white tank top. It's just tight enough to show off the curves of her body and her chest rising and falling as she tries to cool herself down. She could wear that and my shorts to bed every night when she moves in with me ... I won't mind.

And I let my mouth get away from me, "You're eighteen in a year and a half right?"

Her eyes fly open and she studies me. My hands rest easily on her hips; only the thin cotton material veils the heat of her body against my palms. More laughter comes from the rocks above and someone starts yelling my name. *Go ahead, keep calling. You're going to be waiting for a while.* She pulls me back down to her lips and I'm lost in her soft body and heavy breathing. Lust, passion, love and fear rush through me all in alternating waves. What if she's not okay with my career choice and takes off like my egg donor? What if she really does want to go back to University of Illinois? What if she tells me this is mistake? *Scratch that. I can't think about that.* This doubt needs to stop seeping into this perfect moment—it can't deter me.

"A little under two years," she says when she finally releases my lips. "Why?"

I kiss her again, distracting her from my out of place question. It works. She completely forgets that I even asked and rubs against me causing my brain to short circuit. She's going to be the death of me. I'm going to have a heart attack before I graduate high school.

"Ready?" I ask, and reluctantly she kisses me one more time and nods. If someone told me yesterday morning this is where I'd be today—I'd swear they were lying.

She turns and I show her how to position her hands in the crevice and then steady her foot on the hold. Putting my hands on her hips and then her thighs, I push her easily up onto the rock that she slid down from. Thankfully she wasn't hurt, and it led to the most amazing moment of my life, and the realization that she's going to move in with me. I'm going to give her everything she's ever dreamed of ... I just have to convince her.

Jess steals her from me and hugs her tight, "there you are! We were about to send in a search party for the two of you." Jess gives me a knowing look and the corner of my mouth creeps up. Who cares if she knows ... in fact, who cares if anyone knows. I'd shout it from the top of Molden Rock right now for the entire valley to hear.

Evan, Jeremy, Justin, and Ricky come over with ropes and bindings. They've been waiting for me to go up the rock face, but Jeremy knows what a fine line I'm walking right now and he kept the others at bay.

"I'm going to go for a climb with them. Will you be okay staying here with the girls?"

"Where are you going?" she asks and I'm hesitant to tell her.

"Up there," I point to the large rock face across the stream. Lauren's eyes grow wide as she surveys the rock face to the very top. I've done this dozens of times, but this will be the first time she sees it, and it is nerve racking to think she may not be okay with this. But she hasn't run yet, not even after seeing me with another girl, my drunken outburst, my tantrum at the benches or even her party last year—I've put her through so much; it's time I start making it up to her.

"Yeah, it's no big deal. I promise, I've done it before," I say being as passive as I can, hoping to build confidence in her.

"Don't worry," Sara chimes in and spreads a blanket out on one of the large plateau rocks, "they have done it lots of times. Come on, you can chill with us while they go."

Lauren looks at the summit again and just nods. If she asks me not to go, I won't do it ... and I'll get a lot of crap from ...

everyone. "It's okay," I sit down next to her on the blanket and rest my hand on hers, just out of sight of Jess and Sara. She hasn't indicated it is okay that we go pubic, so I'll let her make the first move in that department, although everyone here knows what we were just doing. Maybe she'll start hanging out at my place after school—we can use the excuse that we are running lines, but I really have some other things in mind.

Lauren's hand comes out from under mine and my eyes travel to hers, searching for something, anything to indicate I've done something wrong. But she puts her smooth hand on top of mine and traces the veins in the back of my hand with her index finger. My eyes and hers meet and I'm trapped there again until Jeremy calls for me from the other side of the creek.

"I have to get going," I say, but I don't move away; instead, I lean towards her and wait to see if she meets me halfway. But, she doesn't. We aren't to the *public display of affection* stage yet. I'm not really okay with that and the idea that we aren't brings on a whole slew of self-doubt that I can't be preoccupied with while I'm trying to do this climb. One simple distraction could cause one of us to get seriously hurt.

"Be careful," she smiles and looks out of the corner of her eye to Jess and Sara. At least she's considering meeting me halfway, and that is a good sign.

I grin, "I will. I promise." Being as sneaky as I can, I kiss my fingertips and press them to the back of her hand. She doesn't pull away and the grin she gives me says it was a smart move. "I ..." my mouth snaps shut, ending what my head is thinking, what I want to truly say.

"I'll be right back," I say instead and smile at her lying back on the blanket enjoying the afternoon sun.

L a u r e n

Jess, Jenn, Sara, Alexis, and I lie back on the blanket and enjoy the sun warming our skin. The rushing water echoing through the valley is almost deafening. I can't stop thinking about the feel of his chest pressed against mine, and the way my heart accelerated just by being that close to him. His presence is intoxicating. Waking up next to him this morning felt good, too good. I know I'm going to be in deep trouble when I get home tonight, but right now, all I care about is him and soaking up every bit of this day. My bad memories with Josh have been replaced by the smooth, hypnotic feeling of Danny's hands on my hips and his fingers pressing into my back because he couldn't get enough of me. And I didn't have to be the one to pull away, he did. He was satisfied to accept only what I was willing to give and didn't push for more. It was just enough. In fact, I'm the one who initiated more, and he didn't take advantage.

Danny, Justin, Jeremy, Ricky, and Evan easily maneuver across the rocks jutting above the creek to the opposite side. We watch as they link together their ropes and harnesses and then start snaking their way up the giant, jagged rock face. They look like little ants attached to dental floss. If he gets hurt trying to show off for me, I'm going to freak out.

"How many times has he done this?" I ask.

"He's been climbing with Clint since he was ten. Don't worry. He will be careful," Sara says and smiles. She has to know how I feel about him since it's pretty obvious I stayed in his bed last night.

"So, Lauren, Sara said your siblings live in Illinois still?" Jess asks.

"Yeah, they go to college at University of Illinois," I say, never taking my eyes off Danny.

"Is that your plan too?"

"I don't know. I mean, it's not like they'll still be there by the time I go. My sister only went because my brother did, and this is his last year."

"You don't think your sister will stay?"

"Probably not. If she meets a first drafter, she's out of there."

"What do you mean?" Sara asks pulling my attention away from Danny.

"Lynn only went to college to meet a husband. She didn't really intend on staying there for the education. She's flunking most of her classes right now. If my mom knew, she'd blow a gasket since they are footing the bill."

"Wow, that's harsh," Jenn says. "She only went to college to get married, huh?"

"Yeah, that is the sad truth." The words sting as I say them. That had pretty much been my small town dream, too. Meet the football star, get married by nineteen like my parents and support my husband and children better than my mother did. That is what a wife and mother is after all—the glue that holds it all together. So who could ask for anything more?

"What about you then? College?"

"I'm not sure. I might just get a job after school and try to figure out a plan later." Danny is the changing factor—he is the unexpected wild card of it all. He came out of nowhere and now I don't know what I want. I can't see my future without him, but I can't see my dream life with him. Would he really want to have a wife and the responsibilities of a family? Without knowing his past, I don't know what he plans on doing for the future. And I don't really see him as a white picket fence living, mini-van driving, dad of two, trucking the kids to soccer, football and baseball games, after all.

"You know, the hospital is always looking for volunteers and assistants. If you're looking for a job after school or over the summer I can hook you up."

Mom said I could get a job after the first semester grades are in. Working with Jess would be awesome, "what would I have to do?"

"You'd start off small at first. I work in the maternity ward now, so I'd see if you could help with the babies and stuff. You'd help clean up, hold the babies when needed, organize stuff. Pretty much you'd get assigned to a nurse and do anything they ask you to do. I think you'd love it." It sounds pretty wonderful.

"I'll have to ask my mom, but I'm sure she'd be okay with it." Danny and the group are halfway up the face and making excellent time. If I'm going to get answers, it has to be now. He'll be at the top and back to me soon.

"What about Danny?" I ask Sara. "Do you know what he wants to do?"

Sara and Jess both look panicked and neither answers right away. So I ask, "what is going on?"

Sara swallows hard before answering. I'm hanging on her every word. "He's still not sure what he wants to do. He didn't really have a future until you came along."

"Huh? What do you mean he didn't have a future?" I ask confused. Danny had said he didn't have a future before, but how could his future have anything to do with me?

Jess touches Sara's shoulder. Jenn and Alexis are both leaning forward, now paying attention to the conversation. "Tell her," Jess says.

Sara stares at Danny for a second. "None of you can tell Danny I told you any of this. He will be so mad if he found out."

"Deal," we each say and wait for her to continue. She is battling telling us and I almost wish everyone wasn't listening. It'd be better if she only told me, in case it's something I can't handle.

"Do you remember the months Danny was gone last year?"

"Yeah," I say thinking of the day he returned to school and stopped me from destroying my locker.

"Well, he wasn't in trouble or anything. He was in rehab."

"Rehab?" I almost laugh, "for what? He told me he didn't do

drugs."

"And he never did. He drank, pretty much every day."

Oh. My. God. I'm not laughing anymore; she's serious. "So the night at Jess's..."

"Yeah," Jess chimes in, "he was drunk. He still doesn't remember everything that happened that night."

"Was that why he grabbed me?" I stutter.

"We think so," Sara says and Jenn and I both gasp. That makes sense, considering he hasn't been violent towards me since then. Although, I have frustrated him, I'm sure.

"So, he went to rehab because he hurt me?" I dive deeper into the story, wanting full disclosure before Danny returns. He won't tell me this himself, so I'm relying on Jess and Sara to tell me the truth. If there is anyway for him to be my future, I have to know his past.

"Not exactly," Sara starts, "see, he actually went to rehab because he knew he wouldn't have anything in life with the way he was living. And he figured you didn't want him because of the way he was."

"So the condo, the changed attitude ... all that is my fault?" The realization makes me almost pass out. That is a lot of responsibility —how am I supposed to help him be clean and a better person when my life and future are uncertain. This is more than I'm ready for. More than I can handle right now. More than he can really expect from me, and more than I can expect from myself.

"Basically ..." Jess says as we look back to the rocks. They are at the top, each of them stretched as high as they can, waving to us. We wave back and my thundering heartbeat overtakes my ears and throat. Do I really want to be responsible for keeping him clean?

"If I was so important, then who was that girl he was with?" I ask, digging the hole deeper with every shovel full of dirt.

"He wasn't with her. He never was. We didn't get the full story until later. She was just a favor he was doing for his Uncle."

Oh no. His bookie Uncle ... that rumor was true. Alexis was telling me the truth. What am I getting myself into?

"Lauren?" Jess asks, just before I pass out.

D a n n y

Lauren's head is slumped over in Jess's lap when I run across the creek to give her the flowers I picked for her. Mushy—I know.

"What happened?" Panic drips from every word. There's no way she's still tired after we slept in so late.

"I think it's the high altitude," Jess says, cutting Sara off from what she was going to say. Sara's eyebrows are pushed together and she's biting at her cheek; she knows more than anyone is letting on.

"What did you guys say to her?"

"Nothing," Jess, Alexis and Jenn all answer. Sara keeps her mouth shut.

"Danny, it's just the air and probably exhaustion. She's fine," Jess enunciates every word, almost to convince herself of what she is saying. Jeremy and Evan call to me from across the creek to go into the caves at the base of Molden Rock, but I tell them no. I drape my jacket over Lauren's arms and pull her head into my lap waiting for her to wake up and see if my meddling sister and cousin just messed up the best thing that's ever happened to me. Before the climb, she was definitely mine, so something's obviously upset her and it's probably something about me. Maybe they said something to her about sleeping with me? Or making out with me? It's anyone's guess, but if I can't undo the damage, then they've thrown my chances out the window again.

A half hour later, she starts to stir. She takes a deep breath as if she's coming out of the most amazing dream. She smiles, but it fades quickly when she sits up and looks around. "What happened?"

"I don't know. I was on the summit when you passed out." I glare at Sara. "Do you remember anything from before that?"

Her tiny hands rub her eyes and she glances at Jess and Sara, "I don't remember. We were talking about schools and college and stuff and then I felt dizzy."

"See, I told you ..." Jess says under her breath. No one in our group has ever passed out from the air up here, so I'm skeptical.

"Are you sure?" I push, "no one said anything?"

Lauren snakes her hands around my back and presses her lips to mine for the whole world to see. She lingers less than a second, but the point is well taken and my suspicions die with the rest of my guarded feelings. Whatever upset her obviously didn't deter her from the path we were headed down earlier. I want to pull her to me again, but she seems embarrassed, so I don't. Instead I run my hand down her arm and pick up the flowers I brought for her.

"These are for you."

"Where did you get them?" She pulls them to her nose and smells each one separately as though they are each a delicate treasure.

"They grow up there on the summit. One day I'll get you up there."

She laughs and eyes the steep rock face, "you're nuts if you think I'm going up that."

"Okay, well, maybe not the front side, but there is a much smaller path over there that is more of a hike than a climb." I brush a section of hair off her face for the sun to reflect in her eyes. She's staring just as intent at me and there are a million things to say. But with Jenn, Alexis and Sara all eavesdropping, nothing comes out.

Jeremy climbs onto the rock next to Jenn and claims her hand in his easily. Justin does the same with Alexis and they start talking about going to the Mountain Top café for a late lunch before heading back down. Evan tries to talk to Sara, but she hasn't been the same since Brandon started writing her letters from rehab. I know what is coming—in a few months he'll be out and they'll start dating. I don't think I'll object ... too much. But, Evan will be upset since he's had a crush on her for years.

One more trip into the caves and it will be time to go. I try to persuade Lauren to go with us, but none of the girls wants to go.

So they all stay stretched out on the blanket, soaking up every last minute of the afternoon sun. In a few short months this valley will be covered in snow and ice and the real fun begins: ski season. Since we have a membership to the lodge, my group makes more than a dozen trips each year during the season. The last few years I've been teaching Sara to snowboard and this year she has sworn she'll only snowboard. She said that last year too, but didn't stick to it. Note to self- ask Lauren if she knows how to ski ... if she doesn't—this will be the year she learns. I guess if I plan on her going to the lodge and coming on family trips, it's time to introduce her to Dad and Bev. Yes, it's time.

I bring Lauren back an arrowhead from the cave. It's only the second one I've ever found—the first went to Sara. Jeremy and I help pick up all the blankets, bottles and trash and then head towards the rocks. Alexis and Justin are already at Justin's truck by the time I help Lauren down. Jeremy and Jenn curl up together in the back seat of my truck. Sara joins them, complaining about being the fifth-wheel and Lauren claims the passenger seat. Her hand fits easily into mine across the center console and mindlessly I rub her knuckles with my thumb. Tomorrow is a new day and possibly another fight to keep her in my life. But that is tomorrow. I'll worry about that only when the time comes.

At Mountain Top Café we claim two big corner booths and I laugh when Evan tries to slide in next to Sara, but she moves away and sits next to Jess. We spend the next two hours laughing and sharing shakes and appetizers. I don't warn Lauren how big their burgers are, so when the waitress brings her a plate the size of a serving tray, she looks like she's going to be sick.

"You don't have to eat it all," I whisper into her ear and she giggles and leans into my neck. Jess and Sara are carefully watching my interaction with Lauren. They know what happened last night with Josh and how she ended up here with me. The two of them have every right to think I should be cautious ... but I've always been reckless.

When Lauren heads to the bathroom before we are ready to

leave, Sara scoots in close to me and brings my house of cards down on my head. "Danny, aren't you worried about tomorrow?"

I smile at Jeremy and Evan reliving a trip we took over summer and try not to get mad at Sara for being concerned. After all, Josh was Lauren's Prince Charming yesterday. Sure, I keep wondering if I'm the runner up or just the consolation prize, but those thoughts are like a disease that will attack my immune system if I let it fester. I can't let Sara see this doubt. I can't let her know how worried I am for what the morning will bring.

It's barely six o'clock when we pull into the parking lot of my condo. Sara grabs her things from the living room and Lauren grabs her dress. It's going to suck not having her here tonight, and not knowing how she'll treat me tomorrow. Will I be a nameless to her? Will she act like today never happened? Wouldn't that be ironic?

"So," I start to say when Sara is ready to return Lauren to her story-book life. "Will I see you tomorrow?"

Sara ducks out the door, not wanting to see what's coming. She's sure Lauren is going to disappoint me. I'm not so sure that she won't either. Will she rush back to Josh tomorrow? "Can I drive you to school?"

She chews at her bottom lip and comes close, so close that I can see each of her lashes competing for space over her eyes. It's hard to concentrate or doubt myself when she is this close. I ask her again, focusing on what I want to know, instead of what I want to do, "Can I drive you to school?"

"I'm probably going to be in a heap of trouble over today. My mom left twenty messages while we were up there. I didn't get any service."

"What did you tell her in the message you left this morning?"

"I told her that I was hanging out with Sara and Jenn today at the movies and the mall. She never would've let me drive up the mountain with you." She breaks my gaze and her eyes drift to the floor like she is ashamed. We didn't do anything wrong; she has nothing to be ashamed of. It's about time her parents stop treating her like a child. I'm not going to be okay with them trying to dictate her life and making her feel guilty over what she wants.

"Will they ground you?"

She laughs, "definitely."

"So, I guess driving you is out of the question?" She looks at me with her own expectations and disappointment lurking in her mind. She's made me vulnerable to her charms and needs. If she told me she didn't want to ride with me, I'd be heartbroken, but hearing she's going to be in trouble makes me want to fight her parents because they are the only thing standing in our way now … well, technically. Her delicate palm runs the length of my chest to my cheek and she pushes the worry out of my thoughts and replaces it with her lips and dangerous thoughts I can't act on.

"I'll meet you at the benches in the morning," she says, easing my mind and kindling my desire for the week ahead of us.

"I'll bring you breakfast," I say and press my lips to hers again, not wanting to let her go just yet.

"Mmmm …" she purrs, and gives me several more pecks. "Sounds good to me."

Lauren turns to go out the door and I grab her forearm, stopping her from crossing the threshold. "Will you come over for dinner tomorrow?"

She smiles, "I'll try." Her words are sincere. This is really happening. Walking away from her at the party was a struggle I wasn't ready for, but it's prepared me for this moment, to accept our fate.

I take the stairs two at a time to the bedroom and shuffle all the applications together. I have two very important phone calls to make, the first to Reyes. With the application in hand, and the deadline just days away, I have to make arrangements to hand deliver it to him and make sure all the requirements are met. He is the easier of the phone calls and tells me the acceptance letter was already sent out and the retraction I turned in has been shredded. I should've known he would do that for me.

The next call is to my dad to go over my options for buying a house in Summit Estates. It's a secure community so that I won't have to worry about Lauren and my past colliding. And I'll have two years of payments in by the time Lauren moves in. I'll be investing in our future instead of paying for someone else's, like dad says. Plus, if I have any chance of Lauren's parents approving, I've got to get my shit together.

With the money I have in the bank and Dad's help, the house will be no problem and Lauren will get her dream life—courtesy of the new and improved Daniel Cummings and the death of Mr. Hyde. Can't say it's really sad to see him go, but at least all the pain and sorrow I went through working for Uncle John won't be a waste of my time. The money will certainly be put to good use.

"You want to go tomorrow?" Dad clarifies.

"Yes, tomorrow."

"Are you sure about this? Why the sudden change of heart?"

"I just realized it was time I stopped jerking around with the future. That's all." A partial lie; I haven't told him about Lauren being in my life yet, but if she comes to dinner tomorrow night, he'll find out soon enough.

L a u r e n

I'm in so much trouble that it will take me one whole year to dig out of. I've apologized over and over and faked a dead battery before mom will even look me in the eye over dinner. I can't tell her I'm not hungry because of the huge burger at the Mountain Café. I hang my torn dress in the closet and start taking down most of the pictures of Josh and I in my room. I click open my cell phone a few times and look at the pictures I snapped of Danny at the stream and one that we took together at the café. I would transfer them onto my computer, but mom might snoop and find them. That would be disastrous. I'm already grounded for a month for my little stunt. At least they don't know the extent of it.

I grab my memory box from my closet and dig through it to find the heart shaped charm Danny gave me for my birthday. I toss Josh's stupid ring into an old ring box and set it on my dresser. Eventually he will get it back, but I'm not ready to deal with that right now. I may not know what tomorrow will bring, and maybe I've lost sight of what I've always wanted, but one thing's is for sure—Josh is not it. Not with how he treated me. I know it is careless to act the way I did with Danny today, but I'm drawn to him more than the planets are drawn to the sun. He is nothing I've ever wanted, and there's no guarantee that he's not hiding a billion things from me. The unknown is terrifying. He can hurt me badly and I'm possibly throwing away everything I've worked so hard for in the past year and a half. Not to mention the fact that the rumors of him still haunt my thoughts. Alexis wasn't lying about his criminal past, and how do I know that's not in his future?

The next morning I remind mom I have practice after school and I'll have to start staying later on Wednesdays and Fridays to help with the set designs. I ask if she wants Danny to start driving me home since I won't be out until nine, and she adamantly disagrees. Being grounded for a month includes Danny. But it doesn't include school related functions. Too bad I don't actually have to stay until nine. I'm really out at six ... but she doesn't need to know that.

Danny's truck is parked in a spot right next to the gate when we pull in. That's one of the best spots and it means he's been here for a really long time, probably hoping mom would bring me earlier to school, but we have been running late all morning. She's getting ready for a weekend getaway with my aunt and trying to get a promotion at work. There are reports scattered all over our kitchen table that she is trying to finish before heading off to Vegas for two days.

"I'll pick you up tonight. Do not be late young lady."

"Yes ma'am," I mumble and climb from the van. My pulse races as the benches come into view. Danny is on the closest table, waiting for me with two coffees and breakfast just as he promised. The ice blue v-neck top I wear today is for him, to match his eyes and show off the necklace he gave me, which I slipped on after getting out of the van. He seems to approve as I get closer and his grin turns to a full smile he can't hide. I don't hold back when I get to him. I throw my arms around his neck and breathe his scent in deeply.

"I've missed you," he whispers. The kids around us are already talking about the football princess wrapped in the bad boy's arms. I'm trying to ignore them, but some of the things they are saying are mean and hurtful, including how I'm a wannabe trashy slut. Danny knows it's getting to me; he hugs me tighter. "They don't matter," he says through my hair and my arms cling to him like a beacon at the eye of a storm. This is going to be harder than I thought.

"How much trouble are you in?" he says handing me the coffee and a muffin.

"Grounded for a month," I say pulling off part of the muffin and handing it to him first. "But, I told her I had to stay at school until nine on Wednesdays and Fridays to work on the sets."

He laughs, "I've already corrupted you, huh?"

"Only in the best of ways," I smile and lean in to kiss his cheek. Girls snicker next to us and I glare at them. One of Brandon's ex's, Brenda, is pacing like an exotic cat looking for her next kill. She'll be attacking me soon, I'm sure. I've already heard rumors that she is Danny's female equivalent—fighting and getting suspended at least once a week. I'll make it my mission to avoid her and possibly find a better place for Danny and me to hang out.

"Does that mean I can take you out to dinner on a real date Friday?" Danny inquiries, pulling my attention away from Brenda.

"What else did you think I had in mind?" I say, flirting shamelessly with him.

He seems to enjoy it and leans in to run his nose up my neck, "I could think of a few things. But, I'll settle for dinner."

"Sounds like a plan to me." He pulls back just far enough to barely brush his nose against mine. "Where are we going?"

"It's a surprise." The bell rings before I get to ask him anymore. "I'll meet you here at lunch?"

Sara, Jenn and I get food from the cafeteria and head to the benches. Danny is waiting when we get there. Danny talked to Ms. Nelson this morning and arranged for Jeremy to start helping with the sets, mostly to get time for him to be with Jenn. Ms. Nelson appreciates the extra help, anyway. So Jenn will be helping me run lines tonight too. Talk about life changing overnight. The ring Josh gave me is still looming over me and it has to go back to him before Danny knows I've got it. We never discussed what happened the night of the dance, and truly, he doesn't need to know.

Jenn wraps her arm around mine, "Josh and Mike aren't here today," she says. "The rumors are running rampant though. Mandi already asked me what was going on. Did Jamie say anything to you in Drama?"

"No, I didn't really give her a chance. I didn't sit with her. I sat with Alexis and Danny."

"Wow," she says, "that's a really bold move."

"Well, don't you think after what happened at the dance that the line was already drawn?"

"Yeah, well …" she hesitates and looks at Danny watching us get closer. "I mean, you jumped from one to the other so quickly."

I laugh and blow her off, "like you have any room to talk. What's up with you and Jeremy, again?"

She laughs and agrees with me. She did the same thing I did, so she can't complain or pass judgment on me although I don't think that is what she's getting at. The fact is that she knows my mother and the expectation. Danny doesn't really fall into the plan Mom has for me … especially if all the rumors about him are true. But he's fun and fascinating … and his smile makes me feel like the only girl in the world.

"Hey beautiful," he says and eases me into his arms as if it's exactly where I belong. How can this be wrong when it feels so right? "More junk food huh?" he laughs and points to my sliced apples and carrots.

"Shut up," I laugh. There's no way I'm dropping my routine just because I've dumped that life and the boy that goes with it. However, I'm not sure I've exactly dropped him yet.

"I'm just teasing," he says and glares at Brenda who is hovering, looking for her next meal.

"Maybe we should start hanging out somewhere else." I look nervously at Brenda who seems to be edging her way closer to us with her friend Kristi. Evan and Justin walk up just as I'm about to insist we leave.

"She's just pissed Brandon is gone. Don't worry about her," Danny says and moves over to let Justin sit on the table next to him. "If you want to start hanging out somewhere else, that's cool. But the quad is kind of out right now." His eyes travel to the sidewalk and I look there too. Mandi and Jamie are on the sidewalk studying Danny's hands on my hips and my arms around his neck. I might as well have worn a shirt that says *traitor* on it today.

By the end of the day, mostly everyone is talking about my abrupt departure from the quad and reappearance at the benches and Josh's absence today. I don't know why he's not here, but it has nothing to do with Danny or I, I'm sure. There's no way he's at home pining over me and Danny hasn't really left my side since the dance.

Danny and Jeremy walk around the corner of the theater right on time for rehearsals. Alexis shows up shortly after with Justin in tow. Even though Danny is supposed to help with the sets, he splits his time between painting and running lines with me. His favorite scene is the ending, where we finally admit our love and he gets to kiss me. I'll have to kiss Christian a few times during the play too and Danny warned him not to get frisky with me; he didn't care if it was only acting or not.

"Wear something nice on Friday," Danny whispers as we finish putting away everything. It's already close to six and I have to hurry; if I don't, I'll be in more trouble.

"If I dress up for school, mom will know."

"I'll have Sara bring you something to change into." He looks at the clock, "you better get going. I'll watch you walk up to the parking lot."

We kiss and I rush to mom's van, both excited and astonished to have this day over with and at how well it went. Other than a few people spreading rumors about me and Brenda glaring me down, today wasn't half as bad as I thought it'd be. Then again, Josh will be back tomorrow and it will be a whole new ballgame.

Danny

Dad is ready by the time I get home. I change into the slacks, shirt and tie that Bev pressed for me and get the paperwork together to meet with Walt, Dad's real estate and property consultant. Sara and I grew up with Walt's kids and he couldn't be happier to help me find the perfect home. Buying a house would have been easier if Lauren could have come, but she's grounded and there's no way I'm going to risk getting on her mom's bad side right now. Besides, she doesn't even know about this yet. Hell, Sara doesn't know about it. They are both going to freak out. Shit, even I'm freaking out a little, but this is what I have to do.

Walt is waiting for us at the office when Dad pulls his BMW into the space. The office is normally closed at this hour, but Walt made an appointment with Ms. Anderson to stay for us.

"It's good to see you Danny," Walt says with his southern drawl. He's a short portly man who has always reminded me of Coronal Sanders with his white goatee and unusual suits.

"Nice to see you too, Walt." I shake his hand and wait for him and Dad to say their hellos.

Ms. Anderson is just inside the door with several clipboards, markers and pens. "Hello gentlemen. I'm Molly Anderson. Welcome to Summit Estates."

"Thank you, Ms. Anderson for seeing us on such short notice. I'm Clint Cummings and this is my son, Daniel."

"It's good to meet you," I say and offer her my hand.

She shakes it, but then turns her attention back to my dad. "So, Mr. Cummings, you are interested in purchasing a home for your family?"

Walt and Dad both share glances and turn their focus to me. "Actually, Ms. Anderson, I'm purchasing the home." And I wait for her to laugh. Confusion and dismay overtake her heart shaped face as she looks at Walt.

"I must have misunderstood. You said you were interested in the Community Partners program?"

"Yes ma'am. Mr. Cummings will be joining Mountain Views finest in January. He wants to make sure he gets a prime lot and is able to select the floor plan he wants as well as the amenities," Walt answers.

"My wife and I plan on assisting with the down payment over and above the police grant. We will co-sign, if it's necessary."

She raises both her eyebrows, but offers me a clipboard. "Well young man, why don't we find you a home?"

The next four hours we look at model homes, carpets, floor plans, lots, pre-built homes, homes in upcoming phases, planned parks, planned schools, security options, and community center. The whole experience is surreal, but I've never seen my dad happier. He loves the built in safety of the community, but the biggest draw for me are the parks. All the trees remind me of going to Molden and make my mind drift to Lauren and our make out session on the rocks. I can't wait to bring her here and to show her what really could be if she'd just choose me.

I fill out the application and Dad signs off, although Molly agrees not to include him if she doesn't have to. I want to do this on my own if I can. She agrees to run the numbers and call us next week to let me know what floor plan I can qualify for and what my options are. She gives me several brochures of floor plans and a map of the community with lots to pick where I want the house to be built. With the pre-qualifying, grant application and the time it takes to build, I'll be in the new house in a little over a year, right after I'm out of the academy and ready for pre-service. My life just went into fast-forward and it's making my head spin to think of the responsibility that awaits me, but this is how life should be—dad's supporting my decision confirms it. I'm on the right track.

As soon as I get home, I email Lauren to tell her good night and climb into bed. There are only two things left to do before Friday

—introduce her to my parents and get the ring. Yes, rushing things, I know. But I'm not taking my chances, the sooner I show her I want the things she wants, the better off we will be. Hopefully this will end her confusion and her doubt over me and my intentions.

Tuesday after school Sara agrees to go to the mall with me, but she has no idea why. I listen to her drone on and on about Josh not showing up to school two days in a row and the fact that Crystal put Jackie on the cheer squad—neither of which is my problem. Josh probably already knows Lauren is with me and he doesn't want to face it. And Jackie? Well, I saw that coming. I knew it wouldn't take long for her to aim for the top of Mountain Views social ladder. She belongs in that plastic crowd, but Sara and Lauren don't.

"Are we going to eat?" she asks putting on her hoodie and climbing from the truck.

"Yeah, I figured we would."

"So, what are the plans?" She links her arm through mine and we walk into the main doors of the mall.

"I have some shopping to do." I smile and keep my eyes focused on the far corner of the mall. I hope we don't run into anyone we know. I don't want the surprise for Lauren to be ruined. It's bad enough I'm going to have to trust Sara to keep her mouth shut.

"Danny, what are we doing here?" Sara glares at me as I open the door to the jewelry store.

"Welcome to Diamond Mart, how may I help you?" the sales clerk asks.

"I'm looking for an engagement ring," I say and Sara freaks.

"What? Are you crazy?" It seems she wants to hit me. The poor salesgirl stands there staring at us, totally oblivious to the fact that Sara is not the girl I'm proposing to.

"I need your help to pick one out. I have an idea, but I want to make sure it's something she'll like."

"No, I'm not helping you pick out a ring for her. This is crazy.

You are too young and her parents will never agree, and do I need to mention you've been officially together two days!"

"Do you two need a minute?" the salesgirl asks.

"No, I would like something in a platinum band, something delicate."

"You're nuts." Sara turns to storm out the door.

"Sara, this is happening with or without your consent. I just want to show you what I have in mind and you tell me if you like it or not."

"Danny, you don't even know if she's going to go back to Josh or not." Her words burn through my skin like a thousand bee stings.

"Why would you say something like that?" I ask, hurt and totally deflated.

"Because Danny, you don't. You don't know what she is going to do once he comes back. Why don't you give it some time to see how things go?"

"Sara, since the day I saw her I knew this is where we would end up. I filled out the forms last night for Summit and I'm starting the explorer program in January. She is the only thing missing now." I shrug and hope the truth will help her get on board.

"Why don't you wait until she's out of school? She may leave to go back to Illinois. Have you talked to her about this? About marriage?"

"No, not yet. But I need her and I need your support in this."

Sara stares at me, the clerk and then the dazzling jewelry cases around us. "Okay," she finally concedes and it makes me wonder if she thinks I'm just setting myself up for an epic failure. She may be right, but I don't want to wake up when I'm 50 and regret not following my gut on this.

Sara tries on more than two dozen rings and disagrees with my first choice of a platinum band with a solitaire—she thinks it's too boring and old school.

The last one the clerk shows us is a platinum band with a large cushion cut diamond and antique eternity band. "That's definitely it," Sara says with the ring circling her index finger. "You have to buy this one. She will love it."

"Are you sure? Does this ring guarantee me a yes?" I wink and bump shoulders with her.

Sara smirks, "I can't guarantee you that. But it will at least make her stop and think about it."

"I'll take this one," I say to the sales clerk. I'll take maybe over a no from Lauren any day. Maybe means she's considering.

"Would you like to apply for in store credit?" the girl asks slipping the ring into a blue-velvet lined box.

"No, I'll pay cash."

"What's the plan tonight?" Lauren asks after rehearsals on Wednesday and we are putting away set pieces. I have her until nine and I'm thankful we are getting out of theater early; otherwise it wouldn't give enough time to introduce her to my parents and get her back to school.

"I thought we'd go to my place for dinner?"

"Will we have enough time?" she asks, brushing against me in the prop room. Her touch always ignites fires in me. I don't answer. Instead, I pull her tight against my chest and part her lips with my tongue. We haven't had enough time alone in the last few days, and I want to savor every inch of her body against mine. There are so many things I want to tell her, so much exciting news I want to share. But I don't. Telling her would be a mistake and it'd probably scare her off. It's always been about her for me, but it hasn't always been about me for her. If Josh offered her what I'm about to, I'm sure she wouldn't hesitate to say yes, but coming from me, she may think twice. Everything has to go perfectly. Friday will be here soon and my nerves are shot waiting for her to see the ring. The house will have to wait a few months. It's better not to overwhelm her with everything at once.

"Danny? Lauren?" Alexis calls from the stage. I curse her for interrupting, but we have to get going anyway. If Friday is going to happen, then Clint and Bev need to meet her and love her.

"Coming," I say, and nuzzle my face into her neck and hug her tight against me again. "We will have time. I promise."

Twenty minutes later, I'm trying to steady my nerves as we pull into Dad and Bev's driveway. Lauren might be upset that I sprang this on her, but I want Dad to meet her and see how fantastic she is. Sara already told Bev Lauren is coming to dinner, so they won't be shocked, at least.

"What are we doing?" Lauren asks when I open the door for her to climb out of the truck.

"Dinner," I say passively.

"Isn't this your dad's place?"

"Yup," I respond and her fingers stiffen in mine. "Don't worry, they are going to love you and Bev is the best cook."

"I thought we were going to your place. Why didn't you tell me we were coming here?" She starts messing with her hair.

I stop just before the stairs and take both her hands in mine. "You look wonderful. Amazing. My folks are going to love you. I didn't want you to be nervous about meeting them."

"I don't know if I'm ready for this …" she says and I kiss her to stop her lips from quivering.

"You'll do fine."

Originally, I didn't want Sara to join us for dinner, but it turns out she's a lifesaver. She gets Lauren out of her fake persona that reminds me of her mom. By dessert, she's lazily rubbing the back of my hand and talking about her siblings in Illinois. My dad loves her already. He's harassing her and poking fun at her, and she's giving it right back to him. I've never seen her like this before; she's definitely giving him a run for his money and he is enjoying it immensely.

By eight-thirty, I have his seal of approval and Bev is inviting her to come over on the weekends to watch movies with her and Sara. Lauren accepts, once she's off grounding, which led to a short conversation about her strict mother. She doesn't go into everything, but it's enough for Bev to hug her and tell her she's welcome at their house anytime. Bev will treat her like a daughter soon enough; she won't have to deal with her mother much longer, unless she really wants to.

Bev hugs Lauren tight, "it was so great finally meeting you."

Dad takes his turn, "I agree, you need to come over more often. You are welcome here anytime."

"Thank you. It was great meeting you guys. Bev, I'll see you in a few weeks."

"It's a date!" Bev hugs her again, "I can't wait."

"So, not as bad as you thought, huh?" I ask and kiss the back of her hand as I ease the truck onto the main road. We have less than ten minutes to get back to school and I'm not sure we'll make it, but I don't want her freaking out over it.

"No, I love your dad. He is so cool." Then her eyes drift to the clock, "Oh no! I'm going to be late."

"No you won't, I promise." We turn onto the alley that runs behind the school. The fence around the stadium is open and there's a path she can use to cut across the field to the fence leading into the other parking lot. She gives me a peck on the cheek and runs down the sidewalk. Two minutes to spare. Talk about cutting it close. But she won't be in trouble because of me.

Tonight couldn't have gone better. Dad and Bev don't know about the ring and Sara swore she wouldn't say a thing until we are ready to break the news to everyone. The less people that know, the easier it will be to keep it a secret.

I email her from my phone to tell her good night and drive home with thoughts of being in the prop room replaying in my head. Her skin against mine feels like I'm tempting fate. Friday will be here soon and she will either be thrilled or terrified of me. One way or the other, Friday is the turning point for everything. My nervousness is building and I'll probably get no sleep tonight. What if she says no to everything I'm offering? What if Sara is right and Lauren goes back to Josh? I've already signed on the dotted line and spent six-grand on a diamond ... there's really no going back now. Friday is rushing things; it has only been a week, and things with Josh haven't played out, but I've never wanted something so bad before. The thought I won't get it is too painful.

Rumors are still circulating over Josh's absence, and honestly, it's making me uneasy that he has something planned. It is as if he's just letting me get enough of the new life to want more, and then he's going to sneak attack from behind and rip it all away again.

Climbing into my bed, I twirl the six-grand ball and chain around my pinky. No matter how much I hope she'll squeal and scream yes when she sees it, it probably won't happen that way. She's going to pass out and then wake to tell me no. During the first real conversation we had, she told me how important it was to have what her parents have. It hasn't been long enough for her to change her mind or to show her that she can have more. This Friday, she may or may not be my fiancée, but one thing's for sure: it will be the most romantic night of her life and the most vulnerable of mine.

L a u r e n

Friday afternoon I'm walking from the cafeteria to the benches at lunch. Mom didn't go to the store this week, so Taco-Bell will have to do for today. Danny won't tell me where we are going tonight, but he had Sara bring me a cute strapless black dress to wear. I'm dragging since I stayed up on the phone with him until midnight. Even make-up couldn't hide the potato-sack sized bags under my eyes. I'll have to spend some time in the bathroom later pressing some cool towels to them.

This week with Danny has been easy. Meeting his parents on Wednesday showed me a side of him I never expected. He hasn't told me that he loves me, but it's coming, maybe even tonight. I want him to say it first; I want to hear it from his lips before I throw myself out there. Just because Sara said he loves me, doesn't mean it's true. He may not have been what I've always wanted, but now he is the only thing I want and I can't lose him, not now.

"Where ya going Princess?" Brenda steps in front of me, pushing her two-sizes-too-small push up bra in my face. I guess every group has their *Crystal* equivalent.

"None of your business," I say and try to step around her without spilling my drink or dropping my food, but she moves in front of me again. Her best friend, Kristi, joins her to harass me.

"Big night tonight huh?" Kristi says flipping a section of hair off her shoulder.

"What do you know about it?" I ask and my soda tilts.

"Can't wait to get the whole V thing over with huh?" Brenda asks and gets really close to my face; so close that I can smell her peppermint gum and it makes me nauseous.

"Get away from me," I say stepping to the left, but Kristi blocks me in.

"The thing I don't get is why would you give it up to someone like Danny, when you wouldn't give it up to Josh?" I drop my soda in haste to back away from her.

"How did you know about that?"

"Pu-lease. Word gets around." Kristi lets out a snicker. "I guess Danny will finally get his revenge."

"What revenge?" I ask, playing into their spiteful game. I should know better.

"Don't you think it's convenient that Danny is so interested in the person that Josh Miller is in love with?"

"Oh yeah," Kristi starts, "he'll get what Josh Miller couldn't have. That will really piss Josh off."

"And then you'll be left with nothing. No one to comfort you after he's taken what's most important to you, your hopes of being anything to anybody ever again. No one at this school will have you once Danny's done with you."

"You lie," I say throwing my food down. How dare her talk to me this way. And unfortunately, doubt is seeping deep into every crevice of my mind. Josh ruined Danny's sister. Maybe Josh was so insistent on sleeping with me because he knew Danny's plan? NO. That can't be it. Josh was too focused on doing the deed. Danny hasn't even tried to do more than kiss me. "Get away from me," I shove Kristi away.

"Oooh, looks like we hit a nerve," Brenda laughs. "You'll find out soon enough. Just like half of the cheer squad. Danny has a type and you're it. You will be his MVP soon enough," she gloats and they stride away from me.

It takes a few minutes for me to compose myself. Several students ask if I'm okay as they pass. My lunch is on the ground; I really don't want it anymore anyway. It probably wasn't a good idea to get fast food when Danny is taking me out to dinner tonight. Maybe that's why he hasn't said he loved me ... maybe he doesn't? *Damn Brenda.* Girls like her are the reason I steered clear of the benches last year, and really should've continued that tradition this year.

I'm barely listening to Sara and Alexis as they chatter on at lunch about the play and going shopping this weekend for ski season. I've never been skiing, but Sara seems to think I'll be going on lots of trips with them this year. I don't think my parents will let me go for one. And for two. I don't think they'll spend $300 on a ski jacket either not to mention I'd need ski's and boots and all the other stuff too.

"What do you think?" Danny asks wrapping his arms around my waist and pulling me back to him. "Have you skied before?"

"No," I say, distant. He's probably noticed I'm not contributing to this conversation, but I don't know how he can expect me to if what Brenda said about me is true. I can't think of a more perfect revenge for Danny to have than taking my virginity in exchange for his sister's. *Shit.* Could Sara be in on this elaborate scheme too? That thought terrorizes me the rest of lunch. Danny asks me what is going on while we head to the fifth period. I tell him nothing, but he says someone saw Brenda corner me at lunch. I blow it off that she's just being a cheerleader hater and nothing more. I can't tell him that she's re-ignited the doubts that kept me away from him last year. Thoughts that made me disbelieve he could have true feelings for me. Doubts that make me think if he had gotten his way the first night at Jess's house, he wouldn't be here today. I can't think that way, but it's really hard not to. I've never had a real relationship until these two, and the painful truth is that, if either is using me to get to the other... then I've never actually had a relationship at all.

Danny kisses me goodbye at the door to my classroom and my heart isn't in it. He releases me and stares for several minutes before pressing his lips to mine again, this time quickly, and then, lets go. "Are you okay?" he asks.

"I'm fine, why?"

"What's going on? You were distant at lunch and you won't tell me what Brenda said to you."

"I just have a lot on my mind."

"Is this about Josh?"

"No," *yes*, I say silently.

"I'll meet you after school?"

"K," I say and walk into class leaving him looking after me.

The next two classes I can't concentrate on anything other than Danny and what Brenda told me. He saved me the night of the dance, he slept with me all night and didn't touch me. I don't get it. It's not possible that Brenda is telling the truth. She can't be. But … what if she is?

After the sixth period, I slip into my borrowed dress and pull my hair into a high ponytail. I slick on some smoky eye shadow and lip-gloss. The short skirt shows off more skin than I'm comfortable with considering Brenda's claim today. Did Danny handpick this dress himself or is this just Sara's contribution to the plot?

Danny told Ms. Nelson he would pick up set pieces from her storage this weekend if we can ditch class tonight. He's standing by his truck waiting for me. A huge white bouquet of roses tied with ribbons dangles from his hand.

He takes my arm and lifts my hand to his lips to kiss the back. "You look stunning."

"Thank you." He looks pretty amazing himself in a steel blue button down shirt and black slacks. "You look great, too."

He helps me into the truck and hands me the roses. My hands are shaking and my leg is bouncing up and down on the seat. He's going to know something is wrong with me if I can't get my thoughts in check.

"Are you ready for an amazing evening?" he asks with a hint of mystery in his tone.

"Yup," I say my, tone completely unconvincing.

He trudges on, "you're going to love the place we are going tonight. They have the most amazing food. It's this old steakhouse my dad used to take me to. It's such an intimate place. I think you'll really like it."

"I'm sure I will." However, him saying it's intimate does not help my nerves. This feels like a set up ... like Josh's last weekend.

The restaurant and parking lot are dimly lit to the point they look closed. Danny helps me from the truck and loops my hand around his elbow to escort me inside. He is beaming and it's hard not to be proud on his arm when he looks so handsome; an image that totally betrays the thoughts I'm having of him and his moral compass.

"Reservation for Cummings," Danny says to the hostess with an air of authority.

"Of course, Mr. Cummings. Your table is ready." There is barely an empty table in the restaurant, but it is intimate and quiet inside. The high backed booth is sitting under a makeshift trellis with vines and flowers hanging all over it. It feels like we are eating outside and completely alone.

"May I get you something to drink?" the server asks quietly.

"Could I have a tea please?" I ask and open my menu wondering how long it will be before I'll be running away from Danny and his plan. Will this relationship even last through dessert? Probably not if Brenda is right.

"A coke please," Danny says.

"Great, I'll return in a moment to take your orders." The server disappears around the end of the booth and we are secluded again. I browse the menu trying to get my mind to focus on something, anything else, when I realize there are no prices.

"Why don't they list how much things are?" I ask, mostly to kill the silence that has rested between us. So much for trying to act normal and flush out the truth.

Danny smiles; he's not even looking at his menu. "Don't worry about it."

The server comes back and I'm preoccupied by the missing costs. "Are you ready?"

"Lauren?" Danny asks with his hands folded over his closed menu. How many times had he been here and treated girls to this same luxury? Or worse, how many girls had he brought here before taking advantage of them?

I swallow hard before placing my order. "Could I have the Chicken Alfredo, please?"

"Would you like a soup or salad with your meal?"

"No thank you," I say handing my closed menu back to the server.

"Are you sure?" Danny asks. "You can have anything you want."

"I'm sure," I say, a little embarrassed that he put me on the spot like that.

Danny orders his meal and then orders chocolate cake and an appetizer for us to split.

"Are you excited the play is in a few weeks?"

I fidget with my napkin, trying not to let Brenda take over the evening. I'd been so excited this week for tonight; now to let it go this way is disheartening. "I can't wait until it's over with."

"I can't either. Then again, I can't wait until you are off grounding. Three weeks to go," he says reaching across the table to run his fingers down the length of mine. I turn my hand over and let our palms rest together. Why would he keep bringing up the future if our relationship is just about tonight? But dad always says a boy is lying when his mouth is moving... so who do I believe? A girl with a possible ulterior motive or a boy who has one?

"What about skiing? You didn't seem interested when Sara was talking about it today."

"I don't know. I've never done anything like it." Seeing our hands intertwined on the table makes more than one lump form in my throat. I stare at them for a long time as Danny continues talking about something that I'm sure is never going to happen.

"It's super easy. I'm willing to teach you if you want to try. I mean, I'm not going to force you. There are other things to do up there. There are nature trails, pools, spas, volleyball, mini-golf, and fishing. You name it. It's an amazing place. I can't wait to take you."

"I'm sure it's amazing," I say, wondering if he means it or not. Then again, why would he be so sincere and excited about it if he didn't intend it would happen? "Does Clint and Bev go, too?" I ask mostly out of obligation.

"Not every trip, but they do go sometimes. Dad said you are welcome to come on any trip you want, but if your parents won't let you go without parental supervision, they can go with us." He smiles and rubs his thumb against the back of my hand.

"I'm not sure my parents would be cool with me going, anyway." After all, my parents don't even realize that I snuck out tonight, or on Wednesday to meet Clint and Bev. And if my dad knows anything about Danny's past, he'll put down his foot and ban me from dating anyone until I'm 30.

"Maybe Clint can go and meet your folks so that they are more comfortable with you going places with us. Would that be cool?" He hesitates. I know he's realizing I can't look him in the eye. Josh was able to lie to me, straight to my face... how can I trust someone like Danny? A boy with his tattered past that has left a wake of girls and lies behind him. I doubt if hurting me would even bother him in the slightest. "I mean, I'm not trying to push you or anything." He squeezes my hand.

"I know you're not," I say and withdraw my hand from his. "I really want to go; it's just going to be up to my parents." Curiosity is killing me. I feel like I'm just waiting for him to pounce, but now I want to know. I almost want to bust him in his lies since I wasn't able to catch Josh in his.

"Do they know you broke up with Josh yet?" No, I haven't had that conversation yet, but I think Mom has an idea.

"I haven't brought it up to mom yet."

"Does she know that you are dating me?" He offers his hand to me again across the table, but withdraws it when the server brings a hot basket of bread to the table. No, she doesn't know that yet. She'd be mad if she knew I went from Josh to Danny in a week— this is a Lynn move and totally off limits.

"No," I study the white linen tablecloth and start picking at a piece of the bread.

The waiter comes back to deliver our drinks and appetizer, and then scurries off feeling the tension.

Danny pulls his hand back across the table and rests it in his lap. "Why haven't you told her yet?"

There is steam drifting up from the spinach dip between us and I wish it were thick enough to make a smoke screen for me to escape. I'm so confused, or maybe I just don't want to believe the worst case scenario. There's no way Brenda's right. Otherwise, he wouldn't care. Right? I mean, he'd probably prefer my parents didn't know we are together if he just wanted to ruin me.

So, I tell him the truth hoping it will prompt him to be honest if there is something going on that he hasn't told me. "Because this is the type of stuff Lynn does and last year they got onto me for going back and forth between Josh and you. I don't want them thinking that's what's going on this year."

Danny lowers his head so that his normally crystal blue eyes look like smokey black pearls—both beautiful and ominous. "Do you plan on telling them?"

"Of course," *If this lasts,* I think, but don't add. I almost laugh, but hold it in. "I just don't want them thinking I'm being like my sister. She's always leading a few boys on and mom knows she's only in school to find a husband, though she'll never admit it." I'm rambling and he finally grabs my hands that I've been picking at the bread with. His million-dollar smile returns to his face and the ominous black pearls finally give way to his normally glowing blue pools.

"So, you have no doubts about dating me?" If I say yes, I'd be lying. But they aren't doubts that I want to share with him. They are my own insecurities and rumors that I've allowed to taint him. What if he is being sincere and I'm about to ruin something great?

Truth, Lauren, Truth. "I'm not going to lie to you. I'm worried about the things you won't tell me about coming back into your life, and ultimately, mine. I'm worried that you'll decide I'm too straight laced for you or you'll change your mind about wanting me. And then I've changed my whole life for you and I'll be left with … nothing." He wanted to know what Brenda said; well, he got the result of it.

He gets up and sits on the booth next to me, taking my hands in his. "I promise, that is never going to happen. I swear. I'm here with you as long as you'll have me."

D a n n y

Whatever Brenda told her today has her doubting my motivation for being with her. She was like this last year, but there hasn't been one hint of it in our lives all week. She's said she can't see herself in my life and she's walked away from me before. And right now, hearing her say that she thinks I'll walk away from her is crazy. This has to be what Brenda told her. There is no way this doubt crept in on its own, not after the absolutely amazing week we've had. This morning, she was fine; it wasn't until lunch that she changed. I'll have to ask her tonight; it will ease her fears and show her that I want her around long after high school. If I didn't think it'd freak her out, I'd drive her past Summit Estates to show her how dead serious I am that she has to be in my future.

"I'll be right back," I say after we've both finished our dinners and we are waiting for our cake. I head straight to the hostess stand to order sparkling cider for us to celebrate our engagement.

Maybe I should order a shot of Jack just in case. *Never mind.* I can't fall off the wagon or lose my nerve now.

I'm halfway to the front of the restaurant when Matt comes in the first set of double doors. Aaron is limping in behind him. *Shit.* This is not the way tonight is supposed to go.

My proposal will have to wait. "Can I get the cake to go?" I ask the waiter on the way back to the table and head back to the secluded booth.

The waiter delivers the cake shortly after I return to the table. I grab Lauren's hand and throw three hundred dollars down for the bill. "I'm sorry to cut this short, but we have to go."

"What?" she looks at the cake and the money, "what's going on?"

"I can't explain right now, but we need to get out of here."

Matt and Aaron are talking loud in the foyer. We can't get out that way. "This way," I say and pull her down the hallway towards the kitchen. We find a small supply closet and duck inside.

"What's going on?" she whispers. I haven't told her anything yet and she already senses the urgency. That or she can hear the rattling of my heart in my chest. Her chest is pushed tight against mine and I'm trying to be quiet so that we aren't detected.

"Do you remember the guy that Brandon was with that day on the sidewalk? The day that he knocked you down?"

"Yeah. I think so," she says, still hushed.

"He's my cousin and some of the bad stuff people told you is true. I was working for my Uncle. They don't like that I quit." This maybe an over share, but she's more likely to stay in this cramped closet with me if I tell her the truth of the danger lurking outside.

"They're ..." she swallows so hard that I can hear it, "after you?"

"Basically. They've been trying to get me to come back, but I'm done with it. I swear I'm never doing any of that, ever again."

People walk past the door and she shakes. I'm rubbing her back, her shoulders, her arms—anything to try to calm her nerves until I can get us the hell out of here. But I find myself shaking too. This night has completely unraveled around me; one minute I'm going to ask the most important question of my life, the next I'm hiding like a chump in a supply closet because they've caught me off guard and I don't want to risk Lauren being hurt again.

"Do you mean that?" she asks and slides her hands into mine. I hug her tight, feeling her shallow breathing in time with mine.

"Of course, I never say anything I don't mean, and I love you." Finally the words escape my lips and unfortunately, an engagement didn't come with them. The timing may have been off, but she needs to know that love is the reason we are hiding in this closet, instead of me rushing out to take on my cousins for what they did to my truck and to Brandon. Their time will come, but Lauren will not be present.

She holds her breath, and then whispers the four words that I've longed to hear since the moment I saw her, "I love you, too." She hugs me tighter as more people walk past the door.

Then doubt sneaks in like a thief wanting to steal my bliss, "Do you mean that or did you say it because I did?"

It's an eternity before she finally responds, "I mean it." I want to see the words flow from her mouth.

"Say it again," I say and brush my lips to hers to feel them form the words.

"I love you," she says quietly and seductively ... too seductively. I'm kissing her and ignoring the danger waiting for us on the other side of the door. She's kissing me back hard, harder than she ever has before—almost desperately; her hands are in my hair, and on my chest, then around my neck. It's hot in the closet, and sweat is forming on my back and in the bends of my arms, but I barely notice. She swipes her tongue against mine and chills temporarily replace the sweat on my body. I hold my breath when I feel her lips on my neck and her hands roaming my chest again; her fingertips feel amazing gliding across the fabric of my shirt. The element of the dark is exhilarating and menacing when she starts unbuttoning my shirt and lets the very tips of her fingers slide against my balmy chest. My breathing refuses to slow, betraying my experience in this department. I'd give anything to see her face, but we might be discovered if I search for the switch.

"I love you," she whispers again and pulls my head down to her lips. I'm holding onto her, trying to enjoy every minute and emotion rushing through me. Thoughts of her in my arms are marred by worry that we'll be discovered. The fiends at the gates won't care that I love her. In fact, they'll use it against me.

"I love you too," I quietly respond, as more footsteps go by. She starts running her hands down my arms and kisses me passionately. We are not going to do this now, definitely not like this. But my body is so hot, and she's pressed so tight against me, that I can't stop those thoughts from racing through my head and a few other places. My hands start roaming and I pull her stomach tight against me, showing her exactly what I'm thinking about ... what I want. This isn't going to get any further than where we are now.

Not tonight. Patience is my friend.

When the time comes, it'll mean so much more to both of us
... and I'll undo all those other wrongs for this right. Yes, time and
patience...

"Stop, I can't ..." she pushes me away, her voice trembling.

"Lauren." I grab through the dark for her arm, hand, something.

"Can we go now?" She lets out a deep breath. "Please?"

What the hell just happened? Shit, I've just ruined this.

I finally find her huddled close to the door. "Just a few minutes
and we'll go. Lauren, I'm sorry if I just made you uncomfortable.
Please..."

"I just want to go home. I can't be late."

I comply and peek out the door. "Stay here." I slip through the
kitchen to see if their car is gone. It is; it's safe to leave, but we still
head out the back door instead of the front. Not how I wanted the
night to end. She's upset with me; she can't deny it. I wouldn't
have pushed her to do anything, but with her body so close and her
hands roaming eagerly, I got carried away. She probably just
compared me to Josh in all the worst ways. She never told me
exactly what happened in that damn hotel room and I don't dare
push her about it. How can she compare me to him when I have no
idea what he did? I guarantee he didn't have a three-carat promise
waiting to slide onto her tiny finger. I doubt if I gave it to her now
if she'd realize that the ring was the plan for the whole night. She'd
probably think I'm trying to seal the deal on what we just started.
Sure, there is no doubt that I want her, but our first time won't be
in a freaking supply closet. The fact that she probably thought that's
what I wanted when I told her I loved her pisses me off. She can't
think sex is the only thing between us or that I'd use those words
to get it. Sex isn't reliant on love and I've never used those three
words with a nameless or any other girl for that matter. I don't
need those words to get a girl into bed ... and sure I'd give my life
for her to share her body with me, but I'm greedy—I want
everything else that comes with it, too.

"Can I see you tomorrow?" I ask pulling into the parking lot of
the school with twenty minutes to spare. Lauren is staring out the

window with glassy eyes and if I let her get out the car without a resolution, she may never talk to me again.

She doesn't look at me when she reaches for the door, "I can't. I'm grounded."

"No, I know, but can you tell your parents we have to go pick up stuff for school or something?"

Lauren's legs shift to climb from the truck. She still has to change and the thought of her crying after she leaves me hurts more than I can stand. She can't get out of the truck. I stall her by reaching for her hand.

"Lauren, I don't know what you think just happened, but I swear that life is behind me and I wouldn't do anything to jeopardize my future with you. I meant what I said. I love you."

"I have to go," she says and slips away, taking my heart and my future with her all over again. I watch her slide off her shoes when she gets to the gate. She briefly looks at the truck before running the rest of the way down the sidewalk.

I resist running after her, but that doesn't mean I won't do everything to fix whatever it is that just went wrong.

Lauren

Mom doesn't even look at me when I meet her at nine. The borrowed dress and shoes are haphazardly discarded in my locker to return to Sara on Monday. I guess whether she wants it back or not depends on what happens with Danny. It didn't appear he had any intention of stopping tonight, and honestly if it weren't for what Brenda told me today, I wouldn't have wanted him to. The draw that I have to him is dangerous; it makes me want to throw out all my morals and chase him into whatever danger he wants to get into, but that would get me nowhere except into more trouble with my parents and further away from what little future I have left. But, what I've dreamed of is gone ... now what?

"I found your college applications buried under a stack of books on your desk," she says patting my arm. "The internship application for my company was there too. I thought you said you wanted to start there next month?"

"I don't know how I'll have time, with choir and the play and ..."

She interrupts me, "and Josh's football games?"

How could she not have realized? "No..." I start but she interrupts again, probably figuring she knows where my argument is heading.

"I know you think that the sun rises and sets by activities with Josh, but news flash, it doesn't. You have a whole life to live and I don't want you to have to depend on someone else to support you." She has a lot of room to talk. Until we moved to California, she had never worked outside the home; she was always too busy with schedules and feeding the team. "You have so many opportunities at your feet right now. You can go to college and do anything you want. Life doesn't have to be about pigskins and pizza every Sunday. The internship is a great opportunity for you and it will look great on college applications."

Her work seems utterly boring. Jess's internship at the hospital sounds so much more interesting, but Mom won't want to hear that. "I'll fill it out when I get home." I throw in the towel for tonight. Considering I don't know what is going to happen, I can't bank on Jess getting me that internship.

At home, I sink into an almost-overflowing bath. The heat of Danny's body against me in the closet, mixed with the danger of his cousin finding us, definitely blurred my judgment. If I couldn't sleep with Josh last week, how can it be okay to sleep with Danny tonight? Josh and I haven't even officially broken up either. *Ugh.*

That ring has to go back this week. It's just one more issue I'm avoiding, just like the college applications, the internship and finding a job. It was nice being wrapped in Danny's protective bubble this week, but our pasts collided tonight proving neither of us can avoid what we are or how we ended up making out in a supply closet. He was shaking just as bad as I was. He didn't mean what he said; how can he love me if all the rumors are true? Last year he told me he was a monster ... but what type of monster says they love someone and doesn't mean it? Regardless, I want to believe he meant it. I want to believe I'm enough for him to never take another drink or get into another fight for the rest of his life ... but I doubt that I am.

I wrap into my comfy hand-me-down robe and slide in front of my computer; nothing but spam lingers in my in box, so I shut it down and stare at the pictures of Josh stuck all over my bulletin board from games and rallies. It's stupid tormenting myself like this; nothing is going to be solved tonight. The answer isn't in those pictures. I climb into bed, and open my cell phone to look at the pictures of Danny and I at the café. My favorite picture of Danny with his arm wrapped around my waist is the first of many. I'm leaning against his shoulder looking up at him while his blue eyes pierce the camera. When I tilt the phone back and forth, it seems his eyes follow my every move—so serious, yet gentle when I needed him to be. I hate this. I hate the confusion, but it has come bounding into my life again. I hate Brenda—someone needs to do something about that psycho slut. What did Brandon ever see in *her* when he had someone like Sara by his side the whole time?

Mom wakes me just before eight to let me know she is leaving for Vegas. She'll be back late tomorrow night, and she makes it a point to tell me she wants the internship paperwork filled out and the college applications organized into my top choices before she gets back. At least I'll have something to keep my mind busy the next two days.

It's ironic how she went from pro-University of Illinois to pro-California Universities. The U of I brochure is strategically arranged behind all of the others. I'm not sure I want to go back there anyway; then again, it may take that to get away from the mess I'm in. When mom finds out I've pulled a Lynn, she'll probably ground me for the rest of the year and put me in a military boarding school. Even though she likes Danny, he's not in her five-year plan for me. He wasn't in my five-year plan, either.

My fingertips drum the pile of paperwork on the desk as I scroll through the spam in my in box. In between lottery winnings from India and one hundred ways to lose weight, I have ten emails from Danny and two from Sara. Danny's emails are mostly short, just one or two lines asking me what happened, what's wrong, and if I can call him the second I'm alone. The two from Sara are fishing —asking about school, dinner last night, and what I'm up to this weekend. She's probably feeling things out for Danny to see if I'll respond or not. I don't. I don't answer any of the emails. Instead, I make my bed, then clean the bathroom and grab the vacuum and do the floor. Dad comes in about ten to tell me he is going to the school for a coaches meeting and won't be back until late, so I'm on my own for dinner. So much for being grounded, if I had a car, I'd go somewhere.

I end up at my computer again; five more emails from Danny and more promised winnings if I just provide my banking and identifying information. Yeah, not happening. There's enough crap going on as it is; the last thing I need to add is identity theft to the list. Danny's emails started just after eleven p.m. last night and go pretty much every hour since then. He hasn't been to bed and he's probably exhausted. Or maybe he's not since he's used to staying up most of the night. But, you should never answer emails in anger or frustration, so even though I know he's probably waiting—I still don't answer. I belly flop onto my bed and bury my head into my pillows, trying to still the commotion rattling my brain.

Danny's had so many chances to take advantage of me, and really, would he have stayed around this long just to take something he can't be certain I still have? And would he really have spent four months in rehab just for that? Is getting even with Josh really worth it?

Frustrated, I get up and send Danny a quick email telling him to give me some time to get things straightened out. Nothing more, nothing less. Just time. That's all I want and need right now. Mom expects me to get the applications done, pick a major and a career—all in *two* days.

I crash back onto my bed with no plan of moving for hours. Hours that I need to figure out a few things. First, do I really want to do an internship with mom? Second, what college do I really want to go to? And third, if I'm not planning on being a wife and mother for the rest of my life—where does that leave me? Other than lost, I mean.

Sara shows up barely an hour into my wallowing. Her emails went unanswered, and Danny probably didn't like my response. She holds up two cups of iced coffee and pastries from the local bakery. "Hey want some dessert?" she says cheery, too cheery. Ick. She's not going to help me figure things out and her being here is just another distraction. Besides, you can't really have desserts when you haven't even had lunch.

"You didn't email back, and I didn't know what you were up to this weekend."

"I'm grounded, remember?" I shrug acting coy that I don't know why she's really here. She's Danny's spy and she's trying to dart behind enemy lines.

"Oh," she looks past me to the kitchen. "Where are your parents?"

"Mom's in Vegas with my aunt. Dad's at a coaches meeting. He'll be back soon." I tell the slightest fib. She's not buying it, so I head back to my bedroom with her in tow. At least she brought goodies with her. I hadn't even realized my stomach was screaming for food until I could smell the frosting on whatever she has in the bag. She hands me one of the coffees and I sprawl out on my bed sipping the caramel, frothy, icy goodness.

Sara pulls out the chair at my desk and sets the bag of pastries on my stack of applications. Hopefully she won't drop anything on them. I'm sure Mom would notice sweet, sticky smudges on them —and considering she doesn't keep those things in the house, she'll know I've had a visitor or I've snuck out.

"So, what are you working on?" She picks up the bag and fans the applications out across my desk.

"Figuring out what I'm going to do. Mom is on me to fill out college applications."

"Eww, yeah, I have a stack at home too," she says and glances around my desk and starts opening the bag that I've been anticipating. "Is this part of your grounding?"

"Yup. She wants them done by tomorrow night when she gets back."

"Bummer." She pulls out two apple turnovers and hands me one. "I hope you like these. Danny got me hooked ..."

"Thank you," I say and we chew in silence.

"Is there anything you want to talk about?" she finally asks when the turnovers are almost gone and I'm riding a caffeine induced sugar high that will probably end in a serious crash and a three hour long nap.

"No, why?" I say coyly and look at the pictures of Josh and I on the bulletin board that I haven't taken down yet. I seriously hope she doesn't notice them, but I'm certain she already has.

"Danny said things didn't go right last night," she takes a long sip of her coffee.

"No, I guess they didn't," I glance at the pictures of Josh again and then the stack of applications. If someone would've told me when those pictures were taken that I would be sitting in my room with Sara a little under a year later, I would say they were nuts.

"Danny's afraid that you think he's going to go back to the way he was." She wipes her hands on a napkin out of the bag and starts scrutinizing each of the applications on the desk.

I crumble up the napkin the turnover was on and toss it into the wastebasket. It bothers me that she could be in on what Brenda claimed Danny is doing; plus, I'm sure Danny told her how we ended up making out in the closet. That's not really the image I want out there, or the rumors that go along with it since my dad is always in the boys' locker room now.

"I don't even know what Danny's *old life* entailed," I say rather snarky. "So, how am I supposed to know what he'd go back to? Besides, how do I know, even if he's not planning it now, that it won't entice him back in the future?"

"I already told you, he went to rehab for you. Rehab. And not the fun kind either. The serious detox kind that almost kills you. He didn't do that for any of us, he did that for you and only you." Her tone is pure aggravation, but I almost feel as though she's not entitled to be.

"Sara, I just need some time right now," I say with cluttered thoughts bouncing off each other like bumper cars in my head. Bells and whistles sound when there've hit the sides of my skull too many times. All that sugar I consumed is bringing on a nauseating headache, or it's the argument; either way, I need an Advil and to get her the hell out of here before I get caught.

"What happened that made you change your mind so quickly? Was it Matt and Aaron?" She begs me with her eyes and guilt settles in on top of the pounding in my head.

So I figure it's best to get the nitty-gritty. I ask her, "Did you hear that Brenda came and talked to me?"

Sara sets her coffee down and I scoot to the end of the bed

wondering what she's heard and if she'll let me sneak in some much needed meds before we go any further.

"Yeah, I heard that. But no one would say what she wanted."

I go into the bathroom for the pills and a cup of water knowing if I don't get it now, my head is going to explode once Sara hears what Brenda said. "She said Danny is interested in only one thing. She said Danny only wanted me because Josh did."

"What? That's stupid," she stutters out as though her thoughts can't catch up to her mouth. "You can't seriously believe that." Her voice rises and lowers with each of her breaths. Her pale skin is starting to turn red, like mine.

"I don't know what to believe anymore. Danny seems to say and do the right things at exactly the right time. And, until yesterday, I had no reason to doubt anything he said. But I was naïve to believe Josh too, wasn't I?"

She stands, furious at my comparison. "Don't you dare say my brother is anything like that jerk. Danny has a ring for you ..." Her hands cover her mouth quickly.

Having more than enough of this for one day, I snatch the ring box off the desk and toss it to her, "yeah, Josh gave me a ring too and look what he wanted in exchange for it. I guess Danny and Josh are more alike than you think, huh?" Folding my arms across my chest, I feel vindicated and Brenda was my saving grace.

Sara clasps the ring box, staring at it like it's a bomb just waiting to go off. Her fingers shake pulling the lid off the box. She starts crying the second the ring is revealed. I've hurt her feelings, but she said Danny had a ring for me too. How could I not compare them and what would Danny try to make me give him? Would he expect more than Josh did? Would he tear me apart again like he almost did last year?

"Lauren," she says with a shaky voice, "Josh gave me this same ring the night he suckered me into sleeping with him."

The bells in my head sound louder than before as my pulse races and my knees start to give out. The world is being swept away from under my feet. "What?" I barely squeak out.

"I'm serious," Sara says firmer and wipes tears from her cheek. Her fear and sadness starts to lead to anger. "He gave me that ring. I had it on my finger!" I snatch the box from her hand, not wanting to believe what she is saying. "Did he make you promise to love him forever and be devoted to only him? Did he tell you that he wanted the house and the kids and the ever after only with you?"

"Get out," I practically scream at her as visions of the night at the hotel race through my mind; Josh dancing with Crystal, then sweeping me away to the hotel room as if nothing ever happened and his quick change to wanting me forever. I slam the door behind Sara when she finally goes with her tear soaked face and anger that I'm sure she's dealing with. But I really don't care.

Back in my room, with my skin throbbing from heat and tears rushing down my face, I tear every picture of Josh and I off the bulletin board and desk and rip them into pieces. Colored, high gloss snow flies everywhere in the path of my destruction.

How can I be so stupid? How have I managed to do the one thing I set out to avoid? And the biggest question, how can I bring myself to trust a boy ever again when they are just all out to use me?

D a n n y

I just need time.

That's what her only email to me said. Nothing more. Just time. What does she need time for? Time to get over Josh? Time to figure out life in general? Time to finish school? Time to forget me?

Time is not on my side right now.

I don't have time to give her.

Time away will not get me closer to any of my goals or get her closer to me.

Time is my enemy and giving her it would be like wrapping her in a package to Josh Miller all over again like I did last year.

NO, time is not my friend and I can't give it to her. It's all or nothing now. I can't give her distance and time. I've tried that before and all that has done is get me nowhere except behind the eight-ball.

I email her back, begging her to call me, but it goes unanswered. So I convince Sara to go over there. Lauren is grounded, but her mom probably won't be mad if she sees Sara. Me, on the other hand, would probably get Lauren an extension.

When Sara gets back to my place from Lauren's, her face is red and her eyes are puffy. Something tells me sending her may not have been the best idea, but you can't undo the past, so whatever happened I'll have to deal with. I grab some sodas from the fridge and settle into the couch next to her to find out the bad news.

"Is my life with her over? Is she totally pissed at me or what?"

"We didn't really even talk about that," she pouts.

Isn't that what she went over there for? "What did you talk about?"

"Josh gave her a ring ..." she sobs and I hope I didn't hear her right.

"What? Did you say ring?" The ring I bought her is in my safe. If Josh gave her an engagement ring and she took it, I'm going to take a hammer to the one I bought. I don't care how much it cost.

"Yeah ..." she covers her face and I have to stop myself from ripping her hands away to make her get to the point fast.

"When did he give it to her?" I'm trying to stay calm, but I can feel the undeniable fire building under my skin.

"Probably the night of the dance. It's the same one he gave me." *Wait, what?*

"The same one ... Are you sure?"

"Yeah, I'm positive. The one he said was his grandmother's. It's the same ring." Now I understand why she is so upset. That night at the dance Josh was trying to make his move on her like he did with Sara although Josh kept Lauren around longer than Sara.

"Was she wearing it?" *Please say no...*

"No, she had it in a box on her desk. She compared you to him."

I'm a complete moron. "Because she thought ..." The heat in the supply closet comes rushing back and goose bumps spread down my arms. It's not because of Matt or Aaron or the danger she was in. It's because she thinks I only want her to sleep with me. "She thinks I'm trying to get even with Josh over you?" I say thinking out loud. If that was the only thing she had to offer, there would be no way I would've put myself through all that I have for her.

"What can I do to fix this?" I say hoping Sara can come up with a solution, but really, there isn't one. My past has come back to bite me in the ass once again.

"I don't know Danny. She wouldn't talk to me after I told her it was the same ring Josh gave me. She didn't say what she was going to do."

"Did she say anything else? Or did you notice anything?"

Sara's eyes are bloodshot and tearing again as she strokes the throw pillow she has rested on her lap, "no, nothing else." Something tells me she is lying.

"Are you sure?" I push.

"Yeah, I'm sure." No she's not. There has to be something else, but she's crying again and upset over what's happened. She's probably afraid the first thing I'm going to do is get shit-faced, but it's not happening. This can still be salvaged. My relationship with her will be fixed. Lauren is a smart girl; she will come around and things will be fine. She just needs time, so, time is what she will get, no matter how much I hate the idea of giving it to her.

Time is what I said I'd give, but six hours later I've driven myself insane watching re-runs of bad reality TV. Sara ordered pizza and then went and got ice cream and called Alexis a few times. I check my voicemail, emails and text messages and there is still nothing from her. She hasn't called and Josh giving her a ring keeps running through my head. I punch in her phone number, but I don't hit send.

"I'll be back," I say, interrupting Sara's latest call to Alexis. I climb into Sara's cramped Honda to drive past her house. It'll be less obvious driving by in it than my truck. In less than ten minutes I'm on her street and her house is in sight. Her dad's truck isn't there and neither is their mini-van, but the light in her bedroom is on. The rest of the house is dark. This is a stupid idea; I tend to have a lot of those when it comes to Lauren. I know that—but it doesn't stop me.

Parking several blocks away, I stick to the shadows like a cat burglar, until I'm on the side of her house. I wait to make sure no one on the street has seen me before I knock on her window. I can hear the TV through the window, but can't see anything because of her blinds. I knock again. I probably should've gone to the front door—she's going to call the cops on me for trying to break in.

The curtains pull slightly to the side and her stark green eyes glow at me in the darkness. "Danny?" she finally says and reaches to pull up her blinds. "What are you doing here?" she asks when she tugs open her window.

"You didn't answer my emails, so I got worried."

"I've been busy," she says, but she's lying. She's watching the same show I was.

"Are you alone? Can you come outside so that we can talk?" I lean forward to get a better look at her. Her eyes are blood shot and puffy just like Sara's. There is a white ring box on her desk and torn papers all over the floor that implies she had a major hissy-fit.

"Yeah, I'll be right out," she says following my eyes to the floor and the scattered mess. She just shrugs and turns toward her bedroom door.

I ease onto the small bench sitting just beside her front door and wait for what seems like an eternity for her to come out and bring my heart with her. She's wrapped in her robe and stuffing a wad of tissue into one of her pockets. That's not a good sign.

"What do you need?" she says passively and folds her arms across her chest. She doesn't sit next to me.

"Ummm ..." I'm lost for something to say. This week was the best week of my life; that's what should come out of my mouth, but it doesn't. Something better does. "I want to apologize for ruining last night." I stand, closing the distance between us, wanting to bridge the gap of where we were and where we need to be. "I know I freaked you out with having to hide in that closet. Trust me. That was the last thing I wanted to do." *Yeah I wanted to ask you to marry me and give you a huge ring that would take your breath away. Not to mention, get on with my life.*

"I don't really want to talk about last night," she mumbles and shifts from one leg to the other. She didn't turn on the patio light, but it's easy to see she's not looking me in the eye. She's looking down the street, up the street, at the door, and at the ground ... everywhere but where I need her to look. Lauren has to see the sincerity in my eyes, the pain that she's causing right now. The power she has to crush me.

"Lauren," I say and move closer to put my fingers under her chin. Finally she looks up at me with loss and hurt in her eyes. "Please tell me what you are thinking ... what did I do to make you so upset with me last night?"

"Nothing," and she pulls her face away from my fingers.

This week has meant absolutely nothing. "Don't lie to me. You haven't emailed me, texted me, or called me."

She steps back. "I told you I've been busy."

I don't want to argue with her, but she's not really giving me any choice. "You've made time for me all week. Last night when I dropped you off you barely said two words to me." She's not up for the fight. She turns to walk away from me and I grab her arm, not willing for it to end this way. "Things can't end like this. I refuse to think that everything this week doesn't matter. Just tell me what I did and I'll apologize."

Lauren reaches for the door and my fingers tighten around her arm. My arms and legs twitch from the new found adrenaline rushing through me. This can't end this way. She can't walk into the house and leave me here to wonder what I've done wrong and live with this regret the rest of my life.

"Lauren, please ..." I beg and she pulls her arm, so I let go. It's easy for her to walk away from this, from me. That ring is probably sitting on her desk because she's reconsidering the offer Josh made her and everything I'm willing to give her means nothing— because she'll never know. "Don't leave things this way. Won't you always wonder what might have been? What could've happened between us?" I say in desperation before she can get across the threshold of the house and it stops her.

Lauren turns slightly, still in the safety of her house, and says, "what was going on last night?"

I step forward and then step back when she tenses. "What I told you was true. My cousins showed up. They know it's one of my favorite restaurants. I'm so sorry I put you in danger."

Lauren steps forward, "why are they after you?"

"Because I stopped doing jobs for my Uncle."

Another step. Now we're getting somewhere. "Why?"

I turn and walk towards the bench again and urge her to sit with me. "I knew I was destroying my life and any chance at normalcy I had."

Lauren joins me and I resist taking her hand at first, but when she starts wringing them in her lap, I grab one. "So, what did you do for him?"

She asks the same question she's been asking since we've met and I haven't been willing to answer ... but I am now if it means she'll stay with me. "I collected gambling debts for him mostly."

She sniffles. "So, you really were beating people up for money then?"

I squeeze her hand to keep it in mine. "Yes, but I told you, that is over."

"But you can't just quit it, can you?" The streetlight reflects off her eyes and she's starting to tear up. Seeing her cry kills me.

"No," she deserves the truth. "They vandalized my truck two weeks ago. I've been waiting for them to retaliate. I'm surprised they've left me alone this long." I expect her to worry about herself like Jackie did, but she doesn't. She says the last thing I expect her to say.

"Will they hurt you?" If they get a chance ... they will. But I don't want her to worry about that on top of everything else.

"Not if I can help it." I say and add, "I didn't want to tell you everything I've done because I thought you wouldn't want to be with a monster like me."

Calling myself a monster gets a little laugh out of her. "You're not a monster, but those things make you who you are ..."

"No, they don't." I utter quickly. Her words sting and I'm fighting the balled up emotions that are collecting in my gut. "The things I've done aren't me, they are my past." I say defensively.

"I didn't mean it as a bad thing. I just meant they helped you to be who you are. You are more aware of things and you've lived more than I have. You've had more ... experiences than I've had."

Experiences. The word has so many meanings and in the way she just said it makes me worry about what she's really getting at. I'd kill to be in her head. "I may have had *experiences* you haven't had, but that doesn't matter to me. I don't care." I wanted to avoid it, but it comes out, "I got carried away in the supply closet. I know I did, but I promise you, nothing was going to happen. Not like that. It was just overwhelming, being in there and having you that close to me."

"Sara told you …" Her lips press together and she swallows hard. We both shift on the seat and I move strategically closer to her, wanting to be comforted by her soft vanilla scent, a scent and intimacy that will assure me we can get past this and tomorrow will conclude our first full week together, with the prospect of many more to come.

"I'll do everything I can to prove to you that I'm nothing like Josh Miller. You upset Sara when you compared me to him, but I understand why you did. First we are having a great dinner, the next I'm forcing you to hide in a cramped closet and we're making out. I'm not here because of Josh or revenge or sex or anything else. You are the only reason I'm here … I only want you and if it takes not touching you or kissing you to prove it, then say the word and I won't touch you ever again."

Lauren lets out another small laugh that ignites my hope and finally brings her scent when she tosses her hair off of her neck. My breath is coming easier and I move closer and so does she. She rests her head on my shoulder and I loop my arm around her back to hug her into my side. She didn't run or think of herself when I told her the danger we are in. Extraordinary. Not the expected response, but welcomed all the same.

"Did you mean what you said?" she says, quietly crying into my shoulder.

The entire conversation runs in fast forward through my head.

Uncle John- yes.

Fighting- yes.

Danger last night- yes.

Got carried away in a supply closet- yes.

"Which part?"

She says quieter, "The part where you love me?"

If she only knew; "Yes. I love you." The words roll easily off my tongue, thankful to get one more chance to say them out loud to her. "More than you know." I say and stare deeply into her tired eyes. She's exhausted from today just like me and I want nothing more than to curl up with her and sleep, to put this horrible day behind us ... but that is definitely out of the question.

I love you too, she whispers.

L a u r e n

Monday morning and I'm rushing. Mom has to take me to school before work and she's still hung over from her wild weekend in Vegas. I've never seen her leave the house without make-up, but she's called in sick today, so she's going without.

"We are going to be late ..." Mom calls from the kitchen, hovering over an extra large cup of coffee. Dad is already fed and gone by the time we are ready to go. I barely saw him yesterday and he came in after midnight on Saturday. That's the latest he's ever been out for a coaches meeting, then again, with mom gone he probably went out with the guys afterward.

"Ready?" I ask with my book bag slung over my shoulder. The stack of college applications and the internship application are completed and sitting on the counter for her approval. The major is still undecided and putting them in order was really scientific. I shuffled them together, shuffled them again, and then again. And that's it. The one at the top of the pile is USC, second is UC Santa Barbara and the third UC Irvine. She'll be pleased.

"Are you sure you did everything on those forms?"

"Yes, I triple checked them."

"What about the internship?"

"Yes, that too."

"You know it starts soon."

"Yeah, I know."

"I was talking to my boss and he thinks they maybe able to put your internship in as a part time employee to pay you." That gets my attention.

"Does that mean I can get my license?"

"Once you make enough money to cover your insurance and the gas ..." And it's settled. As soon as I can start working, I'll have a car. Score one for doing what she told me to do this weekend.

Mom drops me off at my usual spot and Danny's truck isn't there, but Josh's Camaro is. "Bye mom," I say but she stops me before I get the door closed.

"Can you get a ride home?" she asks, yawning.

"Yeah," I say. Danny can give me a ride and I can tell him about the internship. If Jess can get me a paying one at her work, I can do it instead and have a lot more fun. Mom is going to know something's up soon when Josh doesn't come over when the other players do. I'll have to tell her soon. She won't like that I've jumped from one boy to the other, but, she practically pushed me towards Danny last year; that has to count for something, right?

I pull the dress from Friday out of my locker and brush out the wrinkles in it to give back to Sara this morning. A group of cheerleaders walk by, snickering at me and giggling. If I tripped one, would they all go down? How much trouble would that get me into? Mom may think it's funny, but the Guidance Counselor won't. The ring box holding Josh's false promise tumbles out of my book bag. It's going back to him today. No amount of talking or rumors can make me go back to him. Nothing. He is nothing.

"Hey sunshine," Mark says rushing past me to his locker.

"Hey, have you seen Josh?"

"I just left him in the quad. He's heading to first period. See you after school?" he asks. I forgot tonight dad is having some of the team over for pizza and strategizing. If I weren't grounded, I'd skip.

"Thanks, see you tonight!" I rush towards the quad with the ring box in hand. This isn't how I wanted to start out my Monday, but, considering I've made my decision, there's no reason to keep the binding trinket any longer.

"Hey, can I talk to you?" I say grabbing Josh's arm in main quad. My old friends, the *deserters,* are staring at me as though I'm not worth their time. But they aren't worth mine. I just have to get this over with.

"Yeah," he says and tells Mike and Ben he'll catch up with them later. "What's up?" he asks when we are finally alone.

"Here," I say holding out the box, "I don't think it's right to keep this." His absence the last week is dancing in the back of my mind, but I bite my tongue.

"Thanks," he says and nothing more. I expected a big show, a big production, a big fight ... I don't know ... something. Shouldn't almost a year of dating lead to more than a *Thanks*.

"So, we're over ..." I say uncomfortably staring at him and the kids around us rushing to class.

"Yeah, it looks like it," he says and nods to a few players that walk by.

"Don't you have anything you want to tell me? Anything you want to say?"

"What do you expect?" he says harshly, "I did everything to make the night special for you and you shit on me."

"What?" I say stunned at his attitude and his tone.

"Whatever, you're a tease. I'm over it."

"I'm not a tease. I loved you."

He starts laughing when Crystal, Lindsay, and Jackie walk up to stand less than five feet from us. They are not giving us any privacy; they probably feel I'm invading their territory.

"I only wanted you because I knew Danny did," he says cupping my cheek with his palm. The words sting through my chest and seep deep into the pit of my stomach. Tears streak down my face. "It was all a game. It's always been a game."

Crystal and Lindsay both start laughing. My teeth bite into my cheek—salty, icky blood blends with the saliva sliding down my throat. Danny is going to kill him for this—I swear. He played me, and blindly, I followed him. Mom has warned me about boys like Josh my whole life ... but seeing it first hand is totally different. It's ... overwhelming.

The flashing fluorescent light in the nurse's office wakes me. Talk about history repeating, this feels like sophomore year all over again. Josh said it was always a game. All of it. Every kiss, every touch, every talk about the future … our future … it was all a game. He never meant one word he said to me.

"How are you feeling?" Nurse Smith asks.

"I've been better," I say sarcastically and sit up from the hard bed. It's already lunchtime according to the clock on the wall. I've missed all my classes and Danny. He'll make things better. He's here for the right reasons. After promising never to touch me again, if that's what it would take to keep me in his life. Only time will tell if he's being genuine or not. Right now, he's the only thing I have, so I hope he isn't lying to me like Josh was.

D a n n y

I've been up half the night worried whether things with Lauren are truly fixed or not after the debacle Friday night turned out to be. She didn't call or email on Sunday, although I suspected she wouldn't with the way her room looked and knowing her mom was coming home. Her deadline to pick a college was yesterday and Sara told me U of I is her top choice since it was the first in the stack of applications she had. I've downloaded the brochure for the school and the application, too. I doubt I can get in, but if she's going there, I will be too ... even if it's just to the local junior college. The house and academy can wait. If she wants me to, I'll drop everything to follow her into the unknown. Today will be the proving ground. If she can get past what I told her about Uncle John and my cousins, not to mention all the crap with Josh, college will be smooth sailing. Maybe I can go to the academy as planned in January and then apply to the Illinois State Police instead of going to college ... I have to keep my options open right now. Flexibility is key, considering how unsure she's been about her plans.

Lauren isn't at the benches when Sara and I arrive at school. No one has seen her either, so I pull out my cell phone and call her house and cell, but there is no answer. She's probably running late, but I convince Sara to head over to her locker anyway while I wait at the benches. When Sara comes back, she brings the world crushing down on my head.

She's crying, something she's done entirely too much lately, and I can barely understand her muffled voice against my chest, "Lauren's back together with Josh."

"What?" I grab her shoulder and push her backwards to see what she's saying.

"I didn't want to tell you, but she has pictures of them together all over her room and posters of his number all over her walls. She's not over him. She's with him in main quad again. Lauren's going back to Josh."

I push Sara away from me and venom courses through my veins. Josh Miller has successfully destroyed every part of my life —my past and present, all of it begins and ends with Josh Miller. That cocky bastard planned this the whole time, although, he never gave me the impression he was smart enough to destroy my life.

My keys cut into my palm as I grind them back and forth with my fingers, wanting to feel this pain rather than the burning Mr. Hyde is calling for. Josh is going to die and Lauren will officially hate me forever for trying to give her a better life than what she's always dreamed of. How can she want the lie her parents have? Why can't she just wait to get the life she deserves? She never expected anything more from me, just like my family when I came home. She's tossed me aside like a bag of trash.

The truck roars to life and I leave half of my tires on the pavement pulling out of the space, down the aisle towards the exit. There are cars blocking my escape, so I go over a curb, across the sidewalk and into the street, cutting off several cars in the process. You should never drive angry, it's dangerous and foolish, but it doesn't matter … nothing does anymore.

Three hours later I feel nothing—not the burning in my stomach, not the walls closing in or the room spinning. The light is too much for my eyes, so I hurl the half empty bottle of vodka at the light switch. When the bottle crashes against the wall—sending sticky, fiery goodness everywhere—I think what a waste that was. The light switch really isn't that far from my place on the floor, and now I have no alcohol and the light is still on. Damn my impatience.

"Danny?" Sara says timidly coming in the front door. It's then that I realize I'm not in my room; I'm lying half in the hallway and half in the living room. I've lost my touch and can't hold my alcohol anymore. That has to be fixed.

"Go get me another bottle. My other one broke. My wallet's on the counter," I command and wave my limp hand toward the counter where I discarded my keys and my wallet. Jeremy pushes the door open and grabs me by the arms and yanks me off the floor, over his shoulder and up the stairs towards my room. Five seconds later he's got my head over the toilet and his fingers shoved down my throat. This is totally killing my buzz.

"You've got to get the poison out of you," he says wiggling his finger around in my mouth until I'm gagging and convulsing. My feet and arms thrash trying to get away from him and free from the bathroom, but he's stronger than I am now. "You can't do this to yourself again. You're going to ruin everything you've been working so hard for." He shoves his fingers in my mouth again and succeeds. Everything from the last three hours comes back up, and keeps coming. Once it starts, it won't stop, and with each lurch the feelings return. Feelings suck.

"Here, drink this," Sara says when my body and skin hurt worse than it has in my entire life. "Be thankful I called Jeremy and not Dad."

"Yeah, thanks," I say taking the coffee from her and tug my hand through my hair. Jeremy is channel surfing on my couch when I finally emerge from the bathroom.

"Sorry," he says standing and shoving his hand into his pockets.

"It's alright. I'm fine now."

Sara lets out a deep breath, dumping glass from the shattered vodka bottle into the trashcan. "You know we aren't leaving you alone for one minute, right?"

"Yeah, I gathered that."

"Sara told me what happened with Lauren. I'm sorry, but you can't control her or what she does. She's made her choice. Now you have to get on with things. You can't go back to the way you were." Easy for him to say; he still has Jenn.

"I know," I say, but hardly mean it. The minute the bottle met my lips earlier, Mr. Hyde was back and ready to stay. Uncle John will have his best crewmember back by the end of the week. Forget this new life, I don't know how I ever thought I'd have more or be more.

Lauren

Danny and Sara aren't at the benches when I get there from the nurses office. In fact, neither is Jenn, Alexis or Justin. None of my friends is here today. Danny's truck isn't in the parking lot either. What am I supposed to do now? I can't go to the quad, and hanging out alone at the benches isn't a good idea since Brenda's there today. I head to the library to work on homework and sneak bites of my lunch in between rounds by the Librarian. This is lame to the tenth power. After lunch, I call Danny's cell and leave him a message to call me. I leave messages on both Sara and Jenn's voicemails, too. Did I miss Junior/Senior ditch day or what?

"How was your day?" Mom asks when I climb into the mini-van after school. She's still in her PJ's and still hung over. She's not happy she had to come get me, but she won't fight me now, so ...

"Josh and I broke up," I say, but she doesn't react. "We wanted different things."

"Like what?" she says indifferently.

Do I really tell her? "He was just focused on other stuff."

"Is this about the dance?" she asks, waiting to merge onto the main street.

How could she have found out? "Not really,"

"Well, I've been waiting for you to say something. Your dad told me last week that the rumor on the team was that you split up and started hanging out with Sara ... and Danny." She looks at me from the corner of her eye, "Is there something else you want to tell me?"

Great ... rumors beat me to the punch. "Danny and I are dating," I admit.

"Don't you think you should've waited before jumping to a new boy?"

"Yes," I say getting quieter. "I didn't really plan on it going down that way though."

"Why didn't you tell me last week when you and Josh broke up?"

"We didn't officially break up until yesterday." Oops ... shouldn't have said that.

"Dad says you hung out with Danny all last week."

"Josh didn't come to school last week. He didn't come back until this week so I couldn't break up with him," I say trying to justify my behavior, which I'm sure she considers inappropriate. Then again, she doesn't know that I ended up in bed with Danny last week. Thankfully, that isn't a rumor that got around at school.

"I mailed your applications to the top five today. I also filled in the *rest* of your internship packet and I'll turn that in tomorrow. I like Danny, but I think you've focused enough on boys for this year. How about taking a break for now?" she says as the final word on the subject.

Dad takes my TV, computer, and cell phone away. My grounding is extended by two weeks for being dishonest about Josh.

On his last trip in, Dad stops and sits next to me on the bed. "So, you know the guys on the team talk, right?"

"Yeah," I say nervously.

"Some of the guys are saying that Josh got a room the night of the dance ..." Oh God.

I start begging for forgiveness, "I swear, Dad nothing happened." He glares at me.

"Is that why you and Josh broke up?" He shifts uncomfortably on the bed.

"Yeah," I admit. "Does Mom know?"

"No, I haven't told her yet. I wanted to talk to you first."

"Please don't tell her. She'll be so mad at me and nothing happened."

"I won't tell her, but you can't put yourself into those situations. That's how rumors and bad reputations start. Mark said you've been hanging out at the benches. Is that because of Sara or that Danny kid?"

I swallow hard; he doesn't want me with Danny, he made that clear last year. "Both. Alexis is there too."

"Mark said Josh doesn't hang out in main quad anymore, so you can go back and hang out with them." Yeah, that's not happening. Just because Josh isn't there doesn't mean that Crystal and Mandi aren't.

"Dad, I can't hang out there again. Those friends took Josh's side after we broke up."

"Because you started hanging out with their enemy. Did you give them a chance?"

No, I hadn't. But I'm with Danny now, so it's not happening. "No, but I started dating Danny."

"Already?" he asks.

"Kind of; we aren't official or anything like that."

"What did your mom say about that?"

"She grounded me for another two weeks and told me no boys."

"Well then, I agree," he says and picks up my keyboard. "Consider going back to the main quad where you belong."

Ugh. I probably don't belong at the benches, but I certainly don't belong in the quad either. After the crap that happened on Friday with Brenda, Danny will be more amenable to hanging out somewhere else, or at least, I hope so. He's not going to like the additional two weeks for my hi-jinx, and that my dad wants me back in main quad ... but at least we are together and free of Josh once and for all. It's such a relief having that ring gone and the pictures of Josh turned into confetti. Today is the beginning of something big ... I can feel it.

The next day Mom drops me at the usual spot and I rush to the benches to tell Danny and Sara everything that happened and find out what is going on. They never showed up at school yesterday and that's making me nervous. Alexis is there, but they aren't. "Hey, what's going on?" I ask and get the cold shoulder. "Alexis?" I grab her arm when she starts to head to her class.

"What do you want Lauren?" she asks annoyed.

"Where are Danny and Sara?"

"Like you care!" She leaves me standing there with my mouth hung open. What the hell is going on?

At lunch, I head to the benches, but I know they aren't there. Neither of them showed up to any classes this morning. I refuse to spend another lunch in the library like the biggest loser on the planet. Climbing into Danny's normal spot on one of the tables, I try to ignore the eyes burrowing my skin. This is worse than I thought. Alexis isn't here and without a cell phone I can't call Sara or Danny to find out what is going on. Maybe Danny changed his mind? What if he's decided he doesn't want to put up with my insecurities, or inexperience?

By Wednesday morning, I'm listless. No word from Danny, Sara, or Jenn. Then again, I have no access to email or my cell phone for another month, so I'm hoping they show up today. Danny still doesn't even know that I've told my parents that we are dating. One hurdle for us is over, and now it's up to him and whether or not he truly wants to be with me.

Sara intercepts me before I can get to the benches. "You're a fool. Danny was so stupid to give you another chance after you chose Josh over him. Now he let you do it again. I loved you like a sister and you betrayed us." I'm shaking my head trying to get the words to come. I don't get it.

"Sara, what ..." she won't let me get the words out.

"If you go near my brother again, you will be sorry."

"I have no idea what you are talking about ..." Panic sets in as she turns to walk away from me.

Then she stops abruptly, "You made Danny think you loved him, and then you crush him by running back to Josh."

"What?" I say with my heart in my feet. "That's not what I did." I follow the rest of the way to the benches. Danny is there, but so is

Jackie … in his arms. My heart stops beating. I'm dying. I've been the fool. Josh didn't want me, now Danny doesn't either.

Danny shows up to Drama, but won't come near me. Ms. Nelson has someone else read his lines for the play and it makes me think that he's dropping out of my life completely. He won't look at me, even when I'm staring at him so hard he should feel it.

"Danny?" I finally say when he comes close enough to hear me, my whole body shaking so badly that I can't control it.

"What do you want?" he says in a cold monotone.

"What happened?" I ask and chew at my cheek trying to keep the tears from coming. "I thought we were okay after we talked on Saturday…"

"Yeah, well, me too. I can't help that you lied. Don't expect me to pick up the pieces anymore. I'm done with your games. I'm done being your consolation prize."

"Mr. Cummings, I need that piece over here," Ms. Nelson says pulling Danny's attention from me.

"Good luck with Josh," he says, "you'll need it."

"No, Danny, it's not like that …" but he's gone. He doesn't hear a word I'm saying. I'm begging him to come back, wanting to find out what Josh told him or what rumors he heard to make him think I'm back with Josh.

He leaves before class is out and he's gone the rest of the day. Jackie, Sara and Jenn are hanging out at the benches during lunch and I'm the loser in the library once again. How did things go so horribly wrong? I don't understand.

I'm working on homework when Dad pokes his head in after nine. "I don't know if you had something to do with it or not, but Danny and Josh got into a fight today. Danny beat the hell out of him."

Dad seems almost pleased with the news, but my first thought is Danny can't get into trouble over me, over this. He's already been to juvenile hall once and he promised me the life he had with his Uncle is over. Then again, he said he loved me too, but walked back to Jackie so easily.

"Is he in a lot of trouble?" I ask.

"No, not too much. They talked about expelling him, but I talked to the Principal and told him what Josh tried to do with you." I rush to my dad and throw my arms around his neck to thank him. "Let's just keep this between us, but I'm glad Josh had to answer to someone for what he tried."

"Thanks, Dad." I squeeze him tighter. Secretly, I'm glad Danny did it too, but that doesn't get me any closer to him. He won't talk to me, and Jackie back at the benches tells me he'd rather be with her. I lost both boys because I wouldn't go all the way with either. Fantastic.

By the night of the play, I've dropped almost ten pounds and barely get out of bed anymore unless it's for school. Hearing everyone gossip about Danny and Jackie everyday stinks. And hanging out in the library at lunch because no one will talk to me, sucks a million times over. Jackie has officially gotten both of the lives I wanted. Not to mention Crystal and Josh are now officially together. She got the Cinderella ending of my dreams too. Go figure.

Nerves shake every part of my body through the entire play. Danny dropped out of the production weeks ago. Rumor has it that he used his job and other commitments to get out of it. He shows up on the last night to help with the sets. Sara, Jeremy, Jackie, Jenn, Justin, and Alexis are all sitting in the front row sneering and laughing when I'm saying my lines. Danny took away my fear when I was on stage with him, but Nate doesn't have the same effect on me and I stumble over my words and forget two lines. My parents and Mark are sitting just a few seats down from Sara and I hope they don't say anything to each other. Sara could rat me out for everything that happened during the night of the dance and the extensive sneaking around Danny and I did the week following. That would just add to everything else and I'm only a week away from being off grounding.

"You did amazingly well!" mom says when she walks onto the

stage after the final curtain. She must have been blind and deaf because there is no way that performance was amazing.

"Thanks," I say and watch Danny cross the stage putting away set pieces. Jackie starts helping him and Sara stares at my parents and me. I've tried more than a dozen times to approach her and Danny, but they won't talk to me or listen to anything I have to say. As soon as I get my computer back, I'm going to email them both and try to figure out how things went so terribly wrong. Danny wished me good luck with Josh—how could he think I'd go back to him after all that he did to me? I miss my friends and hanging out with them. My old group of friends from the quad ignore me, and the people at the benches laugh at me whenever I walk by. I don't fit in anywhere anymore and Mark is the only person who still talks to me and comes over once in a while.

"She's right, you were fantastic!" Mark says handing me a huge bunch of red roses. I barely listen to him as Jackie twists her arms behind Danny's back and rubs her body against him near the prop room. Less than a month ago, that was me. Those arms were mine, his skin was free to my touch, his heart was open to my love … but that's gone and I have no idea what I did to deserve how he turned on me overnight. I seriously don't want to believe what Brenda said, but with the way Jackie is grinding against Danny, I'm sure they've already done it.

"Will you go out with me?" Mark says pulling me back to the smell of the roses and his overwhelming aftershave.

"What?" I say, almost certain that I've hallucinated.

Mark laughs uncomfortably and looks at Dad and Mom, both eavesdropping. "Will you go out with me?" he says, the words cracking.

Danny stops and stares at me like he knows what is going on. Sara stares at me too; they both seem to be anxiously awaiting my answer.

"You can come back to main quad where you belong, and I can help you get through your last classes before I go to USC next year." Mark is following in his dad's footsteps to become a doctor, but he's always been like a brother to me. Can I really force there to be anymore?

"Well?" Dad says when enough time has passed and most of the theater is now empty.

"Yes," I mumble and Danny shakes his head, grabs Jackie's arm and heads down the stairs of the stage. He's practically dragging her behind him. Sara and Jenn both glare at me.

"You won't regret this," Mark says wrapping his teddy bear arms around me and pressing his lips firmly to mine. I regret it already. This is going to take a lot of getting used to.

"Did you encourage this?" Mom asks dad, but I don't get to hear the response as Mark starts telling me how great things are going to be. I don't know how great things can be, considering my heart just left the theater with another boy.

D a n n y

Sara told me Lauren got back together with Josh, but that proves to be false when Josh starts dating Crystal and Lauren is ostracized by every friend she's ever had at Mountain View. The night after I got drunk and destroyed half of my condo, Jackie showed up and said her parents threw her out and she had nowhere else to go. She also told me she can't live without me and she doesn't care about my past. And it was irresponsible, so I took her into my life, into my condo and into my bed. Two days later, she moved in completely.

That was three months ago and we've settled into a systematic routine. We drive to school together, hang out at lunch, drive home and I go to work while she takes online classes to meet prerequisites for college. After work we eat dinner, watch a show or two and go to bed. She knows about the house because of the brochures, but I haven't told her myself, and she hasn't brought it up. Everything in that house is for Lauren, not Jackie. I'll sell it the minute it's finished and be done and over with Lauren McIntosh all together. If Jackie is going to be my future, she deserves her own place in my life and my heart. She can't occupy the place that Lauren did … that's irreparably broken.

At the end of the month I'll start the explorer academy and Mountain View High School will be just a distant memory. Dad arranged for me to take the exit exam and challenge my last two classes for credit. Dad and Bev aren't happy Jackie is living with me, but they aren't fighting it because she's keeping me clean. No one told them what happened with Lauren, but they know it didn't go the way I planned. They want me out of school before it gets worse. I'm just looking forward to getting away from school and Lauren's fake romance with Mark. She went from one jock, to another ... obviously she couldn't give up on her desire to marry the football stud and live the fake life her parents have. Betrayal is a dish best served with a side of Jack Daniels ... but that won't get me anywhere. What did I do that made her run back to Josh and why isn't she with him now? Josh must have been officially dating Crystal by the time she tried to run back to him; otherwise, I'm sure she'd be with him. That was the best week of my life ... it sucks that she doesn't feel the same way.

"Danny?" Jackie says standing at the front door, waiting for me to grab the vegetarian lunch she made. Salads are great and all ... but not every day.

Brandon left early to pick up Sara. It's ironic this is his first week back, and my last. Things have been eerily quiet since he got out of rehab and we are expecting Matt or Aaron to show up again soon. After the night at the restaurant, I haven't seen them. They are like roaches hiding in the shadows, just waiting for the light to go out so that they can wreak havoc. *Jerks.*

"Yeah, let's go." I set the alarm, grab my bag and head to the truck. In less than a week, I'll be completely done with Lauren. That's not really okay with me. At least I get to see her daily, even if she is with Mark. He won't try to take advantage of her like Josh did. They barely hold hands or touch each other at school; it's painful to see her so devoid of all life and excitement. But if it weren't for him, she'd have absolutely no friends anymore.

It's probably hard for her to see me with Jackie, and I'm sure she knows I've taken Jackie in. But I'm not sure if she knows this is my last week since she never talks to Sara or me anymore. It doesn't matter anyway. Lauren has to get out of my mind if I'm going to get through this week.

I leave Jackie in the parking lot talking to Mandi and Jamie, her new/old BFF's that haven't figured out that I hate them and want nothing to do with them. Jackie dumped the team, so why she didn't drop those troublemakers is beyond me. She doesn't hang out with Sara anymore either because she's *too busy* preparing for college, although she goes to Vince's every Tuesday night with the cheerleaders.

"Hey, so are you ready for this weekend?" I ask and pull out a protein bar since she couldn't be bothered with making breakfast today. Brandon, Justin, Jeremy and I are making our first trip to the lodge to celebrate ski season and Brandon's freedom. We all agreed no girls, and Jackie is pissed. I haven't told her that I'm letting Sara go; it's none of her business.

"Beyond ready. You tell Jackie Sara's going yet?"

"Hell no," I say and Sara almost spits out part of her soda. "She doesn't need to know." I glare at Sara, making sure she knows if it comes out, then I'll have to take Jackie too and it'll ruin her weekend as well as mine.

"Damn ..." Justin says, drawing out his A and then whistles. "Check that shit out!" He points to the parking lot as a sleek jet-black BMW with huge rims and jet-black windows pulls into the parking lot. *Someone got a new toy. My money's on Crystal ...*

"That's an awesome car ..." Sara says leaning back on the table to get a better look. Brandon's hips between her knees and hands on her thighs are distracting me from the car. Who the hell cares about a BMW? I can buy one any day, in fact, I drive my girlfriend's all the ...

Holy shit.

A long, lean leg stretches out of the car with a pair of black high heels and pushes the door open. A black coat covered arm holds the handle and she carefully maneuvers her way out of the car in her tailored mini-skirt.

Sara says exactly what I'm thinking, "Lauren?"

None of us says a thing as she pulls a satchel from the back seat and strides easily down the sidewalk, past the benches and towards main quad. Her ever-present, clingy boyfriend is nowhere in sight and his Jeep isn't in the parking lot. She looks as though she's either ready for court or a high powered business meeting; either way, a million dirty thoughts just went through my head watching her curled hair bounce as she struts like a supermodel on a runway.

"Did she break up with Mark?" I ask Sara, walking with her to first period.

"I don't know, but I'll find out." Sara is ready for Jackie to be gone from our lives, so my sudden interest in Lauren is probably welcomed considering I've forbidden anyone to speak her name near me for months.

By lunch, I feel like a stalker. I've made meaningless trips past her locker and went out of my way to go through the main quad several times just to catch a glimpse of her, but she isn't in her normal spots today. The ominous BMW in the parking lot is making me nervous, and the clothes she has on suggests something big is going on. Something... secret. Something I want in on. But after she and Mark started dating, rumors about her stopped spreading because she was no longer relevant.

Brandon and I get to the benches about the same time. "Hear anything?" I ask him, checking the parking lot to confirm her car is still there. There is no way in hell her self-centered mother bought that car for her, and though Mark is well off, I highly doubt he gave it to her.

"Sara said Mark's not here today. She should be here soon." And we both wait, and wait and wait.

Loud screeching and crying echoed from between the portable buildings by the fence line breaks the silence between us. Brandon jumps from the tables and takes off running towards the screaming. It takes me a minute to realize the screaming is my name. I bound into action, rushing after Brandon, around the corner being pursued by dozens of kids wanting to see what is going on. Between one of the buildings and the fence, Sara is crumpled on the ground, her face is bloody and it looks like part of her hair has been pulled out. I blink hard trying to figure out if I'm really seeing things right—Lauren is fighting Brenda. With the differences in their size, it's like a chipmunk taking on a cat. Brenda is the last person I'd think Lauren would take on ... then again, Sara is the first person Brenda would since she thinks Sara stole Brandon from her.

Brandon stumbles and almost falls on Sara in his haste to get her away from the two girls. They are totally oblivious to anything other than tearing each other apart and are getting dangerously close to falling on Sara. I've broken up fights before, but never between two chicks and it proves harder than it looks. Lauren's eye is already pink and swelling, but Brenda has a few marks of her own. Justin intercepts Brenda before she can hit Lauren, but my arms don't fully close around Lauren until she's landed one more punch directly against Brenda's nose. Lauren is kicking and screaming trying to get away from me. Her heart is racing against my forearms as she strains to scream without breathing. Justin is doing all he can to stop Brenda from coming at us, but he can't hold her much longer, and if the Proctors show up, we'll really be in deep shit. Kids are blocking us in the tight space and Lauren is still clawing to get away and cursing at Brenda. It's only the second time she's cussed in front of me, and she probably doesn't realize what she's saying. If it weren't in this situation, I'd find it more than mildly amusing.

Finally, Brandon gets Sara off the ground and heads to the parking lot with her. By the time he gets out the gate, he's got his cell phone out, probably calling Jess. With my arms still tight around Lauren, I push my way through the tightly weaved crowd while Justin starts going the other way with Brenda, who is putting up her own fight to get free. If she does, I'll be in trouble because it's obvious Lauren isn't done with her yet.

"Lauren, stop," I say over the noise of the crowd. The fight has ended, but they are hungry and begging for more; they aren't going to get it though. "Lauren, it's okay, she's okay. You're okay." But really it's not. We aren't out of the pack of kids and if the Proctors come around the building from this way, we will be caught. With my track record for fighting, they will take me to the office out of routine, not that I've actually done anything; then all my plans for getting out of school early could be down the drain. I can't just let Lauren go though, not until she's safe.

When we get to the girls' bathroom near the Science building, I finally let her go, having carried her most of the way, and pull her inside to get the blood off her hands and her face. Her polished image is destroyed. Whatever she was dressed up for is out of the question now and I'm part of its demise by default.

"What happened?" I ask, wetting paper towels in the sink while she stares at her bruised and bloody reflection. "Lauren?" I put my hand under her chin and force her to turn and look at me. "What happened?" I ask again.

"I saw Brenda jump Sara," she stutters, confirming at least part of what I assumed happened. Her chest is heaving, accentuating the lacy camisole that's visible thanks to the three missing buttons on her jacket. She has long thin scratches on her face, up her neck and on her chest; they really need to be looked at. I click open the phone and call Jess to make sure she is already on her way to my house for Sara.

"I'm going to take you to my place so Jess can check these out."

She starts to disagree, "I can't. I'll go to the Nurse's Office. My dad's here today, too."

Lauren looks uncomfortable just trying to breathe. "Do your ribs hurt? Does it hurt to breathe?"

"A little," she says and winces when I press the cool rag below her eye. I keep working to get the blood off her face, but it's all over her lips and in her hair too. Dabbing the rag gently at her cheek, she says, "thank you," without looking at me.

"You're welcome," I say and for the first time in months we are in the same room and it doesn't feel as though she wants to kill me nor do I want to kill her. Everything that happened three months ago is forgotten, even if only temporarily.

"It's not that it matters," she starts to say and loses her nerve and adds, "never mind."

I get more paper towels and turn on the cool water again. "What were you going to say?"

Lauren turns to look in the mirror and whips back around quickly. Her hands are strangling each other. She's probably worried about the huge black eye she's going to have tomorrow and she hasn't even seen the scratches yet.

"Nothing. I've got to go." She slides off the bathroom counter and it crushes me. This is my last chance …

"What did I do to make you not want me?" I'm losing my nerve with each word. This is impossible and if she gives me a crap answer, it will make it all that much worse that I even asked. "I mean, is Josh so much better than I am?"

"I'm not talking about this now." She shakes her head and straightens her coat like she's trying to slip back into her safe façade.

I stop her before she gets to the door. "It has to be now. Wednesday is my last full day at school. I'm leaving."

Lauren turns swiftly and looks at me with confusion and panic in her eyes. "What do you mean you're *leaving?*"

"I'm getting out of school early. I'm going into the explorer academy at the end of the month." I didn't want to tell her about my plans like this, but my chances to get the truth and give the truth are coming to an end.

"You … are you moving?"

"No, I'm going to be on the Mountain View police department, like my dad was."

Her eyebrows curve in towards her eyes, "You're going to be …" She stops and looks away. "Well, good luck, I guess." She takes off her heels, making me tower over her again and reaches for the door as though she's completely unaffected.

"You didn't answer me. I think I have the right to know."

"Why start this now? Why do you care?" She rolls her eyes. "That was so long ago. You're happy with Jackie and I'm with Mark."

"You aren't happy with him." I move closer to her.

She bites at her bottom lip, causing it to do that perfect pout that I love and brings back memories I haven't allowed myself to have in a long time. "I can't hurt him with my indecisiveness. I'm done with all that."

"I'm not asking you to hurt him. I just want to know why I wasn't good enough for you? Why did you choose Josh over me?"

"I didn't."

"Yes, you did. Sara saw you in the quad with him that morning."

"I know she did. I found out later. I tried to tell you what was going on, but you wouldn't listen." She sniffles and wipes gingerly at her bruised eyes. "I told you I loved you and I meant it. I went to the quad to end things, once and for all, and give him back the ring he gave me the night of the dance. He said it was some family heirloom." She half laughs and sucks in a breath as she wraps her arms around herself. "It didn't feel right keeping it and I didn't want it hanging over my head." Her words sink into the pit of my stomach like the Titanic. I know exactly how she's feeling. I have my own platinum and diamond encrusted noose at home.

"I'm an idiot," I say more to myself than to her, but she responds anyway.

"I agree. But, there's nothing I can do about that now." Her tone matches her suit, all business and no feelings.

"You weren't choosing Josh?"

"No." She snickers as if she knows regret is rushing through every part of my body. She is right. "I even told my parents I was going to date you and they extended my punishment by two weeks for it." Tears form at the corners of her eyes. My fingers shake wanting to find their way to her face, but I can't.

I'm a fool. I played right into what everyone else wanted me to think and do. The first sign of trouble and I believed the worst in her. I thought she hadn't given us a chance—and it turns out it was me all along. I am my own worst enemy.

"I have to go. I have a meeting at my job this afternoon and I can't go like this."

I want to fix this. "Please come back to Jess's with me. Her boyfriend is a doctor and you should have him look at your ribs and your eye," I beg, but mostly to make sure she's okay. Okay, that's a lie. Truly, I'm not ready for her to walk away from me. I've been a complete jackass.

"That's okay. Thanks though. I'll see you." She limps out the door and I watch her go, unwilling to stop her and unable to say anything else. She's miserable ... because of me. If what she says is true, I've thrown away my future and no one else is to blame for my insecurities.

Jackie is already home by the time I get there. She's stomping around the kitchen, annoyed at Justin and Alexis sitting on the couch eating *our* food ... that I pay for. Jeremy and Jenn are sitting on my bed trying to convince Brandon to stop hovering by the bathroom door. Jess and Brian are tending to Sara, making sure nothing is broken. Fortunately she isn't seriously injured. Brenda didn't fight fairly and used some sort of weapon because Sara has slits on her arms, two of which needed stitches and one on her stomach. Brenda was out to seriously hurt her; if it weren't for Lauren, she probably would've. . .

"Do you remember what happened?" I ask, interrupting Jess and Brian.

Sara shakes her head; her normally blue eyes are marred with blood and her multicolored hair is matted. A section in the back is missing and I'm not sure if it was one of her clips on sections or not. I've never seen her this way and I'm seriously considering changing my policy regarding intimidating girls.

"Brenda jumped me. She just called me a few names and grabbed my hair ..." Jess and Brian leave me to deal with the cuts on Sara's hands. "I don't know really what happened." Then fear flashes across her face. "Oh my God," she closes her hands around mine. "Is Lauren okay? I know she jumped into the fight. Is she hurt?"

Sara is just as concerned for Lauren as I am. Watching her limp away earlier and hearing her admit she wasn't choosing Josh is still clouding my chaotic thoughts. After all these months would she have any reason to lie to me? Every feeling and emotion I've ever had for her is competing for space in my heart.

"I don't know. I cleaned her up as best as I could at school, but she said she had some meeting to get to, something for her mom's work."

Sara picks at her nails, pulling some hanging cuticle off her index finger. "I have a confession. Danny, I messed up, seriously messed up."

"The thing with Brenda isn't your ..."

"I lied about Jackie's parents. They didn't kick her out," she blurts out.

"What?" I say too loud for the bathroom. We can hear Jenn telling Jackie everything is okay.

"I'm so sorry," Sara says as I yank my hands away from hers. This is one betrayal she won't be able to take back.

"Why would you do that," I practically yell at her. That means Jackie's been lying this whole time too. Sara's eyes grow wide in instant acknowledgment of what I know. They've both been pulling my strings like a puppet master, making sure my life is how they want it.

"Because the day that I told you about Lauren you got that look in your eyes. The one that said I was losing my brother all over again."

Sadness and frustration settles onto her face. I pull back from her further, pressing my back to the bathroom door. Even the fake world I've come to accept is crumbing around me; no earthquake, tsunami, or tornado could compare to the destruction coming my way.

"I can't believe you did this. I can't ..." Frustrated, my fist connects with the plaster and drywall, leaving a pothole in the wall that I'll have to fix ... just one more broken thing to add to the list.

"Danny," she cries knowing the severity of what's coming, "I'm sorry. I didn't want to lose you again and you were slipping away. I thought you would forget about Lauren and fall in love with Jackie more if she were here with you. I'll fix it Danny. I swear. I'll make it right. I'm so sorry!"

I throw open the bathroom door, leaving another hole in the wall from the knob. Jenn and Jeremy are in my face the second I take a step over the threshold. "What's going on?" Brandon bounds up the stairs. Rage, pain, hurt, anger all thrash through me. Both

Brandon and Jeremy recognize it and stop me before I can get to the door. They hook their arms around mine and toss me—kicking and punching—to the ground.

I'm fighting them off when Jackie gets to the top of the stairs. "Get the hell out of my house!" I yell at her. The look on Jackie's face says she knows that Sara told me. We are over. That's all it comes down to; she knows it. Everyone in the room knows it. How many of my friends knew this was going on the whole time? None of them really wanted to see me happy? How can I fix this now? Is there anyway to repair the past? What type of future can I have, when I can't even maintain a fake one?

L a u r e n

Needless to say, I missed the meeting. I call Mom and leave a message that I'm not going to make it. I drop off her boss's BMW to his secretary and catch a cab home. The new suit she bought for this meeting is destroyed ... she is going to be seriously pissed. When she finds out I was in a fight, she'll either pat me on the back or ground me for the rest of my junior year.

Mom comes in the door shortly before five. I've already washed and pressed the suit, but it's missing the buttons, and has a tear in the hem. There is no hiding the softball sized black eye I have, or the scratches running the length of both my arms.

"What were you thinking?" she asks pulling another packet of frozen peas from the freezer and wrapping it in a towel.

"I didn't want Sara to get hurt," I say and wince when she presses it to my eye.

"That meeting was important. Donovan did everything he could to get you onto that project."

"I know, Mom. I'm sorry."

"It's almost as if you want to throw away every chance you have," she says, and then adds, "We came out here and you've had nothing but opportunities for a better life."

"I'm not throwing away my future because of one fight mom. I'll call Donovan and apologize for not making it." My heart wasn't really into the meeting, anyway. The only benefit to working at the payroll office has been getting my license, but I still don't have enough money for a car. I can't see myself working in an office for the rest of my life ... it seems so *monotonous*.

Mark squeals his tires pulling into the driveway, almost taking out the mailbox and the shrubs in front of the house. The doorknob is still in my hands and he's pushing against the door trying to get in.

"What were you thinking?"

"Excuse me?" I ask, taken aback by his demeanor.

"Ben told me you stopped a fight between Brenda and Sara? How stupid! Your mom's going to be ticked you missed that meeting. You needed that project for your USC application, Lauren." He continues to lecture me as I walk back to the kitchen, shuffling my house shoes the whole way. Mom makes herself busy with some reports on the couch. She's not a fan of me dating Mark; she's made that no secret. The only thing she likes about him is I blow him off most nights to work on projects with her.

"You threw away your chance today for Sara? Seriously, Lauren? What the hell were you thinking? We've been preparing for this meeting for weeks."

"You're starting to sound like my mother," I mumble, hoping she didn't hear me and pull out a fresh icepack for my eye.

"Stop." He pulls my arm before I walk away to my bedroom. I don't even try to hide my eye roll. "I don't get it. What suddenly made you decide to help these people that abandoned you?"

"So, are you going to dictate who my friends are?"

"What?" He steps back, looking confused.

Mom's not going to like where this conversation is going. It has me wondering if Mark doesn't realize she's here.

"Josh tried to pull that crap too, and if you're going to start, you can get out." I point at the door and pull farther away from him.

"I'm not saying you can't be friends with anyone. What I'm saying is they aren't your friends. You put all that drama behind you months ago. Why do you want to wreck everything when you are so close to the goal?" He pulls a chair out at the table and motions for me to sit next to him. He tries to take my hand, but I refuse. "If you stay on track, you'll be out of school by December and in early at USC with me next year. Why would you want to jeopardize that for them?"

"I'm not and I didn't. She would've done the same for me." I press the make-shift ice pack to my eye wishing it could numb my brain, too.

"I don't think she would've," he says. Planning for the future and goal setting is all I've heard the last two months. There is hardly a day when he's not mapping out his education and career goals. In fact, the huge chart he made for me is over my desk where he hung it a month and a half ago. He was funnier when he came over and played video games and watched movies ... now, it's all school and his doctor's program. However, secretly, I think he wants me to go to school only temporarily, and then drop out to be a stay at home mom like his mother is, like my mother was. If mom knew the truth of what his plans are—married in four years, house in five, kids in six ...she'd be even madder. That's not on her "Lauren's Plans for the Future" timeline. Even though that is really what my plan for the future had been too, it's just not the same being with him.

"Is this about Danny?"

"What are you getting at now?" I shift away, not liking what he is implying. It's bad enough I've already gotten my butt chewed by mom, but to put up with it from Mark too feels seriously unfair.

"You heard me. Ben said you disappeared with Danny." Oh God. I wish he hadn't said that. In fact, mom isn't going to like what I'm about to say.

"He broke up the fight. He KEPT me out of trouble."

Mark grasps towards my hand, but misses. "Look, I love you. I don't know what I would've done today if that girl seriously hurt you. I'm thankful Danny was there when I couldn't be, but I don't like him near you. How can you so easily forget how he hurt you? How he and all his friends walked away from you and left you with nothing? They didn't stay around or come back to pick up the pieces. I did. I'm the one that fixed what they broke. I hate the idea that you would let them back in. It's like you're addicted to trouble, to their drama."

"I'm not taking them back as friends and I'm not giving up on my life. Why don't you jump to more conclusions while you're at it?"

"Why are you being so defensive over them? Why are you mad at me, when all I'm trying to tell you is I'm concerned."

"Because I already have one set of parents, I don't need another."

"Look." Mark takes aim and grabs my hand firmly. "I don't want to fight about this." Doesn't seem like it—seems like he wants to keep this going. Me? Not so much.

"Then don't try to tell me who I can be friends with."

Mom clears her throat to let Mark know she is there; the look he gives me confirms he didn't know. "Hi, Mrs. McIntosh."

"Mark, I think we've had enough excitement for one day. Maybe you better get going home." She stands from the couch and turns to face us with paperwork still in hand. Mark starts to say something, but she puts her foot down, "Goodnight, Mark."

"Goodnight." He shoves his hands into his letterman jacket pockets. "Call me later," he demands under his breath.

He can wait by his phone all night. I'm not calling him. I can't deal with him right now, because the look on my mom's face tells me I'm about to be at war with her instead.

"So, why didn't you tell me Danny broke up the fight?" She starts questioning the minute Mark is out the door.

"Because I knew you'd be mad."

She laughs and it's unnerving. "I'm not mad that Danny saved my daughter from her own stupidity. But, you know what I am mad about?"

I'm afraid to ask. "What?"

"It feels as though you haven't learned a thing about yourself, or how life should be."

"You don't get it," I say shaking my head and getting up from the table trying to avoid the atom bomb that's about to go off in the kitchen.

"Oh no, I don't get it because I haven't been miserably trapped in the life you are chasing after. I don't get it because I wasn't married and pregnant by the time I was nineteen. Hell, we were small town royalty when your father and I got married; half the town came to the wedding. So, how could things be so terrible? Right? That's what you're thinking?"

"You never seemed unhappy ..." Shouldn't have said that.

"You're right, I didn't, because I was married and had three children that were depending on me. Why take my miserable life out on them? I don't want this life for you. I want you to find out who you are and chase your own dreams instead of depending on someone else to give them to you." Then it dawns on me, the move to California wasn't just for them to start over; it was so that she could reinvent herself. "When Lynn started going down this path, I fought it, but your father was a stronger influence on her. With you, I was determined you wouldn't make the same choices I did."

"Mark wants me to go to college and have my own job and my own life. I'm not trying to get wrapped up in things. I've been focusing on my future and school. You should be happy Mark has helped me so much."

"About that," she takes a seat at the table across from me and puts her hand over mine. My face is throbbing from the ice pack and her hand on mine makes me realize I should've been putting ice packs on them too. Today was stupid, but I did it for the right reasons, regardless of what happened with Danny afterward. "I know you think Mark is the responsible choice, but it's obvious you're not in love with him. In fact, I think it's pretty much written on a huge billboard for everyone to see that he is nothing more than a friend." I dig my finger along one of the long grains of the table, wanting to avoid having this *mother/daughter* talk with her. I'm doing everything I can to be what they want me to be; why can't she just mind her own business?

"It's not fair to Mark that you are leading him on like this. You know he's not your future," she presses her hand down on my roaming fingers and I want to scream at her, but resist. "When I said no boys for a while, I wasn't saying you couldn't be with Danny. I just wanted you to take a break and focus on finding yourself for a while. Danny would've waited for you." I let a sad laugh escape my lips; she's so wrong. He didn't wait for me. He didn't need me like I needed him … especially since he replaced me so quickly. "It's not going to hurt my feelings if you tell me he is what you want," she hesitates, "or if you tell me you want to work with Jess."

My eyes shoot to hers. I never told her anything about Jess's internship. I didn't want to hurt her feelings or shun the offer her boss was making. "I ran into Sara at the store a few months ago. She asked if you were still considering the job."

I shake my head and try to fight back everything. The life I could've had was within reach and I'm still not truly sure why it all slipped away. Why couldn't Danny have waited for me? Why didn't he just give me time like I asked? My connection with him was so strong. I don't understand why he couldn't feel it. But it's clear; mom just gave me the green light to chase what I want. She has an eerie look of relief on her face as I rush to her side and give her a huge hug. Sometimes, I guess she knows what she's talking about. "Thanks, mom."

Dad comes in the door early from practice, ending the conversation, and I'm okay with that. I know what I have to do. College is an opportunity I won't throw away like Lynn has, but it has to be joined by a few things in order for me to be truly happy. Danny is still what I want and I'm willing to wait for him to realize he wants me, too. It will crush me if he chooses Jackie over me, but that's the risk I have to take.

Back in my room I turn on the computer and wait for the introductions to finish scrolling by. When did I get so many pop-ups on this stupid thing? Spam sucks. I click on my in box and there are twenty waiting for me. Fifteen are junk. Two are from Sara: long, rambling and apologizing for everything. One is from Jenn begging me to call her or Sara as soon as I can. The last two are from Danny. The first email just says *call me*. It was sent over two hours ago. The second, sent ten minutes ago, is much, much longer and I'm cherishing every word knowing that he is at least thinking of me.

Lauren,
There are no words to describe how I feel about what you did today for my sister. Because of you, she wasn't seriously hurt. Brian and Jess are both a phone call away if you want them to look at your eye. If you ice it over night, the swelling should be gone by morning.

Hearing you scream my name today was the most horrifying, heart wrenching, experience I've ever had to live through. If I had known Brenda was out for blood, I would've given her mine over yours, any day. I'm sorry you missed your meeting and I know your parents are probably going ballistic. So I doubt you'll email me back, and that's okay. Even if you're not grounded, you probably won't.

I hate this.

I feel like such a fool. It's not that it matters now, but I am so sorry, for everything. I want to finish the conversation we started. Please let me know if I can call you. There are so many things to say, but not like this...
Danny

I'm about to email back when my parents screaming at each other pulls me like a magnetic force out of my room to the kitchen.

"...because your life is so bad? HUH? I've given you everything!" Dad yells at mom and slams his fist into the counter.

"No, I've given you my entire life and it's time for me to focus on what makes me happy."

"What's going on?" I say, but neither of them notices.

"You chose me, remember!" Dad yells, "Don't stand there acting as if someone forced you to be with me. No one forced you to leave Jack for me!" *Huh?*

"What's he talking about?" I ask.

"Your mother has buyer's remorse," he says pulling a beer from the fridge and slamming the door shut. "She's had a wretched life and it's because she chose the wrong guy." He storms down the hallway and slams the bedroom door, leaving mom and me with our mouths hung open. Mom never said anything about dating anyone other than dad, ever.

"Mom?" I say, wanting to comfort her, but also wanting to find out what he is talking about. She doesn't answer though. She rushes past me, pausing only to grab her purse and goes out the front door. Could she have regretted her decision to be with dad so much that she's punishing all of us for it?

D a n n y

The condo is too small. It's collapsing around me while I'm watching my in box like a hawk. I have the computer speakers maxed out and the house is ghostly quiet. I'm growing more aggravated each time the speakers ring that I have a new message and it's only spam. The first email I sent shortly after throwing everyone out of my house earlier, the second after the adrenaline was no longer stinging my skin. I tried to convey how sorry I am and how much I really want to take back everything I said to her. If she calls or speaks to me again, I'll apologize for everything and vow to leave her alone, if that is what she wants. But, the apology comes first ... I'll deal with the rest later.

My cell phone rings just before ten, when I'm debating whether or not to make dinner. It's kind of pointless now. "Hello?"

"Hey, just wanted to let you know Lauren called Jenn," Jeremy says, offering at least some comfort. "She's on the phone with her now. She said she's bruised but she's doing okay. Jenn just said she'll definitely be at school tomorrow."

"Did she say if she's grounded?" I ask although it doesn't really matter. It's not likely that she'll do anything with me anyway.

He covers the phone. "Is she grounded?" he asks Jenn. "No, not yet, she said. I think there is something going on with her parents."

"What's up with her parents? Does she seem like she's okay?" Of course she's not okay. "I mean, it's been a while since she's talked to Jenn."

"I didn't get the story about her parents. They've been talking for about thirty minutes and Jenn has her talking and laughing. Or, at least Jenn's laughed."

"Have they talked about me?" Self-centered, I know.

"In the beginning when they talked about the fight."

I stay on the phone for the next hour listening to the play by play of their conversation. A few times I can hear Jenn laughing and giggling as if nothing ever went bad between the two of them. Jenn apologizes to Lauren for not being there for her and makes Lauren promise to get together soon before finally disconnecting after eleven. Dinner is definitely out now, but this is the closest I've felt to her in months. Even though she wasn't talking to me, it feels like she was.

It's thirty minutes before the campus will be a flurry of students. Sleep wouldn't come last night, so I packed up the remaining stuff Jackie left at the condo and dropped it on her front porch this morning. She lied the entire time telling me she wasn't talking to her parents. With how she was treating Sara, I'm surprised their little plan didn't come out sooner.

I sit in my truck, hoping Lauren doesn't ride with Mark today. But if she were my girl, I wouldn't let her out of my sight after yesterday's activities. And he doesn't. Right before the main bell, Mark pulls into one of the spots reserved for the football team and helps her from the car. She has huge sunglasses on to block her black and blue eyes, although her cheek is still swollen. I doubt she iced it all night, as I suggested.

Sara, Jenn, and Alexis all intercept her at the Jeep and Mark looks instantly annoyed. He's trying his best to be a bodyguard and push the girls out of the way for them to walk, but Jenn is determined, and Alexis will not be stopped. They wrap their arms around her and she winces slightly away. If I offered her mine, she'd wince away worse. At least Sara is comforting her for me; she's brushing Lauren's hair back from her face, and for the briefest moment, Sara's eyes catch mine and we share a moment of acknowledgement. Lauren seems to be accepting their apology; hopefully, she'll accept mine for being such an insecure prick.

"Hey," I say when she comes into the theater for class. One of her eyes is bloodshot from a busted vein and the make-up isn't concealing anything … there's no doubt she got into the first fight of her life. I can't even count the number of times I've woken up looking just like that, or how many guys I've made wake up like that.

"Hey," she says; maybe I'm mistaking her quick response as upbeat, but it seems as though she's almost thankful to be talking to me.

"I emailed you …"

"I know. Sorry I didn't email you back. It was a *really* hectic night."

Yeah, she probably got a lashing from everyone …"Grounded?"

"Not yet." She slightly grins. "Its coming. I'll find out tonight."

"Sorry you got into so much trouble over us."

"No, it's my own fault. I shouldn't have taken on Brenda by myself."

"Yeah, that took a hell of a lot of guts considering she's triple your size."

She laughs, and then covers her cheek with her hand, "Don't make me laugh. It hurts when I smile."

Ms. Nelson comes in and calls for us to take our seats. I sit directly behind her, wanting to reminisce in memories of her delicate vanilla scent, but I get overwhelmed by perfume that reminds me of Jackie. That has to go. That's not who she is.

Ms. Nelson gives each of us the assignments for the day and turns us loose to work on sets and backdrops. Lauren and Alexis are working on stretching muslin while I'm assigned to painting the backdrop. Strategically, I pick the trees at stage left and eavesdrop on the girls. When Christian and Ivan come over to ask about the paint, I blow them off and go back to my not-so-slick listening in. Both of the girls are aware of what I'm doing as I inch closer to the end of the backdrop.

"So, what are you doing this weekend?" Alexis asks, causing me to drop my paintbrush. That's the last thing I want ... especially if Alexis has something sinister planned like she did that first night the snuck out and ended up at DJ's.

"Mark has a game, but I don't even know if I'm grounded yet or not."

"I could come over," she says as I'm cleaning up the mess I made, "we could sneak out." That causes me to kick over the entire paint bucket and gets a laugh from both girls. Alexis just set me up. Bitch.

"We do need to get together. You know, I'm going out with Sara this weekend," she says. When did the plans for the weekend change? Did Sara think I didn't want her going with us to the mountains now? "It'll be so much fun."

"What are you guys doing?" Lauren asks like she's considering ditching her plans with Mark.

"We don't have our plans locked down yet, but Jenn said she's going to go too. We may go to the movies and the mall. Maybe drive to the pier. Do you think your mom would be okay if you hang out with us all day?" *Uh-oh* ... My stomach starts doing back flips.

"It depends on if I'm grounded or not. And I'm really supposed to go to Mark's game,"

"Mark has games every weekend, can't you skip one?" I'm on my hands and knees cleaning up the paint from the bucket spill. Ms. Nelson comes over with more towels, since the one I'm pushing back and forth is already soaked.

"Maybe you should pay more attention to the task at hand," she points to the backdrop, "instead of the girls."

"Yes ma'am." And just like that, the girls are onto another subject. Damn it. I missed her final answer.

"So how are things with Justin?" Lauren asks, switching to a safe topic. I concentrate on finishing the tree I've made look like abstract art.

"Where are the girls?" I ask walking up to the benches at lunch.

"Main quad, hanging with Lauren," Brandon answers and I consider going over there, but I don't. I stay put where I belong. Brandon and Justin take either spot on the table next to me, silently comforting me and steadying my nerves. It may be pointless, considering it's impossible to undo three months worth of hating her for choosing Josh. Only to find out that she wasn't. When she told me she loved me, doubt instantly crept in and never released me. If she gives me another chance, I will never doubt her again. I swear it.

"What time do you want to leave on Saturday?" Brandon asks distracting my glare on the walkway to main quad, wishing Lauren would come running to me. She hasn't let me tell her my side of what happened all those months ago, and it needs to be out there so that she can make the decision to be with me or not. I doubt she'll choose the latter, but I'll regret not telling her everything for the rest of my life. I'm always going to wonder what could have been with her if I don't lay it all out there.

"Early, maybe five? Six?"

"Are we going to stop at Mountain Top to eat?" Justin says pulling apart his sandwich. I'm going to miss times like these, but I'm looking forward to getting into the explorer academy, too. Just another couple of weeks and I'll be away from the rumors, the lies and the high school politics. But, I'll miss lunches and hanging with my friends too.

"Yeah," I say and the conversation Alexis had with Lauren is lingering. "Hey, did Alexis say anything about hanging out with Sara this weekend?"

"No, they're going with us. Why?" Justin confirms.

"Nothing, no reason." He knows better. I don't ask questions without a purpose. Alexis and Sara are up to something; and it probably involves tricking Lauren into going with us. The day at the creek with her is still one of the best days of my life, one that I hope to repeat. All those dreams and wishes from before never completely faded and they easily return upon thinking of her going to the mountains with us again. If the girls can't pull it off, I'm going to be disappointed, even though it wasn't even an option until today. There's no way her mom would let her stay overnight … but what if she's not given an option? There is a huge storm coming after all … maybe I'll pack a few extra sets of clothes. Wait, is kidnapping a felony? What about holding someone hostage at a mountain lodge until they fall in love with you again? Yeah, probably not a good idea either, and more than likely a felony. Both are out.

I catch Sara and Jenn walking to the parking lot after school. I didn't see Lauren for the rest of the day and it's killing me. "What happened today?" I ask, hoping neither of them will make me dig for the answer.

"It's still in process," Jenn says and turns to look down the sidewalk. Lauren is walking up the sidewalk towards us. "We'll see you, okay?" she says dismissing me like the hired help.

I refuse to leave so easily. "Are you guys trying to get her to go this weekend?" I ask Sara directly. She knows I'm still pissed at her, so she better answer.

"Not if you don't out of here," Jenn quickly answers for her, sticking up to me when Sara wouldn't dare.

"Call me," I demand and stalk off towards my truck. That's when I realize why they wanted me out of there. Lauren climbs into the back of Jenn's car. Unbelievable. They went from enemies to BFF's in less than a day; then again, Brandon and I were like that too. Jenn can do it. Lauren will be at the mountains this weekend. The hope spreads through me as the three girls drive past laughing the whole way. Lauren's cheek probably hurts like hell with how hard she's laughing. For the first time in months, she's finally alive, and it's a beautiful thing.

I drive home and pace the rooms of the condo for what seems like an eternity. Brandon isn't home, and Sara hasn't called or picked up her phone either. They're all in on this huge secret, and I'm the outcast. The waiting is killing me. I'm not even sure what they are up to with Lauren, and it's bothering the hell out of me. I call Vince's to order a pizza, mostly just to get out of the house because I'm not really hungry. I take the long way to Vince's, and then an even longer way back. I've killed more than an hour, but still no calls.

Just before midnight, I check my emails again but the only ones waiting are from Jackie. I delete them all, unread. She had her chance and she blew it. It pains me to think Lauren may be having that same thought about me right now. If they tell her I'm going to the mountains this weekend, she'll never go.

"Danny?" It's midnight by the time Sara and Brandon come in the front door. Both look exhausted.

"Have you been with Lauren the whole time?" I don't let her say anything before asking her what I want to know. I've worn out the carpet in the living room; you could literally see a Nascar shaped track around the couch and coffee table and I refuse to wait any longer to know my fate.

"Yeah, Jenn and I hung out at her house with her mom." That's thrilling. They've wiggled their conniving little way back into her life.

"Did they ground her?"

"No, not yet," Sara says and yawns. Brandon heads up the stairs and Sara starts to follow. Yeah, she's slept over with him before, but not tonight. Not until she tells me everything.

"Did Mark show up?"

"No, he had something going on today with USC. Lauren's got this huge chart on her bedroom wall that is a timeline to her classes and summer school so that she can graduate in December to go to USC with him. It's pretty in-depth." That's not a good thing.

"Is that ...," I swallow hard, "...is that what she wants?"

"The truth?" she asks as though I'd want to hear anything different.

"Yeah." Maybe I don't want to hear it.

"No, but I think she's resolved that you and Josh betrayed her, so she's just thankful he isn't treating her like dirt." A deep breath escapes my lungs, showing how deflated I am by hearing she really doesn't think I'm any better than him. Maybe I'm not, but that never was my intention. I've never wanted to hurt Lauren; I guess I never assumed she didn't want to hurt me, either.

"Did you bring up this weekend? Does she know you want to go to the mountains?"

"No, we're hanging out tomorrow on lunch and I'm driving her to school in the morning. Can I go to bed now, Danny? I'm tired and I have to get up early to get my own car so that she doesn't think something's up."

"Yeah," I say and then add, "Thanks. I really appreciate what you're doing."

"Don't thank me yet. I haven't fixed what I did. But, I will."

L a u r e n

Hanging out at my place with Jenn and Sara is exactly what has been missing. Mark's pissed that I told him not to come over. I'm sure he sees the writing on the wall when I tell him Sara is driving me to school in the morning. Mark and I are over. He just hasn't been informed of that yet. He'll find out today. Mom's right: it's not fair for me to continue leading him on when this isn't what I want. Danny may not want me right now, but I'm going to show him he is what I want.

"Hey girl, cute shirt!" Sara says. Little does she know that the locket Danny gave me is hovering just below the neckline, perfectly concealed, giving me strength to get through the day. How can I make the transition from the main quad to the benches when Danny is still there with Jackie and everyone is going to see me as just another groupie slut? Sara and Jenn are my best girlfriends, though. I just need to get through the initial embarrassment and show everyone I'm there to stay.

We pick up Jenn and pull into the school parking lot. Danny's truck is there, and so is Jackie's BMW parked next to it. Jackie is with Danny at the benches when we walk down the sidewalk. "Ummm." Sara looks at them and hooks her arm through mine. "Let's go to the cafeteria for some breakfast." Jenn nods and they pull me away from having to see Danny in love.

Mark watches the three of us cross main quad. Today is going to be a lot harder than I thought. It sucks being so sure of my decision and doubting it so much at the same time.

By lunch, I have no idea what I'm going to do. The benches are calling me, but I can't stand to see Danny with Jackie. I still have to break up with Mark, and Sara is hopeful I'll hang out with them this weekend. I'm not this strong; I don't know if I can do this.

Mom said she would back me ... but she can't save me from the prying eyes at school or the shit talking all the people at the benches will do. Even though Brenda and Kristi were both suspended, they still have allies who would do anything to get to me.

Autopilot sets in, and I head to the main quad, betraying every empowered thought I've had all day. Sometimes, it's just easier to go with the flow. Breaking up can wait until tomorrow.

"How has your morning been?" Mark says with more than a hint of jealousy in his tone. I haven't even seen him all morning and it's pretty clear he hasn't appreciated my absence.

"It's been okay." I pull out an apple from my bag and wish I had taken the time to cut it up. It's going to hurt to try to eat the crispy thing with my face all bruised. Smiling still hurts and it feels like my skin is already stretched as far as it can go.

Mark leaves me to talk to Ben for a while. Mandi, Jamie and several of the other cheerleaders are laughing and talking under their breath about me. I don't care. I'd jump into the fight again to save Sara. None of them would even consider saving each other like that. But after five minutes, and with Mark not coming back, I'm done. I've had enough. It's easier to be by myself than deal with people talking about me. I grab my bag and my lunch and head to the library. I've hung out three weeks in there before, so another day, week, or maybe month ... wouldn't matter.

"Why did you leave?" Mark asks after I've finished sneaking most of my lunch in the library. I'm surprised he even noticed I was gone. He slides into the chair across the table.

"I got tired of Mandi and Jamie talking shit about me."

"They weren't ..."

"Yes, they were. They were laughing at the fact I got my ass beaten yesterday."

Mark takes my hand across the table and rubs his thumb down one of the gashes. I yank my hand away. "You know how I feel about what happened. I meant what I said yesterday. I don't want you near them anymore." That sets me off. He's only starting this now because my mom's not here to intervene. I hadn't planned on doing it now, but I know I have to. I can't keep living this way.

I scrape the chair against the floor, causing all eyes to drift to us. Great, a very public break up. "Mark, we're over. I can't do this anymore. I never should've done this."

"Wow," he says and looks around. "This is about Danny, isn't it? You've finally decided you can't live without him ... haven't you?" No, I hadn't, but the fact is, I've admitted I can't live with Mark anymore. It's too much of a struggle and relationships shouldn't be like this: all about goals and not feeling loved.

"No. It's not about him. I just finally realized I should've said no in the first place. I love you, but as a friend. I can't keep pretending that there is more here."

"I see," Mark says and pushes his own chair back. The hurt and anguish in his eyes is hard to mask. He hates me and I never intended to hurt him like this. But I can't go on being miserable. I refuse to make the same mistake my mom made, now that I know what she's been through. It has changed everything.

Sara is putting stuff into her locker when I approach her after fifth period. "Can you give me a ride home?" I ask and I'm thankful when she says yes and doesn't press why.

After school, I wait for her by the Honda and duck when I see Jackie storming to her BMW. Her arms are loaded down with bags of junk like she's moving. Maybe she's leaving Mountain View when Danny is. Lucky. She won't have to be left behind with no friends and no comfort when he goes.

"How was your day?" Sara asks when she climbs in the car.

"It was good," I say pulling on my seat belt. "Is everything okay with Jackie? She looked mad when she left today."

Sara pulls out of the space just as Danny and Brandon emerge from the gates of the school. "She's leaving to go back to her other school." I shouldn't be happy about that, but I am.

"She doesn't want to hang out after Danny's gone?" I say, trying not to sound jealous that she's taken my spot in his life.

"I heard a rumor today ..." she changes the subject. "Did you break up with Mark?"

"Yeah," I say and keep myself from telling her that I want to fix things with Danny. She'll think it's too soon. Plus, there's still the issue of Jackie to contend with.

"What happened?" We pull onto the street to my house.

"Can you pull over so that we can talk? I might be in a bunch of trouble when I get home, so it's better we not go there."

"Sure," she says and pulls to the curb a few houses down from mine. "So, you wanna talk about it?"

I fidget with the seams of my jeans. "He got so pissed at me over the fight and said you guys weren't really my friends."

Sara looks down at her lap, "Lauren, I'm so sorry. That day at the quad, I really thought you were going back to Josh. After seeing all the pictures in your room and hearing you talk about the ring … I really thought you were going to hurt Danny again."

I try to fight back my own tears. The very existence of my life vitally changed all over a huge misunderstanding, but that doesn't matter now that I'm back on the right path and slowly getting back my true friends, and possibly, Danny. "I know you were just looking out for Danny. We did kind of rush into things after the dance. You had every right to be cautious and look out for him."

Her blood shot blue eyes finally match mine, "Do you forgive me?" she sniffles and swipes the very tips of her fingers under both of her eyes, catching lingering tears.

Really, she didn't do anything wrong. I'd want her on my side, protecting my heart if she were my sister. My sister doesn't even care that this is going on; she's too wrapped in her own drama. "Yes, I do."

She gives me a half smile. "What are you going to do now?"

"I'm just going to hang out and concentrate on going to college. Do you think Jess will still help me with that internship?"

Sara bats away one last tear from her cheek, "Will your mom let you do it?"

"She said she would," I barely finish and she wraps her arms around my neck, solidifying our newly found friendship.

"That is awesome news! Do you think your mom will let you hang out with us this weekend?" She claps her hands together quickly. "We're going to the lodge to celebrate. Danny and..."

I stop her. I'm not ready to see Danny with Jackie ... there; a place that still holds such good memories of my brief, but magical, moments with Danny. "I can't. I'm going to be grounded and seeing him with Jackie is a little too hard ... harder than I want to even think about."

She starts laughing and it's very inappropriate considering I just told her how much I hate seeing him happy with someone else. "They broke up."

"They ... their . . . over?" I practically trip over every word. It can't be.

"Yeah, he broke up with her." She shrugs passively, as if she couldn't care less.

"What happened?"

"The fight," she sighs. "It finally came out that I lied to him to get him to let Jackie move in with him. I was afraid he'd start drinking again after what happened with you."

Danny and Jackie are over. Mark and I are over. There's no way this opportunity will pass me by again. Third time is a charm; it has to be. I know I'm rushing things, but I don't know how long I'll be grounded for this time and boys may be completely off limits when dad finds out I broke up with Mark and I intend on going back to the benches again.

"Do you think Danny still . . ." I hate asking her this because it's going to hurt if she says no, ". . . do you think Danny still has feelings for me?"

Her laughing almost busts the car windows, "you're kidding, right?"

No, I'm not. Three months can change everything and he said tomorrow is his last day at Mountain View. He can slip away without knowing how I feel and getting to air out everything that happened. He said he was a fool ... I hope he truly embraced that and listens to what I have to say now.

"Is Danny home?"

"No, he had a meeting at work, why?" she looks at me perplexed.

"Can you take me to the store?" I'm going to put myself out there and let him decide if he wants me. He may not want to jump into another relationship, but I have to show him that I'm willing to do anything to have him back in my life. If he wants me to wait for him, I will, but I have to know if he will even consider taking me back. By the end of the night I'll either be the luckiest girl alive, or the dumbest.

"Who are you calling?" she asks doing a U-turn to head away from my house. I have two calls to make. The first to my mom to justify why I'm not coming home right after school and the second is to Jess. It's time I embrace what I want, what I've always wanted, and have denied myself. If Danny will have me, I'll do everything I can to show him I deserve another chance.

D a n n y

Lauren getting into the car with Sara is the only thing I can think about all night. Our briefing for a security detail in a few weeks takes longer than it was supposed to, so I'm aggravated trying to get all my equipment back into my locker in the shower room at work. There's nothing waiting for me at home; I'm not sure why I'm rushing. If Sara and Jenn can't get Lauren to go this weekend, I may not go, either. It sucks when you're the only one not with someone. Going to the lodge isn't quiet as fun when you don't have someone to share it with, and Jackie is definitely a thing of the past. Then again, I won't date anyone until I get another chance with Lauren. Everyone can see she's not happy with Mark, but she's probably staying with him because she'd go back to being friendless.

"So, did you hear the rumor?" Brandon asks tossing his stuff into the locker. He's been on the straight and narrow since he got out of rehab and his training is almost done for him to work beside me in another two weeks, although once I start the academy I'll only work part time. Brandon and I will share a new life soon … this time on the right side of the law.

"Nah, what rumor?" I ask and pull on my jacket.

"Mark and Lauren broke up today," he says calmly, but I spin around to look at him and catch my face on the open door of his locker. He starts laughing and I want to pound the locker in his face in return. I resist and wait for him to add more, rubbing the spot on my cheek that I'm sure will be a lump tomorrow. "Yeah, I guess it got really messy in the library today. Didn't hear the whole story though. I'll ask Sara about it when I get home." His phone rings, "speaking of the devil." Turning around he leaves me craving more about the rumors I didn't hear today.

Lauren's charade with Mark is finally over, but I highly doubt she'll come running straight to me. I can't be that lucky. I was such an ass to her I guess I should be lucky she even talked to me at school today. She's focused on college and planning her own departure from Mountain View, probably back to Illinois with her siblings. Then she'll really be lost to me, at least for a while, since I never turned in my application to U of I and I'm committed to the academy in just a few weeks.

"Hey, Sara and I are going to dinner. I'll catch up with you later." He has the biggest grin on his face and I want to slap it off of him. Dinner my ass. They probably want to go some place to be alone and I'm envious for that sneaky, exciting relationship I once had the chance of with Lauren.

His departure turns my focus to the empty condo that awaits me. Jackie may not have fitted into my world, but it was nice having someone there when I got home, someone who wanted to see me and spend time with me, regardless of what a nag she was most of the time. I call Jeremy to see if he can get together and he doesn't answer, nor does Jess. I'm friendless, for the night. It's just me, the big empty condo, and my demons. I consider calling Lauren to see if she's okay, but just like when she left Josh, I doubt she'd be cool with me trying to pick up where we left off. That's the last thing I want her to think, that I'm simply pursuing her to finish what we started at the restaurant. Tomorrow is going to be a busy day for me, turning in all my books and chasing down information about her break up.

Sara left lights on in the condo again. I'm paying for her being forgetful and it's starting to make me mad. I can't really blame her since she's still scared of the dark after I made her watch *Nightmare on Elm Street* when she was ten ... not one of my better decisions, I admit. I open the door and toss my book bag and security belt onto the table just inside the front door. The smell of cinnamon and apples is drifting through the house and my first thought is Sara left a candle burning, until the smell of cooking meat drifts through with it. Sara and Brandon's cars were both gone. I reach under the table to grab the baseball bat I hid there, just in case. I grip the bat with both hands and prepare to take on Matt or Aaron … or both. I guess I should be thankful Brandon got Sara out of here before the village idiots decided to show up. I knew it wouldn't be long until they made an appearance at my place.

I creep slowly against the wall to the kitchen with the bat poised to go. "Hello?" I say, giving them the chance to give up before I take their heads off. Hopefully neither of them has a gun…

"In here," a familiar female voice answers. *There's no way.*

I round the corner into the kitchen to find Lauren, hair in a ponytail, no make-up on, wearing a form fitting white t-shirt, jeans, and tennis shoes; all of which look like Sara's. She bends over and pulls a fresh pie out of the oven. "Do you like apple?" she asks like it's the most natural question in the world. Baked goods aren't necessarily at the top of my list of questions to ask.

"What're you doing here?" I ask and realize I'm still holding the baseball bat with a death grip. I set it down on the table and watch her pull another pie from the oven.

"You didn't answer me," she says completely ignoring my question, "do you like apple pie?"

"Yes," I answer, still very confused at her being in my kitchen … cooking, no less.

"Good," she smiles. "Dinner is almost done." She opens the cabinet with my plates in it and takes out two and holds them out toward me. "Can you set the table?"

Speechless, I comply, putting the plates down, and then pulling glasses out of the cabinet, and silverware from the drawer. "Are you going to tell me what's going on?"

"In a minute. I don't want the food to burn."

I know she broke up with Mark today, but I'm not going to assume anything about her being here. I refuse to get ahead of myself again. That doesn't mean I'm not hopeful that she's here to stay, but I can't fight the voice in my head telling me to be cautious.

I try to help her and she ends up ushering me out of the kitchen. "Nope, I'm cooking, you're ... sitting."

"You're kicking me out of my own kitchen?"

"Yup, for now." She gives me a mischievous grin. "You can come in here later, if you want to clean up. But right now, you are in the way."

I watch her twist and bend getting salad and dressing out of the fridge like she's been here and done it a million times. That food wasn't in there earlier. She planned this, the dinner, the dessert ... everything.

Lauren carefully slides a steak and baked potato onto each of the plates and then sets a salad in the middle of the table. This is almost the exact dinner we had the night... "This looks familiar."

"I thought we could use a do-over," she smiles and slides into the chair across from mine. "Everything is the same except the cake," she proclaims, "which, by the way, we never got to eat."

"Are you saying ...?" Don't get ahead of yourself Danny. "I mean I heard you broke up with Mark today."

"I did," the confidence in her tone makes my head spin, but she doesn't seem affected as she starts to scoop salad into our bowls.

"Why?" I ask cautiously. I want her to say because she can't live without me. However, that is not how things usually work out for me. History has taught me not to get my hopes up, especially when it comes to the beautifully confusing Lauren McIntosh.

"I realized that I don't have to settle for what everyone else wants. I can have what I want." The sultry way she says *want* makes my heart do back flips.

I have to say what I've been feeling the last few months. "I'm sorry for what happened at the restaurant and how I treated you afterwards. Sara convinced me you got back together with Josh and I let doubt overshadow my feelings for you."

"I know." She reaches across the table to my hand. Her smooth hand glides down the length of my fingers, and then weaves through mine stopping every thought racing through my head. "Sara told me what happened." She shrugs. "We all made mistakes."

That is a serious underestimation of the last three months, but if she is willing to say it's behind us, then that's fine by me. However, I'll make it up to her if she'll let me, if her being here means I'm what she wants.

She picks up her silverware and I can't even think about putting the food in my mouth. The only thing I can think about is whether or not she's going to stay this time, or if she's going to let something tear us apart again, even though, really, last time was my fault.

"I can't keep doing this," I say and watch her slump against the back of the chair. I get up and pull my chair close to her. "I want you." I pick her hand up off the table and hold it between mine. I lean toward her and she smells like soap ... my soap. She was in my bedroom again and she showered here. Thoughts of the last time she was here plague me, as I issue an ultimatum and hope like hell I'm not making the wrong decision. "I don't want you to be here because you have nothing else, nowhere else to go. I need to know you're with me because this is what you want." I barely choke out the words. "Because I'm what you want." My nerves are shot. This doubt needs to stop rushing over me like waves pulling me out to sea. I hate to force her into an answer that she may not be ready to give, but tomorrow is my last day at school; I can't concentrate on getting everything else in order if this is unresolved.

"Well?" I ask. Her eyes travel the length of my arms to focus on our hands, locked into each other.

She doesn't answer and the void fills with my heartbeat pounding in my ears. If she changes her mind now, it will be over for good. Then she shocks me and comes forward to press her lips to mine. Her arms wrap around my neck and she pulls me deep into her kiss. The magical feeling of her being here, and giving me this chance, is more than I deserve, but that doesn't mean I'm not soaking it in. Tomorrow will be the end of one life and the beginning of another. One filled with love and possibilities.

There's only one thing left to say to her. "I love you," I say resting the palm of my hand on her cheek and stare deep into her glowing eyes.

"I love you too," she whispers and comes forward again to softly meet my lips with hers. I easily get lost in her kiss, in her breath against my face that makes my heart race and awakens hope and desire deep inside me like no one ever has. If these are the last lips I ever get to kiss, I'll be the luckiest man alive.

Yes, tomorrow is another day ... one I'm sure I'll be ready for, with her finally at my side; hopefully she plans on staying here.

BLACK ROSE
writing™

CPSIA information can be obtained at www.ICGtesting.com
Printed in the USA
LVOW11s1101141213

365168LV00001B/2/P